Cause of
Death

;

Cause of Death

PETER RITCHIE

BLACK & WHITE PUBLISHING

First published 2017
by Black & White Publishing Ltd
Nautical House, 104 Commercial Street
Edinburgh EH6 6NF

1 3 5 7 9 10 8 6 4 2   17 18 19 20

ISBN: 978 1 78530 132 2

A CIP catalogue record for this book
is available from the British Library.

Typeset by Iolaire, Newtonmore
Printed and bound by CPI Group (UK) Ltd, Croydon, CR0 4YY

PROLOGUE

'Fuck!'

When the car hit him, the pain was an explosion – then almost as quickly it drained into the cold, damp ground below, and with it went all sensation. He was just aware that the freezing droplets of rain were making him blink, and that he couldn't move his head to avoid them. He was sure he was dying, but he felt surprisingly calm. Like most people he'd wondered how his last moments would be, but there was almost an anticlimax in the experience.

With the pain gone his mind adjusted to the situation. A uniform bent over him and mouthed something, but it was a silent movie, although he could guess what was being said. Christ knows he'd been there often enough himself as a young policeman – a thousand years ago now it seemed. All you could do was tell the poor sod to be calm and that help was on its way. Well, he was calm but didn't think much could sort his situation. He imagined his own young face on the policeman, and if he could he would have wept. Then he saw Grace trying to get to him. She was crying, her face lacerated with pain, and he realised what she'd become to him. His chest heaved with the effort of staying alive and he said it in no more than a whisper: 'Jesus Christ, this isn't how it should end.'

The young policeman turned to Macallan. 'He's saying something but I don't know what it means.'

She pushed the boy aside, knelt down and put the palms of her hands against his cheeks, her tears dropping onto his face. He smiled at her and thought that he must look a fucking sight. Somewhere in the distance a two-tone blared out its approach.

'Why are they bothering?' he murmured, and she looked up and rubbed the back of her hand across those startling green eyes of hers.

'Jesus, will you shut up and live?'

He smiled just before he slid into unconsciousness.

1

The Belfast Incident

Detective Chief Inspector Grace Macallan cursed the cold. She was in an observation post overlooking the Ormeau Road in Belfast, freezing December rain hitting the pavements like cold shrapnel. High above the streets in a derelict building, she watched the operation against a dissident Republican active service unit – or just plain old terrorists to one half of the good people of Northern Ireland. Years of blood had spilled onto the Ormeau Road during the Troubles, and it had seen all forms of brutality in a war where there were no clean hands, despite what some politicians said.

The road runs from the historic St George's Market, not far from Belfast city centre, and the 'Markets', as it's better known, became part of the Troubles' legend as a stronghold of the old Official Irish Republican Army, until the Provisional IRA and the Irish Nationalist Liberation

Army became the big boys on the block. The road runs past the old gasworks and Donegall Pass, another stronghold, but the murals of King Billy and fallen volunteers marked it as loyalist. The Markets and Donegall Pass are no more than a few minutes' walk from each other but may as well have been in different countries. Of course for the people who lived there, they were.

The road pushes up over the Ormeau Bridge, another flashpoint for some of the darkest days of the Troubles. Orangemen marched and taunted the other side, barricades had been erected, pubs bombed and, on one of the darkest days, marked now by a small plaque, a couple of Prod gunmen had shot four men and a fifteen-year-old boy in Sean Graham's bookies. Catholic and Protestant working-class people had died on the Ormeau Road, and to a stranger it would have been impossible to look at the dead and tell what religion they'd followed or ignored in life. It had been used on too many occasions by paramilitary ASUs as a route from the Markets to their operations, and sometimes it had taken them no more than minutes to leave the area, carry out an attack and be safely back by their fires. Belfast is a small city by any standards, and yet a few yards of territory between two communities represented centuries of mistrust.

Macallan had time to sip some sweet black tea and relax before the high tension hit her when the operation started to move. She looked down at the street again and reflected on how deep the shadows became in Belfast at night. Was it just her imagination? She'd always thought they seemed more threatening in this city, and they'd covered so many tragedies during the Troubles. People were dragged into the shadows and died there, or a dark shape would step out and blast the back of your head off. When you ventured out in this city at night, it was better to stay clear of those dark places.

It was just early evening now and very few of the natives had been brave enough to face the northerly gale that was whipping sleet into the faces of those who had ventured out. She couldn't see any of the police team but she knew they were in place – and just as cold as she was. They were spread all along the route to the ASU's target, which the agent had identified as a uniformed police inspector. The terrorists had located his home address through their intelligence-gathering team and the plan was to kill him in front of his house when he arrived home from his office at HQ. Not so unusual – Special Branch had told any number of officers they'd been targeted and that men with guns were coming for them. Moving home overnight was part of the job, and if it happened – well, you just thanked your God that something wasn't stepping out of those shadows behind you.

Macallan was almost a bystander in this operation, as she was an E Department officer – or what had been known as Special Branch before the Royal Ulster Constabulary had been rebranded as the Police Service of Northern Ireland. It had been part of the deal for peace, a move to make the force more inclusive to the Republican side of the divide. Although the name Special Branch had gone, for the men and women doing the same job it was still the Branch.

She ran the agent who'd provided the information for the job they were working. Wherever possible Branch officers stayed well away from day-to-day contact with dissidents *or operations against them, other than handling the agents who provided so much of the information on their activities. In most cases, the agents had been terrorists during the Troubles or were still involved with the groups who wouldn't give up the fight. They could have been turned by the Branch for all sorts of reasons: sometimes fear, sometimes money, and very often a basic instinct to survive. The majority were hard, dangerous men and women. Without them the Troubles would have been even bloodier, longer, and at one point might have been lost, such was the scale of carnage when it stretched out to the mainland and Europe. As it was, the security forces' penetration of the terrorist groups had crippled their capabilities, and, just as importantly, their will to keep the war going.*

The operation had been handed over to a uniformed firearm team who specialised in these situations. They knew what was required and did it with the minimum of fuss, and if the other side wanted to do it the hard way, then that was fine too. The Branch were loathed by the Republicans, and not always loved by everyone on their own side, who saw them playing by a different set of rules to the men and women facing the terrorists on the street.

The information on this operation had come from one of the most important agents in Northern Ireland, codenamed 'Cowboy'. Macallan had run him for years, and normally would have handed him over to a more junior rank as she picked up her promotions, but he was just too important to lose and provided paramilitary information from the heart of the organisation. It was these dissident groups that were holding up the peace process, and a big push was being made to knock them out or weaken them to the point where they lost the will to fight. Macallan was worried though – Cowboy had been too close too often, and he was starting to panic. Every time she met him he stank of last night's booze, and he was spending too much of the money given to him by the taxpayer. In his world, the only people who had money were either touts or one of the increasing number who transferred their skills into drug dealing and organised crime. The trouble was that Cowboy could never claim to be selling drugs – it wouldn't check out. The peace process was more important than he was; HQ and Whitehall wanted the diehards to hurt as much as possible, and it really didn't matter if the rules were applied when it was done.

At the last meet Cowboy had pleaded with Macallan and her co-handler. He lit one cigarette off another and she wondered how someone with so much time on his hands couldn't clean the crap out of his nails. His fingers were stained yellow and there was a tremor that might have been the drink – or the fact that he knew who was looking for a tout in the ranks.

'For fuck's sake, get me out of this. They know there's someone talking and I'm starting to lose it altogether. There's something in the way the Big Man looks at me now. You know what they'll do if they find out what I've been doing.'

Against her own instincts Macallan had tried to calm him, although she wouldn't have been reassured by the sound of her own voice. 'Look, they're not killing agents now. They're just parading them to embarrass the state and police. This is all part of the move to peace. The top boys have told them that they can attack the military or police but not people who've turned. The worst that could happen is that you'd be ordered to leave Northern Ireland and we'd sort a new life for you.'

She'd stirred her coffee slowly and lied to him again. 'When I get back I'm going to talk to someone, try and get you pulled out so you can start a new life somewhere.'

It had been hard to keep eye contact, to hear the lies from her own mouth. This was what she hated most – the deceit practised on all sides of the conflict and at every level from politicians down.

Cowboy used to feel attracted to Macallan. She was aware of this, played on it, all part of the game. Now he could see it all – he was just the shit on their shoes. He'd filled more than a few cells for them in the Maze and another three volunteers were worm food after an Army ambush for which he'd provided the where and when.

'You know what I think? I think you've fucked me for the last time. I've told you about this job, so just give me my money and I'll be on my way.'

Macallan's stomach had started to rev up, and she'd known the meeting was running out of control. Although Cowboy had been an agent for years, like so many others he was a man bred for violence; agents could and had attacked their handlers when the wheels came off.

Still stirring the coffee that had long since gone cold, she'd said, 'Look, it just doesn't work like that and you know it. I have to know how to get hold of you if there's a problem.'

He'd pushed his face so close to hers that the smell of days-old tobacco and bad Chinese food had nearly made her

8

retch. His eyes had been red rimmed and weary, but she'd been close enough to see what was behind them and had tried to hide her fear. You could never show fear to these men. They would smell it from a distance then turn it on you. Small white flecks had popped at the corners of his mouth, which had become a tight straight line, and his fist had hit the table in front of Macallan.

'Give me my fucking money!'

The co-handler had put his hand on Cowboy's shoulder, easing him back into his chair. He was pure Ulster and knew how to get through to these boys. 'Take it easy, son. We're only talking here. Let me get you a tea and we can all calm down.'

This had been directed at Macallan as much as Cowboy; he'd known she needed to step back.

A few minutes later Cowboy had walked off into the dark. 'What do you think?' Macallan had asked, staring out of a window into complete blackness.

The co-handler had thought for a minute. 'This is Belfast, so who the fuck knows?'

2

Grace Macallan walked through Stockbridge, a bustling, well-heeled artery on the edges of Edinburgh's New Town that led to the leafy playing fields round Fettes College, where Tony Blair claims he first fell in love and played the guitar. She was on her way to Lothian and Borders Police Headquarters to start her new career after her transfer from the PSNI.

She turned into Fettes Avenue and stopped for a moment to look at the dull square HQ building. It was only a short distance from the dominant and beautiful college, which seemed to reinforce the social ladder that separated the haves and have-nots by several rungs in this ancient city.

Even after all her years in the service and everything she'd faced, she was nervous and wished she'd waited another week to stop smoking. But she put that out of her mind. This had to be the new start she'd promised herself when she'd looked back on the

Belfast shoreline for the last time, and there was time for a coffee before she met the deputy chief constable for the script she could probably predict with some accuracy. She'd be welcomed, told she was valued and no doubt there would be a sign behind the DCC's desk confirming that the force was an 'Investor in People'. There would be business speak, a mention of cooperating with partner organisations, but this was the new world, post 9/11, and all the old certainties were gone.

The PSNI, and particularly the Branch, which had been her life, had been insular, suspicious of anyone who wasn't them, and it had been fine to stereotype and hate whomever you wanted. Life in the Troubles had been straightforward, at least in that respect. The peace process and the birth of the PSNI had changed so much, and a new generation of modern police officers had started to elbow the old guard towards the door marked 'retirement'.

Grace Macallan had been born in Bellshill in North Lanarkshire, no more than ten miles from the centre of Glasgow. Her father had worked in the steel mills but ill health and a declining industry had forced him into the ranks of the long-term unemployed. He'd taken out his anger and disappointment with his own life on his wife and daughter, and while his wife had accepted it as a woman's role, Grace had never forgiven him for failing to love her and making her mother's life a misery. Her escapes had been her books, and school, where she'd dreamed of something other than the husband and children that so many of her classmates had clamoured for. Friends had been few but when she was close to someone she had made it special.

She'd stood out as a student to the surprise of her father, who had seemed almost disappointed by her achievements. She'd walked into Edinburgh University to study law and dreamed of making a difference in the world, but after two years she'd realised that she'd taken the wrong road and that arguing fine detail for a living wouldn't make the difference she hoped for. A friend who'd dropped out earlier in the course had joined the police service and convinced her that although the pay wasn't gold plated, working the street made every day an experience.

Macallan had increased the surprise factor for everyone who knew her by ignoring the mainland forces and going for the RUC, not long before the Good Friday Agreement and the drive for peace. She'd loved it, and it had given her a clean break from the childhood and life she'd dreamt of leaving for years. Fourteen weeks hard training in Garnerville in Belfast had only made her hungry for the front line and her instructors had marked her up as a talented prospect. Ulster had still been on a war footing and there'd been enough hard men still in the fight to keep the force's guard up. Macallan'd had to learn fast, and there had been hard lessons waiting for her on Belfast's streets.

Her father died only months after she'd joined the RUC, but she'd never shed a single tear for him. As far as she was concerned, he'd done nothing to deserve her grief. She saw her mother two or three times a year, and more than anything else she pitied her. She'd been as much a victim of her father's bullying as her daughter and was happier without him, although she would never have admitted that to a soul.

Introduced into a world of brawn, Macallan's brain meant she'd been grabbed by SB almost as soon as she was out of her probation. Her flight through the ranks of the Branch had been spectacular for the time, and for a force that had still not come to terms with equality, being a woman had brought some problems. Her rapid promotions hadn't always made her popular, but no one had doubted her ability.

Physically, she'd been on the heavy side as a young woman and the regulation police diet designed for only the strongest arteries hadn't helped. One morning after a heavy-duty retirement party she'd woken up with the hangover from hell and a half-eaten pizza on the pillow next to her. It had been an all-day hangover, and when she'd stared at her reflection in the mirror she'd known it was time for a change in lifestyle. She'd started running the next day and became addicted, and twenty pounds lighter, she looked athletic, her face more angular. She didn't have the looks of a model, but her intelligence showed in her expressive sea-green eyes, and she was often described as 'bookish'. She rarely troubled herself with make-up, and her short copper hair usually left to its own devices, which suited her fine – being a woman with looks in a job knee-deep in testosterone just meant spending your time fighting off unwelcome advances.

Macallan had become a rated agent handler and expert on covert operations against the paramilitaries – covert work her life and her drug. She could hold her head up and know that she'd gained rank through her own efforts rather than by giving it all to the right boss. She'd experienced that kind of proposition and dealt with it by phoning his wife and asking her if it was okay to take up her husband's offer. He'd never troubled her again, and once the story hit the grapevine neither had any of the marrieds.

3

She sipped a bitter black coffee and watched the citizens coming and going in the street outside the cafe almost opposite the HQ building. It confirmed the description she'd had of the area – moneyed and upwardly mobile, for the young smart set. It was a flashy ghetto fifteen minutes' walk from the once drug-wasted schemes on the coastal area of the town that had inspired Irvine Welsh's work.

On time, she walked through the glass doors of Lothian and Borders HQ and entered her new career. She felt a long way from Belfast and its memories as a young, fresh-faced staff officer ferried her along to the Chief Constable's floor. She knew the type. Set aside from the street, kept well away from the bad guys so he could fly up the ladder, train in business speak and talk the same crap as all the other chief officers being churned out of the sausage machine that was command training. She couldn't really blame him –

she was pretty ambitious herself but reassured that at least she'd decided to do it the hard way.

The DCC was on his feet when she entered and did his best to impress her with coffee and a choice between Kit Kats or digestive biscuits. She hated them both but for appearance's sake chose the Kit Kat, and realised she really wasn't that different from the staff officer.

The DCC offered her a seat and she noted how pleasant it was compared with the depressing boxes that passed for office accommodation in Belfast HQ.

'Have you had a chance to look round the city, Grace?' he asked.

She realised she would have to do the pleasantries and indulged the deputy, who was only doing his job. He had an open face, an easy smile and had worked the streets as a detective (and the story was that he was a good one), before deciding he wanted to shoot for the top rather than wreck his liver in investigation. That was fine by her and she warmed to him, but she was waiting for the crucial point, which was where she was going to be placed in the force. Given what had happened in Belfast, she thought they might stick her in a nice, safe administration job and keep her away from problems, but he managed to surprise her.

'You're probably anxious to know where you're going. Well, I'll be frank with you – I know you had a difficult time before you left Belfast.'

She nodded. *Difficult*, she thought. *Is he fucking kidding?*

'What matters to us is that you have a brilliant record in covert operations, and, in relation to the incident in Belfast, you acted with complete integrity. I know it would have been easier for you to keep quiet, but you did the right thing. We've just formed a new major crime team that incorporates all the elements required to take on the top organised groups.'

Macallan found it hard to believe it was that easy and waited for the punchline – but it didn't come. 'It has the full backing of the executive and will be led by Superintendent O'Connor, who's on his way back from a foreign posting in Germany. He's been working as a liaison officer with the BKA – very smart and better than good. He's a big task to get this off the ground and start biting the legs of some of the criminals we've got now. Your work in Belfast will give us experience we don't have, and you'll work closely with Mr O'Connor. How does that sound?'

She found it hard to hide her surprise, but her expression told him she was somewhere between astonished and wanting to give him a hug. She held back on the latter. 'I'm more than happy, sir, and I'll give it my best.'

'I want nothing else. I'm going to put a detective sergeant on your shoulder for a while just to get you used to the native customs – call him an aide or advisor, just to get you into your stride. He's a dinosaur, an absolute pain in the arse – treats everyone senior to him as probably incompetent, but he's one of the best investigators this force has ever produced. He's put more skulls inside than anyone I've ever come across. Don't expect him to love you, but he'll look after you, and just keep clear of him when he's had more than four drinks.' He offered her another Kit Kat but she refused this one. 'His name is Mick Harkins and he's waiting for you down in the main office. Listen to him. He's got his fingers on the pulse of the troops at the front, can smell a problem three days before it ruins careers and the criminals take pride in being abused by him.'

She saw the humour crinkling at the corners of his eyes and decided she liked him.

'Thank you, sir. I've a feeling I know the type. Every force seems to have one.'

He extended his hand. 'Good luck, Grace. Do us proud.'

She left the office and the deputy leaned back in his seat with the feeling that he'd just been in conversation with someone special. She'd said next to nothing but he'd seen what all the fuss was about, looked again at her record and shook his head. She'd done more in her years in Northern Ireland than most would do in ten careers. He'd often wondered how so many of those Northern Ireland officers had kept sane during the Troubles but knew enough of them to understand that they'd paid in alcoholism, broken marriages and too many suicides. He wondered what had made Macallan bypass Strathclyde and opt for the extreme dangers she'd faced in Belfast.

He put her file into his out tray and hoped he'd done the right thing sending her to Major Crime and Mick Harkins.

4

After managing to walk into the wrong office and collecting glares from a couple of computer operators eating lunch, Macallan found the new office for the MCT. It stank of fresh but cheap paint and looked about half-finished given the desks being humped into place. The windows were wide open and she guessed the scruff gnawing a mince pie and gulping a full-strength Coca-Cola was Mick Harkins. She wondered whether these guys were all descended from the same primitive form of life and smiled at the thought. The truth was that they were the backbone in an investigation and seemed to be allowed slightly more leeway than the rest of the gang.

He looked up and then back at his racing section, although he must have guessed who she was or he wasn't the detective described by the deputy. 'Sorry, love, the Family Protection Unit's along the corridor,' he said.

She realised that in this man's universe the Family Protection Unit wasn't part of the real police world and might as well have been staffed by social workers. Macallan knew she was going to like him – it took class to act that well – but she decided to let him do his thing. 'Please don't feel sorry. I'm DCI Macallan and I wondered whether there were any police officers about – but I'll leave you to get on with the furniture removals.'

He looked up and the inside edges of his eyebrows pulled together in a sentiment which, if spoken, might have been, 'I do the cynical fucking jokes, dear.' No apologies, but he did manage to stand up and put the pie and Coke down. 'I'm DS Harkins and thought you might be having a bit of lunch with the deputy.'

'I've seen him, Sergeant, and was just keen to get on with it. Is there somewhere we can sit or do I have an office?'

She started to note the small details on the man and thought he must have been quite a looker at one time, but the years, untipped cigarettes and spending too much time in darkened bars had roughed up his face. Still, he had a full head of hair that was thick, short and heavily flecked with silver, and the dark brown eyes with a touch of the hangdog in their angle reminded her of John Hurt – minus a few million wrinkles.

'Your office is only half done, but there's a couple of chairs in there, and I'll get us some tea.'

She was pleased that he seemed to have dropped the old cynic act so quickly, and she hoped they wouldn't need to do the nose-to-nose thing to confirm who was boss.

Her office was small but looked onto playing fields, and she had to admit that she'd worked in a lot worse. She imagined getting the room into shape with her own mementos gathered over the years and could see her awards, plaques and pictures making the best of the thin white paint underneath. Some people called that kind of decoration an 'ego wall' but it would make the room feel like hers in this new, and still strange, world. She started to relax and realised that she could survive at least this first day.

Harkins handed her a steaming cup of leather-strong tea and she wondered how long it had been since the cup had been washed. There was a touch of lipstick round the edges and she tried to ignore the other stains.

'Can I call you Mick?' He nodded and waited for her to speak. 'Just brief me as best you can. I know this is all up in the air at the moment but tell me what we've got, what we're getting and whatever you think I need to know. While we're at it, I need you to tell me when I'm about to walk into a cupboard rather than finding the way out.'

He smiled. It was a tired but good smile and, having heard the stories of what this woman had been through, meant giving her a break. He was wise enough to know that whatever her sins, few of the men and women he knew could have taken her journey. That didn't mean he would go easy on her. *Fuck that,* he thought, *I'm not changing the habits of a lifetime.*

21

Macallan hardly spoke for the next hour as Harkins gave her more than she could have asked for, delivered by someone who knew exactly what he was talking about, with not the slightest hint of bullshit. There was no pretence, no self-promotion, just a man doing what was asked. She realised that the deputy had known exactly what he was doing pairing them up, and although there would be a few tussles along the way with Harkins, it would be a price worth paying.

He looked at his cup and asked her if she needed a refill. She decided that her immune system didn't deserve whatever was lurking in her mug but told him to go ahead. She knew he'd be a smoker, would be ready for a blow, and told him to take the break. 'See you back here when you're ready, Mick.'

He'd given her enough to get on with, and when he came back she would take a chance and get the cards on the table early, as she guessed Harkins would just want to get to plain talking as soon as possible. She headed for the ladies and wondered if they would be as bad as the tea mugs. She hoped not.

When Harkins returned, she leaned forward and looked at the floor before trying to fix eye contact with him. 'Tell me about yourself. No crap.'

That tired smile again as he started to tell the story he wore as a badge of honour. 'I guess the deputy will have told you something, and it'll be along the lines that I'm a problem.'

She stopped him.

'He told me that you were a pain in the arse but one of the best investigators the force has ever produced.'

'One of the best? That ungrateful bastard should have said *the* best!'

They both smiled.

'You came from a tough force, so you'll know someone like me. I was a young star, promoted to detective sergeant in front of a line of great detectives, and I thought I was the Messiah. I was just too good, it came easy to me and I just loved mixing it with the bad guys, so played it hard but loved it. Ruined a few relationships and ignored the advice of a few older heads. I could have climbed right to the top, but I'm basically bolshie just for the sake of it. You'll hear the legends from others, but it became an annual event that at some function or Christmas drinks I'd make a point of collaring whoever was the most senior officer and telling them exactly what I thought. As I was always pissed at those things, it was normally a load of shite. I'd wake up in the morning and realise that the next promotion was moving further and further towards the horizon. I still do it, and with only a year to go I'm definitely not going to be chief constable now. That kind of sums me up, but you'll hear more versions from other people. I would say that about half of the stories about me are true and I suppose that's bad enough. You could call me an underachiever in some ways.' He looked straight at her and shrugged.

'Okay, and thanks for being frank. I'll learn the rest as we go along, but please be gentle with me if we go for a drink.'

'No chance, Chief Inspector. I've a reputation to maintain.'

They both smiled again and realised they could work together with a bit of forgiveness on both sides. Macallan relaxed and asked the question.

'What's the reaction to me then? I know you'll have checked me out and would expect nothing else. I want this to work and won't hide behind the desk.'

He looked at her and saw the small premature lines at the corners of her eyes. 'Look, these guys have heard the stories and like all good policemen are making up a load that never happened. Some will just tar you with sticking in another cop, but they live in the now. If you do the business then they'll soon forget, and you know that's how it is in this job. We all deal with too much shite to ignore something that's good. You do the job, and you'll get them behind you. You can't hurt me because I'm too close to the winning post, and believe me, if you fuck up, I'll be the first one knocking at the door. It's easy: just don't fuck up, or if you do, make sure you've fucked up for the right reasons.'

'What about O'Connor?'

He took his time, considering whether it would stay in the room. She knew what was going on, and with good reason. These conversations rarely stayed in confidence and tended to be thrown in someone's face during a battle of egos. It was how the job worked. Finally he said, 'Repeat this and I'll use all my dark powers against you.'

She raised her hands and smiled. 'You have it, Mick. I've heard some of the stories you've not disclosed to me, such as you eat criminal's babies.'

He smiled. 'That's only partly true, like most of the stories about me. O'Connor is seriously smart. Academic background, and when he talks he knows his subject. I've done quite a few jobs for him in the past, and he tends only to have success. He's a deep one, though, and tends not to mix off-duty. As you well know, that's not the norm for criminal investigation. It confuses the troops, so as always they make up what they don't know. He's not married and has never tried it on with a woman in the job, which has to be one for the *Guinness Book of Records*. Of course, for a few guys this is evidence enough that he's gay, but like some of the stories about me, it's crap. I know he keeps his love life away from the job and has had a few short, meaningless relationships that went absolutely nowhere. My guess is the guy just wants the job and there's no real time for anything else. He's ambitious, and apart from the force he's done all these high-profile secondments to the Met, the UN in the Balkans and now this job in Germany with the BKA. He's not used to anyone being anywhere near as smart as he is, so you'll be a challenge for him. I like him, and if there's a problem, it's that I've not seen him deal with a case that isn't getting solved. He might be fine, but that's how I think the great ones prove themselves. There's no test in the easy cases. Will that do you?'

'Last question. Why do they call him JJ?'

'Just one of those things. He used to be John O'Connor, then when people realised that he liked jazz, he became Jazz O'Connor and then they joined it all up and he became JJ. I should have mentioned that I see that as a problem, because, to be quite frank, who the fuck likes jazz in criminal investigation?'

Macallan nodded. 'I'm with you there.'

He looked at his watch. 'We should have a drink, and I can bore you with some war stories about why I'm actually the best detective this force has ever produced.'

Macallan nodded, trying to buy time, assessing whether it was a bad idea when she was just in the door. 'Okay, Mick, but don't think it buys you any favours and you're on the bell.'

Harkins grinned, pulling on his jacket. 'Let's do it. I know the very place.'

Macallan opened the door of her rented flat after four drinks with Harkins, then remembered the advice she'd received from the deputy. She was knackered. It was a mixture of the adrenaline crash after her morning nerves and her introduction to 80-shilling ale. She didn't even drink beer and wondered how Harkins had managed to convince her to try it. But she felt relaxed for the first time in weeks and realised she had a chance to make a new life, when that had seemed such an impossible dream only months before.

She had just enough energy to kick off her shoes and flop back on the bed before she fell head first into the land of sleep and dreams.

The Belfast Incident

After the meeting with Cowboy, Macallan headed for HQ to report the planned attack on the inspector. The room doors in the E Department corridors were closed, as usual. A door left open where men and women were poring over intelligence reports from agents and bugs could cost someone their job. They'd learned through bitter experience that the security of secret material had to be absolute. Agents had been killed after poorly handled meetings in public places or sensitive material being handed over by rogue elements in the service. The problems had been taken on, and no excuses were accepted for loose talk or failing to protect the information that had saved lives in both Ulster and the mainland.

Macallan pleaded with her commander to extract Cowboy. 'He's coming apart, sir. I just don't think he can survive scrutiny from the team looking for the source.'

The man opposite her was a bear. Born and bred in Ulster, he feared his Protestant God but nothing else in this world. He'd fought the paramilitaries who'd made two attempts on his life and always regarded him as a top target. It would have made most men lose the odd night's sleep, but not him, and he took it as a compliment that they bothered to try. Macallan didn't impress him at all. He felt that this was a man's war; they could put women on the front line, but as far as he was concerned they were passengers who caused more bother than they were worth. This one was even worse – an academic record in law and to his mind she should have become a lawyer, where she could have spent all day in a wig defending the indefensible.

He sipped a fresh tea and made sure that she'd not been offered one.

'Chief Inspector Macallan, I think the problem is that you've been handling this agent too long, and to an extent that's our fault. He was just too good, and in the past we'd probably have pulled him by now, but times have changed.

The war's over. It's just that some of those boys don't know it yet. To be honest, it'll finish with or without him and the push from London is to get whatever results we can. When this is over I'm going to retire and plant vegetables, so I'm not going to argue with them about it.' His voice rose a tone and some colour crept through his normally pale cheeks. 'I really don't care about this agent. We're nearly done with him anyway, so let's just get what we can from him. If he ends face up in the gutter with flies laying eggs in his dead eyes then so be it. Is that understood, Chief Inspector?'

Macallan knew a lost cause when it was explained by a police commander who was close to his God. 'That's clear, sir, but I would have been failing in my duty not to bring this to your attention.'

The colour in his cheeks deepened, and he thought that she was just too smart. 'Your duty, Chief Inspector, is to close the door on the way out and hopefully we'll have a good result tonight with another two locked up or apologising in front of their Maker.'

She gave up and tried not to scream as she left the room.

Macallan opened her eyes and thought she was back in Belfast before recognising it was just the dreams again. She was soaked with sweat and realised she must have left the heating on. She swore tiredly, struggled out of her clothes and dropped them in a heap next to the bed before she padded into the tiny bathroom – described by the estate agent as 'nicely proportioned' – and splashed water on her face.

'It's fine, Grace,' she mouthed into the mirror.

She slept again and didn't dream.

5

Setting up the new unit was just what Macallan needed. It gave her something to bite into before O'Connor arrived.

Gradually the new team drifted in, a few at a time. It was ever thus and the good ones had to be prised out of the hands of their old bosses. When someone didn't turn up on time, it was normally followed by a call from their gaffer explaining why they needed to keep them for a while. But Harkins, like a member of the old Royal Navy press gangs, would pull on his jacket and come back a few hours later with the missing man or woman in tow. Whether it was true or not, the story was that Harkins had the goods on the vast majority of ranked officers and wasn't afraid to use a bit of friendly blackmail. Macallan thought it was probably his powers of persuasion, but she knew that the legends worked to his advantage so no one was sure what was true. She was certain he'd started some of them himself, just to keep in the canteen headlines.

The new squad room started to buzz with the energy of so many young men and women who just wanted to get out and do the job. In some cases, the ambition was to be another Harkins, although in the modern service that was probably best discouraged.

Macallan stared out of her office window, feeling the energy of something new. Her emotions lifted by the day. She knew enough to realise that they were close to starting their operations, that there would be tough days ahead and, in fact, tough would be okay. It was avoiding Mr Fuck Up that was the real trick.

She folded her arms, closed her eyes and, as she did almost every day, thought of her mentor and friend Bill Kelly, and her promise to him. He had been her inspector when she'd first joined the RUC, eventually rising to the rank of assistant chief constable. He had transferred from the Met as a young man looking for a challenge. He got it and was shot by a PIRA gunman after only a year in Northern Ireland. He was one of the lucky ones – he survived and was back on the job after only three months, though the gunman still visited him in the odd dream. He'd known when he met Macallan as a raw recruit that she had something – the bonus was that she was a thinker in a war that lacked thinkers. His advice was always given quietly, and through time she had come to rely on him when she had a problem that needed a wiser head. She'd never felt any physical attraction to him, just absolute trust in his friendship and his ability to fill in the gaps left by her father. He was the only man in her life who'd never let her down, and he'd kept her sane in the darkest days of the sectarian war.

She opened her eyes, took a deep breath and called Harkins into the office. As always, he kept her waiting; it was all part of the ritual to show the troops on the shop floor that he actually ran the squad.

'Grab a seat. I just wanted to get your thoughts on how ready we are if the sky falls on us.'

'We're good, almost there, got some good people and a great mix. The surveillance and investigation units are ready now, although we're still waiting on some intelligence analysts, but they're on their way.'

'Good. I'm going along to see the chief and tell him where we are. I know there are a pile of jobs the divisions want to pass to us, and requests for joint operations with other forces and agencies.'

The door opened and John O'Connor walked in.

'Mick, I thought they would have jailed you by now. You might actually make your pension.'

Harkins shook his hand, but O'Connor was already turning to Macallan. 'You must be Grace. I've heard so much about you – it's great you're on the team.'

He pushed his hand out and she had to admit to being impressed. He looked more like a city lawyer than a working detective, and standing next to Mick, the contrast couldn't have been more striking. The shoes were actually polished, while it was hard to tell if Mick's were suede or just dirty. The suit was designer, the greying hair side-parted and just a bit old-fashioned. He was a big man, and she could see how he would dominate a room. What worried her was that he reminded her of someone in Belfast ...

Macallan had only had a few brief relationships in Northern Ireland and kept them away from the job. The boys in the RUC were fit but they faced danger every day, sometimes having to scrape up the remnants of a human being after a bomb blast. They saw their friends maimed and killed, and tried to squeeze as much life into any time off as was humanly possible.

When she had finally become involved with a man it had been unexpected – overwhelming. She'd first met Jack Fraser through the courts. He was a barrister, and a good one, working for the Crown Prosecution Service in Belfast. She'd bumped into him a couple of times at functions and his body language had told her all she needed to know. He was attracted to her but he was married, although it seemed to be common knowledge that the marriage was in trouble. He was physically attractive, tall and a lifelong rugby player, so built to please. His nose had been broken on the rugby field, but if anything that just added cream to the cake. He was everything she wasn't: upper middle class and educated at the best school money could buy. If there'd been a problem it was vanity, but she'd known that this type of package came with vanity built in to the genes. She could forgive that. The big bonus was that he could make Grace Macallan laugh – and that was no easy feat. He'd eventually asked her to go for a drink, and they'd become lovers by the end of the first evening. She'd regretted going that far that quickly and had thought it would just be one of those one-night stands that she'd so carefully avoided. She hadn't realised that he'd recognised her as someone different from the pack and had heard through his RUC connections what had made her stand out in the dirty war being fought in Ulster. She'd never been involved with a married man, but she'd believed him when he'd said his relationship was all but finished. The Troubles meant that he could always find an excuse to spend a night with her and they'd started to discuss a future together. She warmed at the thought of those nights sharing a bed. She'd adored those times after they'd made love, when he would lie behind her with those huge arms pulling her against his warm belly, his breath on her neck as they drifted off together...

As O'Connor closed the door behind Harkins he smiled broadly. 'Sorry I've arrived so late in the day, Grace. I'm not going to get in your road today. I just wanted to see how we were placed to start work. I'm going to see the Chief and if we're not ready, I'd rather just tell him.'

He made notes as she briefed him and she could see that this was someone who didn't miss things. She promised herself only to lie to him when she was sure she could get away with it. He seemed to be impressed with her progress, and a little surprised that they were on schedule.

'You've done a great job; it's going to make my life a lot easier. To be honest, I've been in Germany for nearly three years and feel a bit out of touch, so I think we're both going to be on a big learning curve. Is there anything I can do for you at the moment? And before you answer, I'm going to buy you a pub lunch tomorrow so we can talk a bit more.'

She thought that his accent was pure public school, and a good one. The Scottish accent was still there but almost concealed beneath the small fortune his father must have paid for his education.

'A pub lunch would be good for me. I honestly thought the canteen in Belfast HQ served the worst food on the planet, but this one runs it close. Otherwise I'm fine, and I have to say that Mick Harkins has been worth his weight – and we've not fallen out yet.'

'That's just him luring you into a false sense of security, Grace. Keep letting him think he's the boss and you might survive without needing major surgery. I've had him on a few cases in the past and he keeps order among the troops when things get hard. I can tell you that he's not got long to go and getting this lot beaten into shape will be a personal-pride issue for him. This is his legacy; I pity the poor detectives out there who don't pull their weight. I'll see you tomorrow for that lunch and pick you up here.'

Without waiting for an answer, he was out of the door. Macallan tried to put her thoughts together and decide what she thought of O'Connor. He seemed to have breezed into the office and left, leaving her slightly dazed. He was that type though – big projected image and absolute belief in himself. No bad thing. Through the force of his personality, O'Connor would get resources where others might fail these days. She hated to admit it but he was attractive, and given her love life in Belfast, she realised that his type must push her buttons. Well, she wasn't going there again.

She decided to stop off and have a drink on the way back to her flat, so she headed down the short set of steps to the Bailie in Stockbridge, which had been a favourite drinking hole for a generation of CID and Crime Squad detectives. She felt relaxed in the semi-darkness of the bar and climbed on a bar stool as far away from the nearest drinker as she could get – she just wanted to read the paper in peace. She ordered a large glass of red wine, spread the paper on the bar, then shook her head and muttered at the latest antics in Westminster. On page four, she noticed a few paragraphs about a paramilitary attempt to kill a policeman in Londonderry. She locked into the text and felt her heart beat just a bit faster. It still had that effect, and although the attempt had been disrupted and arrests made, it stirred the memories…

The Belfast Incident
Cowboy had identified an arms stash to Macallan and said that two paramilitaries had picked up weapons from the dump to carry out the attack. There was enough firepower hidden in these streets to stop a train, and if there was a skirmish, then those Republican heroes would lose. That didn't stop her worrying, because these operations never went to plan. She did what she always did in these situations: wondered what the fuck she was doing there in the

first place. She was in a stinking disused industrial building and the only company she had was some dead pigeons and a security service officer with personal hygiene problems. She was tired of this war, but then everyone was. Peace, whatever that meant, had arrived in Northern Ireland, but there were still a few lunatics who couldn't see what the smart paramilitaries had seen years before. Some still wanted to play the game – they just missed the war and what it gave to them.

During the height of the Troubles, PIRA were disciplined and operated along military lines, but you just never knew what would happen with these nutters. She'd often thought about all those men and women she'd helped put in the Maze and Maghaberry prisons and whether it had done any good or just made the situation worse. She lit another cigarette that she didn't want. HMP Maze – the name always brought a rueful smile to her face. Christ, the INLA even managed to hit the loyalist Billy 'King Rat' Wright in the Maze. You had to give it to them – they had balls! That stark collection of H Blocks had become an asylum taken over by the lunatics. Discos, Christmas parties with your choice of drugs thrown in and paramilitary parades in full uniform. It was all possible in there.

The adrenalin pumped her back to reality as the radio hissed into life with a message from the surveillance team. The two targets were reported moving towards the car identified by Cowboy as the transport for the job. Macallan breathed more easily. That was a big boost. Identifying the car made their life easier. It had been bugged so that the surveillance team could keep well back until the arrest was made. She was only an observer, but her nerves were firing up – she couldn't get Cowboy and his problems out of her head now that the operation had started.

They listened to another message from the surveillance team. One of the targets had placed a heavy bag in the boot of the car. In Macallan's mind another piece of information clicked into the picture. The bag had to be the 'weps', so it was going to plan, but they were dealing with a bunch of psychos – every time they were involved, the operation had to fly by the seat of its pants. It didn't really make any difference; she'd delivered the information to the arrest teams and it was now out of her control.

'Stutter' Doyle placed the loaded bag into the back of the car as he'd been told to do by the paramilitary intelligence officer. His partner for the job was Bobby Connery, who closed the door of his small red-brick home in the Markets, blew into his hands and pulled the collar up on a paper-thin jacket that did nothing to keep out the cold. As he always did when he left his home, he looked all around the area for any sign of Peelers. Doyle was agitated, but then he always was. 'Will ye move yer fucking arse, Bobby, and let's get this done.'

Connery smiled. 'Yer a bad tempered fucker on a good day, Tommy.'

No one called Tommy Doyle 'Stutter' to his face, and the last man drunk enough to try it had lost an eye. Doyle got his moniker through a stammer that only got worse when his stress levels were high, which was most of the time. The stammer didn't fool anyone who knew him though, and certainly not Connery, who often described Doyle as a 'violent cunt', which, coming from someone who'd delivered two men to their Maker and damaged a few others, was praise indeed.

Connery walked over to the car and got behind the wheel. He was too confident by far for most, but he could drive a car with a blindfold on and was born to the trade. As a younger man, he'd driven on a few post-office robberies and made his name leaving a police pursuit vehicle on its roof after holding up a small bank on the outskirts of Belfast. After a couple of spells inside, he'd decided it would be more of a kick to get into the war. PIRA thought he was a nutter but welcomed him with open arms – he was their kind of nutter. He got on Doyle's nerves and wherever possible he tried to ignore him.

Doyle levered himself into the front passenger seat and slammed the door shut. His guts hurt again and the cold had drained his face of colour, apart from the roadmap of broken veins that testified to his weakness for cheap whisky. He couldn't say he liked whisky these days; he just needed it to deaden the reality of what his life had become. He hoped Connery would shut the fuck up and not ask too many stupid questions, but he knew that wasn't going to happen – certainly not on this night.

'Have you figured out yet, Tommy, why we're taking a bag of scrap metal for a run round Belfast in this fuckin' weather, 'cause I certainly don't know?'

Doyle thought that Connery was too fuckin' thick to work it out, but he knew full well what it was about, although the Big Man hadn't told him. He lit a cigarette, which just annoyed the pain in his gut. He'd been in the paramilitaries a long time, done some years behind the wire and didn't know anything but the war against the Brits, plus some feuding within the organisation itself that had taken a few lives to settle things down again. He was getting weary of it, just too old now, and for the first time in his life he worried about the future. The thought of peace terrified him, and he'd no other purpose or use in life. He couldn't change a fuckin' light bulb. He never had more than a few notes in his pocket, and when he did, it went on booze and the odd bet that just kept the bookies happy.

Tommy Doyle was short, had been stocky but was starting to look worn at the edges; what had once been hard muscle was beginning to sag through lack of use. His hair was like a wet black hand slapped on the top of his head, and no matter which way he tried to comb it, there was never enough to go round. The pub fights plus a bit of boxing when he was a younger man had thickened his eyebrows, and his nose had been broken so many times it had retreated into his face to hide from the next bout. He wondered what they were fighting for now though, and it choked him that those boys who'd been proud to serve in PIRA were sitting down with the Brits and making sure they were in a good place come the day. Worse still if they were filling their wallets with tout money. He was still trying to put up a fight, although every time they moved there was a team of Peelers in the way. There was a tout somewhere close and he rubbed his eyes, trying to get the thoughts out of his head. There wasn't a single good thing in his life and people wondered why he'd such a short fuse!

They'd been told to run around specific roads with the bag and had only been briefed less than an hour before. No weps were to be carried and, if they were stopped, they were to keep it shut with no lip to the Peelers. They were onto a tout – no doubt about it – and this run on a cold winter's night was the bait. The Big Man must have a suspect, must have fed him some shite story to give to his handler and they were on their way. Well, that was all right with Doyle. He just hoped they made the bastard suffer before they put one in his brain.

'F-fuckin drive will ye, B-Bobby, before we die of old age,' he said finally.

The car moved slowly forward towards the Ormeau Road, and the electronic device plumbed into the car's undercarriage flicked into life, telling the surveillance team exactly where Doyle and Connery were headed. Macallan knew all about them. As far as she was concerned they were both unpredictable nutters, and if they were stopped they would kick off unless an awful lot of guns were stuck in their faces.

She decided to try Cowboy at the agreed number, but the voice that answered was someone else. It asked her who she was looking for and she tried a bogus name and the wrong number routine. The voice said that the person she was looking for wasn't available and had been taken away on urgent business. The phone clicked dead on her and she tried not to panic. She grabbed the mic to call for an abort on the operation, only to be beaten to it by the firearms leader calling for the team to close on the car and detain the occupants.

6

O'Connor arrived at Macallan's office right on time. She'd expected nothing else. *Okay*, she thought, *he's the boss, but it's nice to go for a pub lunch with a man and it's been too long.* It dawned on her that this was a good sign – the problems in Belfast and then the break-up with her lover had dampened her more basic instincts almost to extinction. It was one of those rare occasions where the sun shone in Edinburgh so they walked through Stockbridge and filled in some background for each other with small talk. He was easier company than she'd imagined, and despite his reputation of being a very private guy, he was interesting – though the conversation always came back to work. She got what Harkins had told her about him and his ambition: anything less than reaching the rank of chief constable would be failure for this man.

They managed to find the last two seats in a decent pub and she thought she'd make the right impression by having the veggie option, when what she wanted was the steak pie and chips. O'Connor chose the salad and she thought that was probably what he wanted – definitely not a steak-pie man. There was no doubt in her mind that he was very controlled, disciplined and quite a contrast from a lot of the alpha males she'd worked with in Northern Ireland. This was the future face of senior policing.

O'Connor liked what he saw in Macallan and had spent a lot of time looking into her background. She had the most outstanding record he'd seen in a long time, and that might have worried him, as he instinctively mistrusted anyone with a CV that came near to matching his own. There weren't many about that could do that. Macallan was educated although she'd dropped her law degree, and, unlike his education, hers was not paid for by family wealth. She'd done it all against the paramilitaries and had received a string of commendations. However, he knew about the incident in Belfast, so she was unlikely to overtake him in the promotion race and there would be caution for a while before she was considered for another rank. He liked her though, and her reserve appealed to him. He preferred to stay clear of the job off-duty and it was rare to feel so comfortable in police company. Her eyes were striking, the tiniest slant suggestive of Slavic blood somewhere in her family genes, and he thought she was good-looking rather than pretty or beautiful. She didn't smile enough, but when she did he saw something he liked, and when they were discussing something she cared about, there would be a small blaze in the eyes. O'Connor was enough of a politician to realise that she'd attract friends and enemies; her talent and intellect would trouble some of the less gifted who happened to outrank her. In that strange way that men can self-deceive, it didn't occur to him that he might be in both camps.

O'Connor opened up about his background – it had been privileged, and the family had made a fortune in a transport business. His father had humble enough beginnings but realised as a young man that he knew better than his boss. He'd been right, and it seemed that O'Connor had inherited his father's driving ambition. Like Macallan, his decision to join the police had surprised his friends – and infuriated his father, who'd wanted him in the business. He'd always been fascinated by police work and admitted to being a fan of detective stories.

Macallan relaxed with his mild soul-bearing and decided an admission to liking detective stories made him at least half human. She wondered if that's why he liked jazz – life imitating art. There was still a gnawing worry that she seemed to be hitting it off with both Harkins and O'Connor and she just didn't think it should be this easy. She promised to protect herself and not get too close too soon – she was still dealing with the wounds picked up in Belfast.

The plus side was that whatever was coming the way of the MCT, it looked likely they had the right mix of people to handle it. As for O'Connor, she thought he was too ambitious, but that whoever led such a high-profile team had to be. In this service there was a constant battle for resources and she knew that O'Connor could probably outmanoeuvre anyone who stood in his way. If she could stay on board with him, she knew that he'd be a powerful ally. She'd spent her career doing it her way, but she was wise enough to know that to succeed, you had to be part politician and make sure you didn't piss off the right people.

Real politicians knew this already. How often had she heard a talking head from Westminster say that little can be achieved in opposition? Still, she was what she was, and where it mattered, her instincts were to face up to a problem. If it meant a bit of a battle, then that's where it would go.

They left the pub after a couple of hours, walking slowly back to HQ without saying too much. They didn't need to and just enjoyed the lowering sun, which painted the damp trees and streets in reds and gold. They had become comfortable with each other in a short time and relished the moment. Both O'Connor and Macallan had few close friends and both could fairly be described as isolated characters, so this had been a good afternoon.

Macallan watched the citizens pass her by and realised that she was starting to see them as just other people rather than trying to read every face that might be giving her too much eye contact or pulling a concealed weapon. She knew she would have to accept that this was a different place. She wanted this new life so much – to trust people again – and she was starting to ache for physical contact. No one had put their arms round her since Belfast.

The Belfast Incident

She gripped the edge of the window and looked down on a textbook stop – everyone in the right place, and Doyle and Connery stepping out of the car, doing exactly what they were told. It proved she was watching one part of a set-up. She called the 24-hour duty desk to get backup out looking for Cowboy, but she already knew it was over.

Macallan had been right to worry about those shadows. Far enough away not to be obvious but close enough to see the Peelers do their best, the dissident intelligence officer saw everything he needed to see. This was no routine stop – a firearms team had been waiting for the volunteers and that was case closed. He spoke quietly to himself, using Cowboy's true name: 'Well, that's you fucked then, Bertie Gallagher.'

At that very moment, Gallagher was being transported in the boot of a car to a safe house, where as much information as possible would be extracted before he was given his red card.

Doyle and Connery were lying on the ground while the arrest team checked the car for weps or explosives. When they opened the bag, no one needed to explain that the operation had been organised on shite information or a set-up, but that wasn't their problem and meant they could get an early finish away from the streets.

One of the arrest officers was Jackie Crawford. Not the smartest of God's creatures but hard, fit and perfect for the 'heavy team'. He was popular with the boys, built like a light heavyweight boxer, which was exactly what he was at amateur level, and a top amateur at that. Like so many others he came from a police family that had sacrificed much during the Troubles. His father had been a uniformed sergeant in Londonderry and lost part of his left leg in a sniping job in the city. He survived, but worse was to come for the Crawfords when his brother, Billy, a constable in Bessbrook, South Armagh, was ambushed on his way to the station. He'd been taken alive by a PIRA active service unit and his body bore the signs of torture when he was found over the border in the Republic.

The firearms team leader was satisfied that the car was clean and the boys in the car would be taken to Antrim Serious Crime Suite to be interviewed; CID would take care of that end of the business. They'd be delighted at that, knowing the whole fucking thing was a set-up – that Doyle and Connery could just sit there and laugh in their faces.

Doyle was handcuffed and the team leader told Jackie Crawford to take him over to a van for transport back to Antrim. Doyle recognised Crawford right away, remembered watching the young boxer who was quite a handful and had seen him when they were scouting the Peelers for targets in Belfast. He knew all about the Crawford family but felt nothing about that particular tragedy other than 'fuck them, they're Peelers'. The Big Man had told Doyle to say nothing if they were stopped, and he'd meant it. 'Shut the fuck up, smile and you'll be back on the street in no time. Do you hear what I say, Tommy? It's important.' Doyle had heard what the Big Man had said, but he was cold, felt like shite and this was too good a chance to miss.

Macallan watched the scene from her OP, trying to work

out what would be the best move for her. Branch officers would already be on the job, trying to contact agents who might know where Cowboy was being held. If they got him alive, she would take him away from Belfast herself and the commander could stick her in a uniform – it didn't matter any more. She wished again that she were in bed with Jack.

She watched the young officer walk Doyle towards a van as the rest of the team either stood down or tried to get the car off the road to let the traffic move again. Doyle looked like a child against the bulk of the Peeler who was guiding him. She wondered how someone the size of Doyle could have caused so much mayhem, but that was often the way and most Peelers agreed that the 'wee men' were the worst.

Doyle looked up at Jackie Crawford and realised that when the war was over he would no longer be the enemy or a 'legitimate target'. Well, fuck that. He smiled when he spoke to Crawford. 'I saw you f-fight, young man. B-boxed meself, so like to see a good fighter. You still doing it then?'

Crawford didn't really want to discuss life with Doyle, but then nothing had been found in the car and he'd be out on the street the next morning. The man looked ill and past his best, so why not humour him? 'Still fighting and love it. Best sport in the world. Where did you box then?'

Doyle ignored the question. 'Know your family as well. That cunt of a father of yours, has he grown another leg yet?'

Doyle arched his back in pain as his arm was squeezed. Crawford was built like a gorilla but remembered the training. 'Don't let them get into your head – that's what they want.'

Although Doyle felt like his arm was breaking, this

47

would make a good story for the boys over a drink; he could take an awful lot of pain. 'Y-you know what I heard, young man? I heard that when the boys hooded that b-brother of yours, he squealed like a f-fuckin' girl before they stamped his ticket. Pissed in his p-pants, he did.'

They were beside the van now and Crawford's training couldn't stop the anger welling up from the soles of his boots. He hit Doyle twice in the belly – and realised how frail the man was. Doyle went down on his knees, gasping to get air into his lungs, and his aching guts hit him with more pain that he'd ever endured. Crawford had to hand it to him; he was a tough little fucker – just knelt there on the ground dealing with what was surging through his body. Crawford leaned over Doyle and whispered in his ear, 'How did you like that then? Sting a bit, did it?'

Macallan watched this little incident in shock and real- ised the whole night was turning to rat shit. She'd tried to ignore the spook as much as possible that night, as he'd made it clear there was nothing in it for him and that he was only there under orders as an observer, but now ... 'Did you see that?' she asked him.

He had been putting his gear together. 'Sorry no, getting my stuff wrapped up. Anything interesting?'

She looked round at him and lit another cigarette. 'One of the support team just floored Stutter.'

The spook looked bored, sighed and carried on packing his bag. 'In that case, I definitely saw fuck all. I'll be on my way.'

Doyle vomited on Crawford's boots and the pain came under control. He'd never let any man see him fall over and cry. He looked up at the Peeler's face. 'Give me a hand up there, son. I'm f-freezing me bollocks off on this street. When we get to the cells, I'll have two s-sugars if you don't mind.'

In the rear of the van, he rested the back of his head against the cold wall and prayed that this would pass quickly so he could get back to the street. He knew he had a long night ahead of him. He would be grilled by the CID asking the same stupid questions over and over again. Still, it was what had to be done for the cause. The only problem was that he was having trouble with what that cause was supposed to represent.

Macallan thought of all the training that went into keeping these guys from crossing the line, but Doyle had obviously hit a raw nerve with the young Peeler. She'd had enough, would leave it to CID and pick it up first thing in the morning. She'd head back to the office to see if anything had come in on Cowboy, but she knew the answer to that already. The following day would be hard enough, and the thought of explaining it all to the commander meant she'd have a very large drink before hitting her mattress tonight.

By the time Macallan was opening her front door, Cowboy's body was being dumped near the docks in Belfast. They'd wanted it to be found to send a clear message to the Brits that there were volunteers still in the fight.

7

Macallan hardly noticed the next few weeks passing, and getting the MCT working burned up all the time anyone on the team had. She found that O'Connor tended to let her get on with running the MCT while he played his politics. They worked well together, but there was no time for socialising and getting to bed at night was enough until the team was running smoothly. There was warmth when she spoke to him, and they both knew that somewhere down the line there was more to discover. She was starting to remember and feel those small human emotions that had been numbed in Belfast – the banter in the squad room that was barely politically correct, Harkins pretending he wasn't human then giving her a wink, and most of all, the way she had to try and break off eye contact with O'Connor. It felt good, healthy, and she realised how lonely she'd been and that she didn't want to hide herself from the human race again. She was starting to gain a reputation as a doer in the force and someone with a fearsome range of skills.

Harkins did more than anyone to beat the raw material of the team into shape, and Macallan came to care what happened to him. She could see that looming retirement could end up as a tragedy for the man; she'd seen it before – divorced from his two families, who'd moved on well without him, drinking habits that just stayed marginally on the right side of a serious problem and not a friend outside the force. He'd lived the job as if it would never end, but now the end was in sight and she knew that in the quieter moments, it was getting to him.

They'd started having a regular Thursday night drink, which served two purposes: it allowed Harkins to tell Macallan how well she was doing or whether she had, in fact, fucked up. It also let her talk to the man who had to some extent taken up Bill Kelly's mantle, even though they were two very different men. She knew he cared about her (but there was no chance of an admission), he could make her laugh and he was the closest thing she had to a friend so far.

They tapped glasses and, as always, he threw the first one down in one gulp.

'Cheers, Mick – and thanks for what you've been doing. God knows what we'd do without you.'

He signalled to the barman for a top-up. 'It's going well and from top to bottom we're in good shape. That's the easy bit, and sooner or later it'll get hard and then we'll find out what the team is made of. The guys like you, so keep it going, just relax a bit. I know why that's hard for you, but it'll come. You're a talented woman and you need to share yourself with people, because they'll like that person. Leave the past behind you and get on with life. One bit of advice though.'

She looked up from her glass. 'What's that then, Mick?'

'Don't do it with JJ. He only wants a long-term relationship with the job. Don't get me wrong, if you want something short and sweet that would probably do the both of you a bit of good, then fair enough. It's just he's not going to do the cottage in the country with a smiling family and loveable dogs. You know that but thought I'd mention it.'

She considered him for a moment and probably should have torn a strip off, reminded him who the boss was and that it wasn't his business. He was right though, and she knew it, but nothing had happened with O'Connor so no damage done. She decided that no answer was best. 'Do you fancy getting pissed and telling me some war stories?'

He straightened his shoulders. 'Did I ever tell you about the flashing minister?'

She smiled, and her green eyes lit up. 'Perfect, let me get them in.'

Around midnight, Macallan walked along the chilled, quiet street a few minutes from her flat, aching to just climb into bed. She was pleasantly drunk, but considering what she'd put away with Harkins, she knew the following day was going to be hard going. It had been a good night, funny, with an endless exchange of stories, and she'd surprised herself by starting to tell some of her own. Harkins had seen the human being gradually trying to re-enter the world again.

She was in sight of her door when the man stepped out of the shadows. Cursing loudly, and with adrenaline exploding through her body, she fumbled for her personal firearm – which she didn't carry any more. The man moved towards her and raised his arm. She closed her eyes and waited.

'Could ye spare a bit change, darlin'?'

She opened her eyes, gasping for air, and stared at the wino. 'What the fuck do you think you're doing?' She hit him hard right below the heart and he fell backwards. She ran the rest of the way and slammed the flat door behind her. She stripped, stepped into the shower and cried as she washed the day from her body. The warm stream of water calmed her and she sobered up as she rubbed herself dry before slipping into bed and a troubled sleep.

The Belfast Incident

The phone blasted Macallan awake, and when she looked at the clock face it showed 5.30 a.m. That was bad. She was expecting bad news, although not this quickly. Her mouth felt like a tramp's sock, but that was down to the second large nightcap and the couple of slices of chorizo grabbed from the fridge before she'd crashed out around midnight. She picked up the phone and swung her legs round to plant her feet on the floor. She knew sleeping was over for the day.

It was one of her team giving her the latest bad news. 'Sorry to bother you at this time of the morning.'

She didn't want pleasantries. 'Is there any good news?'

'I'm afraid not, ma'am.'

'Well, let's have the bad.'

The man calling her was one of the best and didn't deserve a hard time from her. This was as close as she could get to humour at such an early hour.

'Bertie Gallagher was found near the docks this morning by a couple of locals going to work. He's pretty badly marked up and finished off with one in the head. No one's claiming it so far, but it's early days.'

She dragged her fingers through her hair and thought for a moment. There should have been a question or direction but her head wasn't ready to cope yet. This was a mess and it was going to be a bad day at the office.

'Ma'am?'

She apologised and explained that she was thinking. He told her there was more.

'How bad?'

'Tommy Doyle collapsed and died in custody just after they started interviewing him. The doc's not sure but thinks there are signs it was down to some form of blunt force abdominal trauma. Apparently it's hard to spot – it might have been an injury of some kind picked up much earlier. They're going to post-mortem him first thing.'

The caller didn't realise what this meant, but she did. What she'd seen from the OP was blunt force trauma alright. She just hoped that something else had killed Tommy Doyle or she was in a very bad place – and so was Jackie Crawford. Her head hurt and she had to think, make choices that needed to be right. There wasn't going to be a second chance if she made the wrong call. It hadn't really occurred to her at the time of the incident because this was Belfast, always the front line of the war, and people got hurt. The Tommy Doyles of this world would never admit that they'd been hurt by a couple of shots from a young Peeler.

She walked through to her small kitchen, pressed the button on her kettle, rinsed last night's whisky glass and filled it with water. She gulped it down to lubricate her tongue, which was scraping the roof of her mouth, then leaned on the edge of the sink, staring at nothing, and tried to slow the carousel spinning round in her head. Jack – she wanted and needed Jack, but that wasn't an option at this time of the morning. She'd try to get to Bill Kelly before the commander started to take her apart; alarms would be going off in a lot of corners of the force after a death in custody. Macallan's problem was stark: if Tommy Doyle had died as a result of the incident she'd witnessed, she could say she saw nothing, but that strategy wasn't straightforward. She didn't want to think about the other option.

Bill Kelly was in his office at 7 a.m., as he would have been anyway. When Macallan arrived he had the coffee ready, and, unlike most policemen, he had cups instead of cheap inch-thick mugs. Although they'd known each other as friends for years, he was an ACC and she still knocked at his open door.

'Come in, and close the door behind you. You still take it black with half a spoon, or have you given that up as well now you're an athlete?' He smiled at her.

The sight of him improved her mood, and she noticed

for the first time that nearly a quarter of a century of the Troubles was carving some lines into his face. 'I've not given everything up, and that includes good malt. Long time since we shared one or two. I miss those days.'

'Sit down, Grace. Of course I know what's happened overnight, and in about half an hour I'm going to have the press, Republican politicians and London thinking that the PSNI is still the RUC and killing good Catholic boys for fun. Use this half hour, because I've a feeling you need to. I guess you'll be seeing your commander, and I don't envy you. This conversation is not taking place, so fire away.'

Macallan really didn't know how to get to the point, and everything looked like a bad option. 'I'm assuming you know that I ran the agent who's been killed?'

Kelly nodded.

'I wanted to pull him out. I know the commander will deny all knowledge, but I'll take care of that myself. It's Tommy Doyle's death that's the problem.'

Kelly didn't expect this and put his coffee cup back on the saucer. 'Tell me.'

'I was in an OP – I watched a young Peeler whack Tommy pretty hard in the guts and he went down hurt. There's no doubt about what I saw.'

She gave every detail to Kelly and he forgot completely about his morning coffee. He never interrupted her and didn't need to. He knew exactly what the effects of a high-speed fan and a lot of shit produced.

'I trained you well enough for you to know what I'm going to tell you already, and you know that whatever you do is going to cost you. If you say you saw nothing and it comes out later that you did, you'll do prison time – or at the very least lose your career. You can't do prison time! If you say you saw it then you're going to put Mr and Mrs Crawford's only remaining son in prison, and nearly everyone in the PSNI will think you're worse than a terrorist. Even then, they'll hit you with failing to report the incident and a lot of Republicans will think he might have lived if you'd intervened, which of course is nonsense. That's quite a pile of problems to be getting on with.'

Macallan tried to interrupt. He put his hand out, palm up, and leaned forward in his chair. 'You came here for my advice; well, I'll give it to you. This country has to change, the war's all but over apart from a few dissidents, and unless all sides change with it we'll end up in the same sewer we've been in all these years. You know this, and the first mistake you made was that you didn't report it right away. Showing people on the other side we can do the right thing will help to get us to something like peace. You saw a prisoner in custody assaulted and walked away because that's how it is. We used to operate using noble cause as justification for certain actions. Those days are gone, Grace.'

Bill Kelly lit a cigarette and broke his rule about not smoking before breakfast. Macallan stayed quiet; she knew that he was far from finished.

'My heart will ache for the Crawfords, but thousands of families have been hurt in this fight, and the days of closing ranks are over. A few years ago, I would have done what you did and looked the other way. We have to show we're better than that, which means we'll take casualties, and we won't be loved for it.'

He saw the effect he was having on Macallan, and a half-smile cut across his face. 'Christ, I told you a long time ago that no one loves us in this job anyway! Jackie Crawford was trained like everyone else, and in a fair world his family wouldn't have to take another blow and that's the truth. But this is bigger than you or Jackie Crawford; the fact that he might do time and you're going to be as welcome as Martin McGuinness in an Orange lodge is not the point. I'm not telling you one way or the other – I'll leave it to you. Your commander won't like the truth, and God knows how you'll get round him. He's not a bad man – in fact, quite the opposite in his own way. We needed men like him at the height of the Troubles and we'd have lost without them. He saw so many of his friends die, and two attempts on his life means he deserves a bit of understanding. He'll tell you the opposite of what I've said, but he's the past and that's the decision you have to make. Do the right thing and there will probably be some form of discipline for not reporting it right away. You'll survive, but I'm not sure if you'll survive in Ulster.'

Kelly sipped his coffee and realised it was cold. They both stood at the same time and he walked across the room and held her in his arms. He'd never done this in all the time they'd known each other. She left the room without speaking, thinking she'd have a cigarette before facing the commander. She'd cut her smoking to two or three a day, but this wasn't the time to worry about her tobacco consumption.

The commander looked at Macallan without a smile or welcome when she walked through the door of his office. 'Have a seat, Chief Inspector.'

Macallan had made her decision, and this was no time to let this man walk over her. She'd tried to get Cowboy pulled out, he knew it, but the agent wasn't the real problem – and he didn't know what the real problem was yet.

He took his time sorting out something that looked like tea, and once again made sure that he didn't offer her one. He sat, pretended to look at some papers in front of him and spoke without raising his eyes to her.

'Bit of a problem last night with your boy. Well, he's not the first one we've lost and there'll be some flak, but we'll survive that. As for wee Tommy Doyle, well, that man fought all his life and was a born drunk, so no doubt there'll be a reasonable explanation for his death. There'll be an investigation, but from what I can see he was handled properly and there are no reports from anyone that there was a problem. No doubt you'll be seen as part of that investigation, but nothing to worry about, Chief Inspector.'

He'd said exactly what she'd expected and avoided her concerns about the agent. 'The agent was set up, sir,' she replied. 'That's a problem, and we let him down.'

She avoided pointing the finger directly at him, because he could always argue that he'd made a decision for the right reasons and to save lives. She decided to get to the point. 'There's also a problem with Tommy Doyle's death, and I'll have to report it to the investigation team.'

The cup was halfway to the commander's mouth and stopped about there. Macallan definitely had his attention now. He put the cup down on the desk, picked up a pen and tapped the table, looking straight at her. Keeping eye contact with this man was no easy matter but she did her best – knew she needed to be strong.

'I think I said to you, Miss Macallan, that there were no problems that I'm aware of.' She knew this was getting serious if he was using her name. He paused for a moment. 'So if there's a problem, it must be with you then?'

She tried to keep her hands still on the arms of the chair. 'After Doyle was arrested last night, he was walked to the van by a young Peeler and I saw him give Doyle two hard digs in the stomach. I mean hard digs because Doyle went down and was hurt. No doubt about it. I know the Peeler is young Jackie Crawford.'

The commander did not want to hear any Peeler's name connected to an assault on Tommy Doyle the night he died – but Jackie Crawford was the last name he wanted up for discussion. He'd served with Jackie's father as a young recruit himself and knew exactly what price the family had paid in the Troubles.

'I want you to think very carefully before you say any more. You know exactly what the Crawfords have been through. You know exactly what this evidence will mean if that's what you think you witnessed. Tommy Doyle was a fighting drunk who probably should have been dead a long time ago given the life he led. No one will shed a tear for Doyle – not even those in his own organisation. Jackie Crawford has a family; the PSNI and the majority of the people of Northern Ireland are behind him. Think, Chief Inspector.'

She knew that she'd already passed the point of no return and guessed that there would be days ahead when she'd wish that she'd looked the other way. Too late for that though, and she straightened up in her chair.

'I'm sorry, sir, but that's what I saw. And before you say it, I should have reported it at the time; as an SB officer I wanted to stay away from the street in case we were spotted. I was wrong not to report it and I'll accept the consequences, but there was no doubt about what I witnessed – Tommy Doyle was assaulted after his arrest.'

The commander took a deep breath and realised they were in a stalemate. He had to be careful he wasn't accused of orchestrating a cover-up. He was too close to retirement for that.

'You have to do what you have to do, Chief Inspector, and I would imagine the investigation team will be seeing you later today. I'll make a note of this conversation. So is there anything else?'

'No, sir.'

The tension in the room calmed, and she left wondering where this would go.

The commander stood up from his desk and looked out at the dark, fat clouds dropping rain on Belfast. He knew there'd been no point in going further with Macallan – she'd made up her mind, and he couldn't change that. Nevertheless, what she was going to do to Jackie Crawford was a betrayal. The boy had been stupid, but he could guess what had happened and the Crawfords would have to take another blow for the peace process and Ulster. The commander could do something though, and he decided to change Grace Macallan's life for ever. He picked up the phone and told his secretary to call Jack Fraser, and ask him to come to HQ.

Jack Fraser arrived at his office late and thumbed through the pile of messages left on his desk from the previous day. He saw the call from the commander and didn't make too much of it. He had regular meetings with senior Branch officers to discuss cases or provide guidance on whether investigations should go ahead or be dropped. He'd heard a news report about a death in custody, and a body found near the docks, so it could be one of the many problems law enforcement had to deal with in the city.

Things were reasonably quiet so he decided to take care of the commander's problem early, and with a bit of luck he might bump into Grace. He would call her anyway and arrange something for the evening. He thought about how good they were together, and although she tended to be a bit serious, he could always make her laugh. But then she was entitled to be serious dealing with life in the Branch; it was hard enough for the men but even tougher for the women.

When Fraser arrived at the commander's office, he knew it was something serious as the secretary had laid on biscuits and coffee in a pot rather than stirred up in a mug that hadn't been washed properly in a week.

'Sit down, Jack, and I'll fix your coffee. White and no sugar?'

Fraser nodded and wondered what was up – because the commander didn't do nice. In all the years he'd been acquainted with the man, all he'd ever known him to do was work. He seemed to live in the office. In fact, there was a standing joke that the commander had never actually been seen in daylight and slept hanging upside down in an office cupboard. And now...

There was something wrong in the atmosphere.

'What can I do for you, Commander? I know there were some problems overnight and presume you need legal counsel?'

The commander gave Fraser his coffee, offered the biscuits and seemed disappointed when he refused. He took his seat. 'There's a problem, and it's a delicate one. I'm a blunt man as you know, so we'll get right to it as we're both busy men.'

He explained what had happened overnight and that an investigation was already underway. Fraser relaxed, thinking that this was just another tough day at the office; all these things had happened before and would be resolved one way or another. This was their business, but then his train of thought was stopped in its tracks.

'The problem is Grace Macallan.'

Fraser ran his forefinger under his left eye, and the commander was pleased to see the nervous gesture.

'She ran the agent who died, and on top of that she's going to tell the investigation team that she saw a young Peeler assault Doyle shortly before he died in custody. The Peeler concerned is the brother of Billy Crawford, who you might remember was abducted by PIRA and killed down on the border.'

Fraser knew the case well and had been involved in giving legal advice to the murder-squad detectives who'd investigated the killing. He knew the commander was playing some game and was losing patience. 'I really am sorry but I have a busy schedule today so if you could tell me what you need from me?'

The commander smiled, which was another bad sign, and Fraser became uncomfortable, an unusual feeling for a man who was always in control. He knew that bad news was coming, and he wanted the commander to get to the point.

'You've done great things for the police service, and the people of Northern Ireland. You worked with us, guided us on the legal problems we've had to resolve and helped put a lot of terrorists where they belong. You come from good stock, and you're needed here. You more than most know what we do and what we were faced with during the height of the Troubles. This province was under the most intense surveillance of any country in the developed world during the Troubles and we have agents everywhere, from the top to the bottom of society. We intercept and bug, and we do all this because we have to do it to save lives. We only ever use a small part of all the information we gather, and in among it we pick up information about otherwise law-abiding people that we tend to leave alone.'

Fraser was smart enough to think he knew where this was going, but he didn't. The commander took another sip of his coffee, and Fraser completely ignored his.

'You've been having a long-running affair with Grace Macallan, and it's probably time it stopped. You really don't want to be associated with the woman who puts Jackie Crawford in prison. You have a lot of friends here, and we provide your business, so think about it. You're a married man and have a future. No doubt when this is all over, you'll get yourself a judge's wig and your backside on the bench.'

Fraser was surprised, but of course in a small part of the world like Northern Ireland he'd known that it would eventually come out. He cared deeply for Grace, and his marriage was just a show until one of them plucked up the courage to admit that it was over. He felt a small sense of relief because he could handle this – and knock this ill-educated plod off his perch. Against his training for the bar, he even allowed himself to appear annoyed before putting the man in his place. Maybe it was all for the best and he could move his life on, although in reality he wanted his marriage over more than he wanted to live a life of domestic bliss with Grace. They worked well together, but being lovers and being partners were two different things, and that could wait.

'I have to say, Commander, that I find this whole meeting an insult. My private life is just that, other than to admit to problems that are well known to our friends. I don't count you as a friend, so I don't need to say anything more on that subject. As for Grace, as far as I can see she acted properly apart from reporting late. If she'd asked me for advice as a lawyer, I would have told her to tell the truth. What else are we here for? Don't approach me again on any of this, or I'll make sure there's a price to pay.'

He sat back and waited to revel in his small victory, and at least an apology from the man sitting opposite him. But the commander was completely unruffled and the only change in his expression was that a small thin smile had opened up on his face. The bastard was keeping something in reserve, and as a barrister he had to admire the tactic.

'I'll continue. I'd hoped you'd be reasonable, and you will be. I've told you already about all this other information we pick up, and for the last two years we've had an agent reporting on you. Nothing too serious you see, and as I said we have them at all levels. You mix with the best people in smart circles and you think you're immune. However, the businessman who supplies you with your odd packet of cocaine is one of ours. I know it's recreational, and all the best people are doing it, but as a trained lawyer you'll remember that it's against the law even here in Ulster. Now you have a choice, son: that information will never see the light of day and you can carry on serving the good people of this province, or you can wreck your career and live with a woman who no one in this place will come near for years. You'll have no friends in the PSNI watching your backs when the paramilitaries come looking for a Branch officer and a lawyer who put so many of their boys behind the wire. It's your choice, my friend. Do the right thing, Jack.'

Fraser's face had paled, and he leaned back in his chair. 'Is that all, Commander?'

His voice lacked the angry edge of his last delivery. The commander thought that it had all gone rather well, but he'd been a bastard for a long time and had a lot of practice. He'd always thought how naive these lawyers could be. Huge brains and they lived in a non-reality bubble where they actually believed that their law books contained the answers. Welcome to the real world, son. The commander knew that the lifeblood of a man like Jack Fraser was his position in life. A ruined career was a death sentence. Ultimately, men like him would choose their careers, being far too selfish to choose the love of a woman ahead of the spotlight of professional success. 'You be on your way now and think about what I've said to you, but don't take too long. I'll expect a phone call.'

Fraser got to the door of the office and turned to the commander before he left. 'Grace had no idea about the cocaine. You do know that, don't you?'

The commander smiled. 'Don't worry. I know that and she's got enough to be going on with. Just don't mention *any of this to her – and that's non-negotiable. Are you sure you don't want one of these biscuits? It's a terrible waste.'*

Fraser closed the door behind him without saying another word.

8

Nancy Park dragged her feet through the damp, rust-coloured leaves that covered the street on her way to the house where she worked as a cleaner. It was a quiet street lined with beautiful old homes in an affluent district of Glasgow, half filled with old money, the other half with new business stars and the odd lawyer. Nancy Park worked in the house owned by Peter Yip, who'd come from Hong Kong as a young man with barely the price of a coffee in his pocket. Like so many of his countrymen he only knew how to work hard, starting as a cook in a third-rate carryout shop in the East End of the city. He'd grafted his way to owning three of the best restaurants in Glasgow and branched out to Edinburgh and Dundee.

Nancy liked Peter Yip and his family, although her husband resented immigrants doing well, missing the irony that he'd barely done a day's paid work in his life. Nancy had filled that role. She loved the old-world charm of the street and the trees that lined its edges. She would dream that she lived there with a husband who loved her – and her dreams were all Nancy had now. She was getting old, worried about the arthritic pains in her legs and how they would live if she had to give up work. Peter Yip and his family were good to Nancy, and she loved the children who were so courteous to her, all so different from the world that she inhabited. Their life was a contrast to hers, and it made her ashamed, so she would manufacture a different life and she would tell the Yips about her tradesman husband, how well her children were doing and that her lovely grandchildren were a joy. The truth was that Nancy hadn't seen her son since his last spell in prison, and although she was close to her daughter, she'd ended up with a man about as useless as her father.

When she opened the gate, Nancy was surprised to see Peter's Merc in the driveway, as he was normally off working before the rest of the family were up and about. She marvelled that given all that Peter had achieved, he worked as if he was still climbing the greasy ladder.

The door was still locked and she frowned because the Yips had the most ordered life. The front door was always open at this time of the morning and she'd had no message from Mrs Yip that they were going anywhere.

She fumbled through her bag and found the key to the door. Her instincts were firing up as soon as she entered the house; it was too warm and there was a barely perceptible smell that she couldn't identify but which was ringing an alarm deep in her subconscious. She would normally have called out but walked slowly through the hall trying to rationalise what was starting to frighten her.

The house was too still and seemed to be holding its breath until Nancy was startled by a cry from upstairs – a child's voice. She called up the stairs, praying that her imagination had run away with her and all was well, but it wasn't that kind of day. There was another cry and she recognised it as belonging to the eldest of the children. She padded upstairs as quickly as she could and pushed open the bedroom door, trying to work out why the room was empty. Another cry made her put her hand to her mouth as she realised it was coming from a cupboard in the room – and that it was locked from the outside.

The children had recognised Nancy's voice and were begging her to open the door. The key was still in the lock and, when she opened it, the three children grabbed her as if their lives depended on it. They were in shock but told her enough for her to realise that something terrible had entered their home. Nancy knew that there was a question she didn't want to answer – where were Peter Yip and his wife?

She made the children sit on the bed and tried her best to calm them. 'You sit there and I'll go and get your father.'

The children were still terrified and she dreaded what they had seen. She walked slowly down the stairs, pressed the three nines on her phone and told the operator the story so far and that she was frightened. The operator was good and started to get what was needed, steering Nancy on what she had to do next – but she was already pushing the lounge door open. The blood spray on the walls caught Nancy's eye first, and although they would tell the scenes of crimes officers a great deal, they just added to her sense of horror at what was waiting in the middle of the floor.

Peter Yip and his wife were neatly tied up and seated on antique dining chairs that she'd polished just a couple of days earlier. She dropped the phone and the operator knew enough to press the right buttons and get the cavalry on its way. Nancy stared at Peter Yip, who couldn't answer because he was dead – she didn't need any medical qualifications to know that. The right side of his head had been beaten to a pulp and something had flowed from the open skull. He hadn't been able to scream because his mouth was taped. Elizabeth Yip had the same sort of mess for a head. It was a horror, and as Nancy hit the floor, somewhere in her dimming consciousness she could heard the two-tone sirens approach.

When the intruders had entered the Yips' home through the French windows at the back of the house, Peter had tried to put up a fight, but they were three very hard guys and had more practice than Peter in hurting people. They gave him a couple of cracks in the ribs and a good slap had sorted his wife. The biggest of the three gave the orders. 'Up the stairs and take care of the brats.'

Elizabeth Yip panicked at the thought of what might happen to her children. 'Please don't hurt them; we'll give you what you want.'

The big guy seemed to be enjoying it – and he was. Seeing fear was what worked for him, and wielding power over people who had so much more than he did. 'Think we're animals? They'll be left alone as long as you play ball.'

They wanted money and their research had told them that Peter should have plenty in the house. As far as they were concerned these Chinese fuckers kept it under the bed so they didn't have to pay tax, and all they had to do was hand it over. The problem was that Peter was a straight peg and kept it in the bank. But they'd come a long way and spent a lot of time on this job and that wasn't what they wanted to hear. The big man put his face close to Peter's and all Peter could see beyond the balaclava were his eyes. But Peter Yip was no one's fool and decided to try and get every detail possible; he looked at the dark brown eyes and saw that there was an unusual black fleck on the left side. He was a law-abiding man but this was an attack on his family and anger boiled in his chest.

The big man gripped him by the throat. 'Now listen carefully, Mr Egg Foo Yung.'

The second intruder snorted a laugh.

'You hand over the money or we're going to spend a bit of time hurting you and your lovely wife. Don't take too long because we're a bit rushed and want to catch the pub.'

The second man snorted again and ran his hand through Elizabeth Yip's hair. She recoiled and looked across at her husband, who wanted to kill another human being for the first time in his life. If he could track these men down he knew some Triad boys who were always happy to oblige and get the meat cleavers out for a few notes.

The big man walked over to Elizabeth Yip and taped her mouth closed. Her eyes were bulging and seemed to be screaming at her husband to find an answer and get these predators away from her door and children. The third man came back into the room. 'There's a big cupboard up there and they're locked in it. They're going nowhere.'

Peter Yip tried to explain over and over again that there was only a couple of hundred in cash in the house. The problem was that the intruders didn't believe him. He told them to take some of the antiques but this team was professional and knew how easy it was to trace them. They did cash only, and maybe a bit of jewellery at a push. The big man just couldn't be bothered fucking about and offered a last chance.

'Right, you give us the cash or we start to hurt the missus.'

Elizabeth Yip was hyperventilating. Her husband realised that these were men who took pleasure in hurting, and if they didn't get the main prize then there was a consolation. He'd never pleaded in his life and it was all he had left, but it didn't work. He strained at the rope that held him to the chair as they taped his mouth and one of them held his head and made him watch as they tore at Elizabeth's lower clothing.

After a few minutes they ripped the tape from his mouth and asked him again about the money. Peter Yip knew that this had moved too far past the point of no return for him and the intruders. He spat in the face of the big man, who didn't even seem surprised. In fact, he was happy enough – and this was all the justification he needed. He stood up and pulled the iron jemmy from a side pocket. 'Fuck it and fuck you!'

The last thing Peter Yip saw was the big man raising the jemmy above his shoulder before smashing it into the side of his head. He didn't die with the first blow but was beyond pain and feeling. He was making a snoring noise and the second intruder wanted to get the job done. 'Finish him. We can't leave them now.'

Elizabeth Yip tried to scream through the tape.

The big man took the two paces towards her and used the jemmy again. They made sure with another few whacks and then checked the place to make sure they hadn't left any traces.

The intruders were professional and burned the stolen car on the outskirts of Edinburgh. They picked up a clean set of wheels and managed a few pints before calling it a day. The big man, or Billy Drew to his friends, directed his last order at his younger brother. 'Frank, you take the boiler suits with the other gear and burn it.'

The big man thought his younger sibling was a complete arse, but he was family and he had to give him something to do. Frank Drew was happy and loved working with his brother, who was a bit of a legend, but he knew he had to be careful, as he tended to fuck up on a regular basis. He got the bin bag from the car and walked the few hundred yards to his house, where he would have a couple of shots of vodka before turning in.

Billy Drew spoke to the third man, Colin Jack, as they stood outside the pub. They had worked with each other for years and had become friends after a spell in Barlinnie prison together. 'Keep an eye on Frank for the next few days. I'm going to look at another job. He's a mouthy fucker and I'm worried he'll land us in it one of these days.'

Colin Jack slapped his friend on the arm. 'No problem, Billy, it's done.'

They walked their separate ways.

Frank Drew had his shots of vodka and the next morning his head felt like he'd been hit with the jemmy and not the Chinese fuckers they'd turned over. He had an old tin drum outside and got it fired up, thought about the job the night before and how good it had felt. He tossed the gear on the fire a bit at a time and was glad they hadn't got the money. Doing the Chinks had been a laugh.

The fire began to die, and it started to piss down as he tossed the last balaclava and boiler suit into the drum. Running inside, he got his face into the racing section – he felt lucky and thought he would put a few bets on the horses.

9

Pauline Johansson shivered under what passed for a blanket, realising it was just another day as the pale sun tried to force its way through the grime and the torn blind on her window. Sunshine just wasn't enough to lift her spirits. She reached for a cigarette, trying to steady her hand long enough to get a flame to it. She dragged on the fumes and coughed wetly, like almost every other morning, and tried to run through the previous night. Nothing much ever changed in the script, only the players.

She rubbed her eyes and looked round to see if anyone was next to her, but she was alone. She got out of the bed, swore at the freezing bare wood beneath her feet and tried to tiptoe through to the kitchen. She flicked on the kettle, looked at the pile of crusty dishes in the sink and decided they could wait as she dropped a tea bag into a cracked mug embossed with the Glasgow Rangers logo, which like her was fading with age.

She tugged on a woollen pullover and tried to stop shivering, but there hadn't been heating in the flat for weeks since the gas had been cut off.

She sat on the toilet and sipped her tea, trying to work up enough fight to manage another day and avoid thinking about the future, unless being a working girl with a smack habit gave you something to look forward to.

By most standards, Pauline hadn't had a bad start in life; her parents were true working class and just wanted their only child to have a bit more than they did. Her father had worked long, hard hours labouring, never complained once, and always managed to put food on the table and clothes on their backs. They were only able to have one child although they had wanted more, but at least the budget hadn't been strained by numbers.

Pauline's mother had worked for years as a school dinner lady and the extra money had given them the chance of the odd small luxury and bargain summer holiday.

Pauline had been brought up in the heart of Leith when it had still regarded itself as separate from Edinburgh; for all its faults this ancient port had a unique sense of itself and the people took pride in being its sons and daughters. At school she'd been an outstanding pupil, so her father had saved a small amount of money every month for what he dreamed would be a place at university and a profession. He would happily settle for that.

Pauline was tall and athletic, with classic Nordic

blue eyes and blonde hair, which echoed the seafaring tradition of the port where so many foreign sailors had come and, in many cases, settled. Like most of the young women from that part of town, her dreams were to escape; it was an age where television and magazines seemed to suggest that a perfect life inhabited by perfect people wasn't that far away – all you needed was money, and stacks of it. Easy.

When she was sixteen, everything had been on track; for her teachers and family it had been a formality that her grades would take her to the next natural step on the higher-education ladder. Then she'd met Danny Fleming, who, like most of the young men around at that time, was hooked on the sight of her long legs, blonde hair and sky-blue eyes. He would try and chat her up on the street, but everyone knew he was bad news, headed for a career in prison just like his father and most of the male members of the Flemings. However, they counted in Leith and the name Fleming, even for someone still young, demanded a degree of respect.

Danny was a couple of years older than Pauline and had started his career as a shoplifter or doing occasional drug deliveries for the family business. He was a Fleming in looks as well as career choice, touching six feet by the time he was eighteen. His shoulders were filling out and he walked like someone who owned the streets – or at least would do some day. Cocky and hard, he wore his hair marine short over a good-looking face that few of the women in his world could ignore.

The problem with Danny Fleming was that he didn't give a fuck for anyone but himself, and that was typed into his DNA so no one was going to change or save him; his sole aim in life was to get as much as he could as quickly as he could.

He'd persisted with Pauline, but she'd managed to pretend that she wasn't interested; it was pretence because, despite what she'd known and what everyone had told her, Danny Fleming had stirred something in her that she couldn't quite explain. When he'd tried to chat her up, giving her that sardonic grin he practised in the mirror, she had felt her legs shake; it had frightened and intrigued her at the same time. He was a predator and had read her body language perfectly. He'd known he could wait and his chance would come.

When he was with his team, he'd promised them it was only a matter of time. 'Just wait, it'll happen. I'll make that stuck-up bitch regret knocking a Fleming back.'

He was patient, and when the time came he was as good as his word. Pauline's friends had arranged a party for the end of term and, better still, there was an empty flat where one set of parents were away for the night. Some beers had been arranged, nothing too dangerous, but the problem was that Danny boy got to hear about it and decided to invite himself. Who was going to stop him?

It had only taken a couple of drinks and all of Pauline's defences had come down. Danny had introduced her to vodka and she'd never been able to make much sense of the rest of the night. She'd woken up the next morning as if she'd burst through the surface of a dark pool, her heart banging against her chest.

It was the first of many panic attacks, and when she'd looked round she'd found Danny Fleming lying next to her, both of them naked. She'd been sore and worried about her mother and father, who would be frantic and probably walking the streets looking for her, and she'd realised that whatever she did – even if she tried to lie – they would know that something bad had walked into the life of their only child.

Fleming had woken up and grinned. 'What a fuckin' night! You were away with it.'

He'd known she probably remembered nothing, and his grin had widened at the thought of what he'd done to her. He couldn't wait to meet up with the team, give them the full story, all his little moves included. Naturally he'd add a bit on that she loved it and couldn't get enough, but that's how it was with women. She'd seemed upset, but he'd supposed that was natural and he'd decided to give her another turn before he pushed off to the streets. She'd tried to stop him but he'd been having none of that. She just hadn't the will to fight, too weakened by alcohol and shame, so she could only lie back as Danny Fleming groaned on top of her and started the process of destroying her future and her dreams.

As she lifted herself from the toilet, Pauline thought back to how quickly she'd self-destructed. After that first morning, she'd gone back to her parents, and although they'd been frightened and upset, they'd forgiven her – but that had been the easy part. When they'd found out where she'd been and whom she'd been with, the certainty that had always been Pauline's future, and theirs, seemed threatened for the first time. She'd been fine for a few days, but it was as if Danny himself was a drug – selfish and dangerous – and when she'd realised that she'd survived that night, she'd become excited at the thought of what had happened. She would have to go back and try a bit more, see what it was like to break the rules that had bound her life so tightly.

Danny had enjoyed breaking her up bit by bit, and of course part of it was that she had something he could never have, and his natural desire was to take it away. When he was bored with the sex, he'd introduced her to her first experience of smack. That initial rush that took her somewhere Danny's rough fumbling never could, and she wanted more. Once she'd stolen the money that her parents had saved, Danny had explained to her why her only option was the street if she wanted to pay off her drug debts.

She looked in the mirror at the face that was ten years older than her age; the eyes that had once sparkled with light were dull and the whites tinged with a yellow edge. Her hair was darker and the sharp edges of her face had blurred, but despite all that she still had a look, faded though it might be, and some of the punters kept coming back to her. What she needed was a fix to keep the nausea at bay for a while. First things first, she had to spend time cleaning herself up.

She did the occasional freebie for a guy who worked at the local swimming pool and would wash and shower there before tracking down her dealer. Eighty notes from the previous night would keep her going for a couple of days, as long as some horrible fucker didn't rip her off, but that was a risk of the trade.

Pauline thought briefly about her parents. Sometimes she would wait until it was dark and just watch the light in their windows. She never saw them; she lived most of her life in the night. Going back was impossible now – she'd taken all they had but would die rather than let them see how far she'd fallen.

She knew that they would have loved grandchildren but couldn't even do that for them: she'd aborted twice and was no longer capable. During the brief moments she did consider her life or what it meant, she realised that she was completely alone, and would stay that way until she injected a bad deal or some half-mad punter decided on the ultimate sanction.

Dressing quickly, she pulled the door behind her as she headed for the pool and decided she'd go out on the street as soon as it got dark.

At the same time Pauline Johansson was washing the previous night's misery from her body, the man who would beat her unconscious later that night was at his gym, working hard on his arms and shoulders. He'd always liked to work out, was proud of his shape and liked the vain atmosphere of the most expensive gym in the city. He caught a thirty-something woman giving him the look – and why not? Everything about him spoke of vanity, down to the trainers that he'd bought because they were the most expensive rather than the most practical.

As he pushed the barbell over his head he smiled back at the woman, who wore a wedding ring but gave off all the right signals. However, he would not make any moves here – he wanted to get onto the streets and find someone to entertain. He'd travelled the country for months picking up girls from the street and getting used to inflicting pain. He'd done enough to be sure of his next actions; it was time to step up the game. Some lucky girl was going to meet him tonight and life would never be quite the same for her.

After his shower and sauna, he pulled on a crisp new shirt, then an Armani suit and admired his reflection in the full-length mirror. What surprised him was that he enjoyed what he was doing to the women he pulled off the street. That hadn't been the reason behind the plan, but he was good at it and knew exactly what he was doing. There were still those flashbulb moments of reality, when he remembered that in almost all other things he was a failure. He had money, all the chances in life, but his plan was helping to block out the truth. Everything was set; but first he would have dinner.

10

The winter sun was just struggling above the city skyline as the MCT gathered for their morning conference. The buzz increased; as always, the banter would start, and there would be the outbreaks of laughter at the stories of overnight drinks or the latest rumour on who was doing what to who. In other rooms, analysts and intelligence officers had been putting together summaries of events from across the force, and where they were of interest from further afield.

Harkins looked round at the faces filling the room and wondered which ones would emerge as stars. They would rise to the top quickly, and he'd be there to put a hand on their shoulder before they made the same mistakes he had. In his day he had got away with stretching the rules to breaking point, but the world had changed and the days of closed ranks were over. This was his last job, and he was going to do all he could to leave something behind that would be worth remembering.

He smiled, thinking of his early days, where the morning conferences had been carried out in a fog of smoke and hangovers. This new breed were a lot fitter and subject to more control, but they were human and still capable of making the mistakes that had gone before. He remembered his first sergeant doling out words of wisdom: 'Drink, women and mishandling other people's property are what'll cause you the biggest problems, son. The first two will only cost your health and marriage. The third one will cost your job.'

He was right, and Harkins had taken his share of the first two but took pride in the fact that he'd never taken a penny that wasn't his. He lived under the code of 'noble cause', which meant that there were certain areas where you could commit wrongdoing or break the law to get the right people put away. However, taking money or property was still a crime. It was just doing what had to be done. That was the code and that's how he played it.

He really needed a cigarette and wished the conference was over, but it was part of modern policing and everyone had to be kept in some kind of corporate loop – which he thought was just a form of thick make-up to keep the image makers happy.

He looked round and watched Grace Macallan sip her coffee while she skimmed through reports from the previous night. She looked like she was settling in, and although this was just the start, the team were taking to her, and he liked the way she carried off the role. She had a reserve and would never be one of the 'boys', but whenever someone wanted to speak to her, she had time, and a half-smile that warmed her face when it happened. Being good in her role was a constant balancing act, and the trick was to keep some space so that if arses had to be kicked then she was entitled to do it.

The team was brought to attention when O'Connor burst into the room. He didn't do 'quietly entering' and true to form he walked in and controlled the place immediately. Harkins and Macallan looked across at each other and smiled in silent applause at the way O'Connor projected his image to both the high and low in the world he owned.

'Good morning, ladies and gentlemen. I know you all want to get out and about so let's keep this to the point. We'll try and keep these conferences short and relevant and the form will be that DCI Macallan will present the relevant information prepared by the intelligence office. If there are requests for assistance or updates from our own jobs, that'll be done once the DCI has done her part. Any questions?'

Only a fool would have asked a question at that point, and Harkins had already warned a few suspects to shut the fuck up till the adults were finished. Macallan ran through the bread and butter then the more unusual incidents or crimes. She had marked up the ones that might need a bit of extra attention and Pauline Johansson was near the top.

'There was a serious attack on a known prostitute

last night down in Leith. We're still waiting on the full extent of her injuries but it looks like a punter worked her over with some form of blunt instrument. This is more than a simple beating – the medics said she looked like she'd been through a grinder, and at the very least we're talking about lifelong disfigurement and who knows what damage to the brain.'

Macallan looked round the office; she had their attention and most of the men and women in the room could visualise what exactly this meant. They'd all been up close and personal with wrecked human bodies.

'Hopefully, this'll be cleared up quickly by the local CID. There's a team working on it at the moment, and although it's unlikely she'll prove fatal, it's as bad as it can be. We'll keep an eye on it and if there's any request for assistance that'll need to be put through to Mr O'Connor.' O'Connor nodded and let Macallan carry on.

'It may be pure coincidence but the intelligence office has picked up reports that there seem to have been a number of serious attacks on prostitutes in other parts of the country, although not on this scale. However, there are some features that look similar and this'll be researched just in case there's a pattern forming. None of the attacks have been fatal.'

She ran through the other matters of interest then came to the highlights from other areas of the country. 'There is one that may well involve us at some stage and I think Mick will comment when I'm finished. An ethnic Chinese couple were killed during a tie-up job in Glasgow. The murder squad aren't sure why it went as far as it did but the couple involved were almost unrecognisable. Now I can run through the script but I've just joined the force and don't know the history that might involve us in this case, so I'll hand over to Mick.'

Harkins shuffled some papers in front of him but didn't need a script – he knew the history quite well. It had been a long-running sore in the force.

'It's possible that there's no connection but I doubt that. For years we've had a team working from this force specialising in break-ins and the occasional home-invasion job, usually on restaurateurs and in a number of cases from the Chinese community. It's been happening for around fifteen years, and there's never been a conviction.'

Harkins had O'Connor's full attention. He could spot an opportunity when it came and this story had all the ingredients he needed.

'The main guy is Billy Drew and a few of you will have come across him over the years. I've known Billy since he left the army, where he'd a good service record in the Paras, and to be fair he was a likeable character in his own way. He went back to his roots and ended up as part of a housebreaking team and they were good, very professional, and Billy made them even more so. However, he learned a hard lesson because I ran a good informant at the time, and eventually we rounded them up. I remember him telling me that was the last time he'd take a fall because of a grass. He did his time and he was right – he's never been caught again. He worked on his own when he came out and never went in with a big team again. After a few years he brought in Colin Jack, who was part of his old team and big mates with Billy. We've never been able to lay a glove on them since, and they do the jobs like a military operation. Over the years Bill's turned into a nutjob, and his father went the same way. Runs in the family.'

O'Connor interrupted. 'Mick, can you do me a summary of this when we finish the conference.'

Harkins' brow lowered at thought of more paperwork but he continued, 'We don't know how Billy targets his victims but he seems to spend a lot of time researching the jobs concerned. What he does to beat us seems remarkably simple, but he leaves a bit of time between jobs and never does more than one operation in the same region, at least not for a considerable time. In other words, he'll wait till we've moved on to the next problem and then he'll travel to the other end of the country to do the next one. He leaves almost nothing on forensics and no DNA. He studies police methods and is ultra careful. He only goes for cash, which we can do almost nothing with if we recover any, and only occasionally will he take jewellery, which he moves on within twenty-four hours.'

O'Connor interrupted again. 'So how do we know it's him, Mick? Surely there must be more than one team doing this. I remember him myself but never dealt with him personally.'

Harkins continued without answering. 'What

we have is enough to say it's down to him but not enough for an arrest and conviction. He's been pulled in a few times but he looks at the wall and won't even give his name. As I said, he knows how we work. What we do know is that he's been spotted near a number of the jobs before they happen – but that's not evidence on its own. The other thing we have is he has a brother who's basically a halfwit and likes a drink. He's opened his mouth to informants but again not enough to get us an arrest. So the problem's been that he targets restaurateurs who in some cases don't like to report what's been stolen in case their friendly IR officer takes an interest. The forces, including ourselves, do a cursory investigation, move on and forget.'

O'Connor interrupted again. 'But if this has gone on for years why suddenly take this step up and attract so much attention?'

Harkins wanted to say that the reason the Chinese couple were dead was because the problem had always been in the 'too-hard' box, and if they'd done their job it would never have got this far. But he decided not to antagonise O'Connor.

'What's changed is that Billy's wife died about a year ago, and despite what he is, they were close and from what I've heard, she was the only thing in this world that he cared about. They didn't have any children. He's not the same Billy Drew since she died. He's an even bigger nutjob now. Other than that I'm not a psychiatrist but I've no doubt this is Billy's team.'

Macallan interrupted this time. 'Mick, according to the report from the murder squad they think that three men were involved, from the footprints outside and in the house.'

Harkins nodded and fumbled with a cigarette packet for comfort. 'Well, I think that's where we might finally have a chance as it seems Billy's started to take his idiot brother, Frank, on the jobs. If that's the case then he's losing it – he'd never have done that in the past.'

O'Connor was now giving Harkins all his attention – rounding up a gang who were a problem across the country had everything the team needed to lift its profile. 'What would it take, Mick, that we've not done before?'

Harkins knew this was a chance to salve an old wound. 'It would take time but conventional surveillance hasn't worked in the past and trying to follow him just won't work. He's wise to that so we need fresh thinking.'

O'Connor made some notes and the room waited for direction. 'Okay, let's get on this. Grace, I want you to lead, and Mick to support you given his previous knowledge. Set up a meeting with the Strathclyde murder squad and let's see what we can do. On top of that, I'd like a meeting after this briefing with you and Mick, plus the senior analyst and DI Forbes from the surveillance team. I'll sit in but you'll be chairing, Grace.'

He looked across at her and smiled. She nodded and her brain started to rev up, trying to make sure she would cover all the angles. Her pulse jumped up a few notches, realising this was the test that she needed. Harkins winked at her and gave her that worn smile that meant he was with her on this.

She looked in the direction of Jack Forbes, who gave her an acknowledging nod, as did Felicity Young, the senior analyst. Young was the known as 'the brain', was slightly eccentric and easy to like. That's what made her what she was – someone who could sift through a small mountain of crime reports, shreds of intelligence from good and sometimes uncertain sources and make sense of the whole mess. This could give the detectives a direction and on occasions steer them away from blind alleys.

Macallan's office was cramped, and once they'd squeezed a couple of extra seats in, she got the meeting moving while O'Connor scribbled notes at her side.

'Can I please ask that what's said in this room stays in this room for the time being?' She gave everyone in the room some serious eye contact to make sure they got it. 'We know this is going to be difficult so we have to come up with a way of taking Billy Drew on. The MCT is in place to take on these "too-difficult" problems, and Billy and his team seem to fit the bill. We're going to get the murder squad all over us for help, so let's get going. Mick, you're the man that seems to know them best. What police action tends to take place against Billy Drew, and where are we wasting our time when we start an operation against them? The other thing is, what will he expect us to do given that he knows that we'll at least suspect him and his crew?'

Harkins had a headache and wanted a bacon sandwich so it was a normal morning for him. He knew this was an important moment for the team and the individuals in the team, including himself. For Harkins, it was securing his reputation and for the others it was about building futures, but in any case he had made up his mind that Billy Drew was a bit of unfinished business. He would make it his mission to see him pulling Christmas crackers in HMP Barlinnie – or Bar-L, as its customers affectionately called it.

'It's a waste of time getting a warrant to search his house and pulling him in. He won't even admit he's in the room and never keeps anything incriminating. You make a good point in asking what he'll expect us to do. If we do nothing it'll spook him, so maybe we should run through the normal script to cover whatever else we come up with.'

The coffee arrived and Harkins thanked God quietly.

Once they'd settled down, Macallan kicked it off again, feeling alive, even excited about the challenge, and the ideas were crackling through her mind. 'So you think we should let the murder squad pull him in to give us cover?'

Harkins nodded and knew that they were entering difficult territory but hoped that Macallan had the balls to take this where it needed to go. He'd watched too many bad guys walk away because someone in her seat was more worried about their next move up the ladder than keeping Joe and Jessica Public safe in their beds. 'I think we have to do that, but of course that means in part we have to restrict what we tell the murder squad before they do their job. We don't want them dropping our interest into his lap.'

O'Connor had known Harkins long enough to feel uncomfortable at this, and despite his promise to sit in the background he asked Harkins what he meant.

'I think we should keep our operation on a need-to-know basis because we don't want one of the Glasgow gorillas letting anything slip when they speak to Billy or his team. I know we're supposed to be all caring and sharing, but if Billy gets the slightest hint that anything else is going on, then we're fucked before we start.'

Young moved uncomfortably in her chair at Harkins' choice of expletives. She regarded him as a bit prehistoric but at the same time worryingly attractive, and Harkins knew this. He'd decided that before he left the job he'd show her what she was missing by spending half her life at a badminton club.

Macallan decided to get hold of the meeting. 'Okay, that may cause difficulties but I'll discuss that with the Super after the meeting and before we meet the murder-squad bosses.'

She looked at O'Connor and he nodded without looking too concerned. She turned to Harkins again. 'Okay, that's what'll not get him a stretch, so if there's a weakness, where is it and how can we exploit it?'

Harkins was encouraged and began to feel that they might get somewhere. 'Well, Billy's been doing it for years and survived, so he must think he has it cracked, but as I said in the meeting it's because no one has really committed to getting him. What we do know is that he researches the jobs himself and spends a lot of time making sure everything's right beforehand. If there was a way to keep tabs on him, we could at least get a head start. Just before a job they'll steal a car and that's disposed of right after the turn. Presumably they do the same with their other gear. The fact that he's now got his brother, Frank, on the team is definitely a chance for us because that guy makes Terry Fuckwit look like Stephen Fry.'

Young shifted in her seat again and Macallan tried her best to look serious as Harkins steamed on. 'Frank Drew talks in drink. We could get an informant onto him in short time. He's a gambler, and we have a number of low-life informants in the area that could hook up with him without attracting too much attention. We'd have to be careful though, because Billy and Colin Jack are sharp – we'd have to concentrate on Frank.

'The last thing is that if it was them for the murder then they probably didn't get much out of it. Peter Yip was a straight shooter, not the type to hide his money round the house, according to the report from Strathclyde. So I can't imagine they'll wait too long for the next job. To sum up, following Billy is a waste of time, as is interviewing him without evidence or searching his property. Whatever we do though, we need to spend time on it and get serious about putting this team away.'

Macallan started to spin the options and problems

and was certain it could be done. It just needed commitment. 'Okay, we know the problems, so we need to agree how we do this. First of all could I ask you, Felicity, to comment on what you've heard? I know that you've looked at the reports of the previous jobs across the UK thought to be down to Billy.'

Young was still thinking about Harkins and how he disgusted and excited her all at the same time. She sat up and looked at her notes. 'What we can confirm is that the victims are the length and breadth of the country. If they carry out an attack in the central belt of Scotland then the next could be in the Midlands or south of England. We've never had any information on how they select their victims other than that in the vast majority of cases they are restaurant owners and mostly ethnic Chinese, so the answer is there somewhere. The victims tend to live in large homes and affluent areas. As Sergeant Harkins has suggested, it seems they steal a car just before the job and burn it out after so we lose any chance of forensics. If we can track them, I think we should look for any cars stolen in the areas they've been in. If we could identify the car just before a job then it would at least be a start.'

Macallan thanked the analyst and turned to Jack Forbes, who was the DI in charge of the surveillance team and regarded as one of the best in the business. Surveillance was an art form, far removed from the TV detectives who carried out surveillance about fifteen feet behind the bad guy and yet were never spotted. It was hard work and took intensive training and selection with a high failure rate. It was about blending into the street and Jack Forbes was a good example. He was a hard leader but his team would jump through walls for him.

'I've worked on Billy Drew before and confirm everything that Mick has said. It would be a waste of time trying to follow him conventionally. Even when he goes out shopping he spends his time doing counter-surveillance to test if anything's there. We could get an OP set up to cover his house, and the same for Colin Jack and Frank Drew. At least it would give us an idea of when they were out and moving. We could take on Frank with conventional surveillance at least till he gets anywhere near Billy.'

Macallan had heard enough and knew what needed to be done. 'Okay I'll have a closed-door meeting with the Super as soon as we're finished here, but what we'll get going is a meeting with the murder squad, offer them all assistance within reason. Mick will arrange an informant to get onto Frank Drew, Felicity will do an in-depth analysis of all the information on the previous jobs including the murder, and, Jack, you'll arrange visual coverage of the targets' homes and the hard one – requesting the authority to get an electronic beacon on Billy's car and bug his home.'

The room straightened up as one and Harkins realised that she was going for broke. It was ambitious and there would be a raised eyebrow or two and probably a comment in the chief's office that this wasn't Northern Ireland, but it was good.

Macallan turned to O'Connor, expecting a frown, but there was a spark in his eyes and a smile of encouragement. He put his notes down. 'I said I wanted fresh thinking on this and that's what I hear. We want success for the team and so, Grace, I want you to make the case for this on paper and I'll do the fighting upstairs to get the authorisations. The rest of you know what you've got to do, so let's get on with it – and the first round's on me if we get this one in the bag.'

They all relaxed and Young decided that she might miss a night at badminton the next time there was team drinks. She felt conflicted by Harkins but wanted to get to know him. She could never take him home to her mother but that wasn't what she had in mind.

11

About the same time the MCT were deciding what to do about Billy Drew and his team of hooligans, the man who'd beaten Pauline Johansson into a life of pain was finishing shaving. He ran the razor down his face and splashed it clean. His skin was plump, well nourished and he knew he looked good. His grey eyes were clear and his teeth were good, almost too straight, and had cost a fortune in private work. He held out his hand and marvelled that there wasn't even a hint of a tremor. He felt calm and doing the whore had gone according to plan.

He smacked some Italian cologne round his neck, smiling at the memory and the pleasure he'd felt in the act. That was what had surprised him most: the original plan had not been about pleasure, but once he'd hurt the first one, the feeling of power had almost overwhelmed him. It was as if something was growing inside him and needed feeding, but for now it was all good – he had his day job to take care of and perhaps a visit to the gym later to work on his pecs.

He pulled on his shirt and fixed his tie into a Windsor knot. As he left for work, he picked up his briefcase and, although it was cold, a watery sun was lighting the shadows on the city streets.

While he walked, he ran the whole thing through his head again; he had to learn where to improve the plan if possible. He felt light and well, studying the faces drifting by him, wondering what their particular secrets were. What would they have thought if they'd known that the man who brushed past them to buy his morning paper was going to be headline news for punishing the dregs of society? Most of them would be shocked of course, but there would be friends in the crowd somewhere, people who'd understand what his mission was really about.

Pauline Johansson had relaxed when she saw the polished Merc cruise past her for the second time. She was out of her tree but knew a nice set of wheels when she saw one, stoned or sober, and the dark shape driving the car was wearing a suit.

She turned and looked to see if there were any other girls nearby but the street was empty. She'd no idea what time it was, other than late, and she'd been planning to call it a night, but if it was a business type then she might hang on to see if he was up for it. Most of the other girls would be away so he was limited for choice. She whispered to herself, which was a habit she'd picked up on the long, lonely waits for punters. 'Business type, that'll do for me. Come on, my son.'

The Merc pulled into the kerb and the window slid down noiselessly. 'You working?'

She stuck her head in the window – it smelt nice, was warm and she just wanted to climb in before she froze to death. 'I was just going to finish, honey, but if you're up for it then I'm available.'

It was dark but she could see that this one was money. The downside of these guys was that they made her realise exactly how cheap and fucked up her life was. When it was the average punter in his clapped-out wheels trying to get the thrill he wasn't getting at home, then in a way it was okay. They were all just circulating in the same vat of pigswill. These business types paid well and really didn't want anything too daft, but it was as if they'd come from another planet.

She tried to focus her eyes but she was zombied after the hit she'd taken earlier. She inhabited a place where every single day was a struggle to get enough together for powder that would keep the stomach cramps away for another few hours. The powder came first and that would be bought before toothpaste or toilet paper. She felt like one of those hamsters that just ran on a wheel to get absolutely fucking nowhere. She needed this punter's money so she gave it her best smile and ran off the prices, hoping it would all be straightforward and he'd drop her off back at her flat. She wondered what his wife was like and what she would think of her husband being with a junkie who was frightened to go to the doctor because of what he might tell her.

He handed over the notes. She tried again to focus on his face, but the heroin and exhaustion reduced the man to a mushy shape rather than a set of features and expressions.

'Where's the best place to go?'

She could hear enough in his voice to know he was educated and it occurred to her that if Danny Fleming hadn't managed to fuck up her head, she could have had the life she deserved and ended up with a man like this. She guided him to an old industrial estate where the local police wouldn't bother them. She thought he was unusual because the normal punters were always a bit nervy, but it was like this guy was going for a walk in the park. She liked him, but then she liked everyone after finishing a packet of brown.

They pulled in behind the old warehouse, she told him they'd be better in the back of the car and she opened the door. She didn't see him pull the tyre jack from under the seat as he stepped out of the car. She was half into the back seat when he'd walked round behind her and grabbed a handful of her long blonde hair.

His first job was to shut the bitch up. He snapped her head back, tightening her throat, pulled her round and hit her as hard as he could just under the rib cage. She collapsed, struggling to get the air back into her lungs and moaned into the wet muck under her face. She was in too much pain to focus or make sense of what was happening but felt the man turn her over. He was strong and she was helpless.

Johansson had been hurt before by the odd punter, but the way this guy had put her down was enough to tell her there was more to come. She saw him take his jacket off and put it in a bag then roll his sleeves up. She managed to say the word 'please', but when he produced the tyre jack she tried to curl up into a ball.

He looked round; it was dark and quiet apart from the bitch moaning on the ground. He got to work – although he didn't want to finish this one, only take it as far as he could.

Johansson lapsed into unconsciousness as the dark shape above her grunted with the effort of ruining her face.

At 9 a.m. the following day he strode into the office and shouted good morning to the whole room. At least two of the women working there spent a good percentage of their working days wondering how they could get the man who had visited Pauline Johansson into their lives. Most of the others regarded him as a creep.

12

Harkins had primed the informant and promised him that this would be his last job before he retired.

The informant was a respected man, but way back he'd had to take out police insurance after getting involved with a piece of nonsense and having a visit from Harkins when he was in the Serious Crime Squad. He knew all about Harkins' reputation and between them they'd struck a deal which kept them both happy. He kept his life on track as long as he threw Harkins the odd carcass – although he always had to buy the drinks when he met the detective. He regarded the arrangement as a good deal considering what he could have lost if the detective hadn't stepped into his life.

Harkins asked him to see what he could get on Billy and Frank Drew.

'Okay, to be honest Frank Drew's a cowboy and better off the street. I know he's doing a bit with his brother, Billy, at the moment. The trouble with Billy is that since his wife died, he's decomposing and someone's going to get messed up, so what do you want me to look out for?'

Harkins gulped on the beer that had been bought for him. 'Concentrate on Frank because he's a liability. Just listen for anything he's up to or how he's doing it. Anything he mentions about his brother would be handy.'

The informant was as good as his word and the same afternoon he wandered into the bookies where he knew Frank Drew wasted most of his money. Drew wasn't there, but it was just a case of waiting, and he chewed the fat with a few of the local punters, all trying to find the magic formula that would make them happier than the bookie. He was a patient man so he could wait, and sure enough Frank Drew eventually breezed through the door as if he owned the place, although he'd certainly put enough through the grille over the years to buy the shop.

Drew didn't see the informant at first, so desperate was he to get his money onto a loser, but once he'd finished with that, he looked round the shabby little betting shop and perked up immediately at seeing someone who meant something, rather than the usual collection of living dead.

'What the fuck, man? What brings you to this dump?'

The informant chatted with Drew, playing on the fact that he was someone and Frank Drew liked to imagine that a real name actually gave a fuck about him. It didn't take long to work out that Drew was skint, and despite working with his brother, he hadn't learned to be discreet. He didn't push too hard, didn't need to; he arranged to meet Drew later for a couple of drinks, but it was clear that the boy wanted to blab and try to impress.

They split up and Harkins got the call from the informant filling him in on the story.

'Good man, don't rush it, and you're sure he's boracic?'

'The bookies get it all. The boy's a twat and God knows why Billy Drew has him in his team, but I suppose we all do things for our families.'

The informant enjoyed making these little oblique comments, knowing that Harkins didn't actually have what most people called a family. He'd come to like Harkins over the years and felt sorry that he'd end up as the old pisshead at the bar that everyone tries to avoid – even his ex-colleagues. Still, that was life and he guessed that Harkins wouldn't have swapped it even if he could – the man was a born thief catcher but fucked without the job.

Later that night he hooked up again with Frank Drew in a smelly little boozer that was safe and still sold a pint at real-life prices, unlike in the centre of town, where you could spend a week's wages on a few drinks. The informant had told Drew that the drinks were on him. After the second beer and chaser, he just couldn't shut the boy up; although he hadn't got to specifics, he'd blabbed that he was working with Billy and Colin Jack, and they were busy. He just let the boy talk – it would come in time.

'So, Frank, how's the big brother? I was sad to hear

about him losing his wife. I knew her. Terrible disease cancer.'

Frank Drew had hated his late sister-in-law because she saw him for what he was and was constantly warning her husband about having anything to do with him. He'd had to play the part though, and in any case, he couldn't say anything against her that might get back to his brother. Billy had adored his wife, nursing her right up to her last day, and anyone stupid enough to insult her memory would definitely get a visit from big Billy Drew – and a pickaxe handle.

'She was a wonderful woman; she never complained once about her illness. Trouble is that Billy's definitely been wrong in the mind since she died. He seems to be alright most of the time, but every so often somethin' just snaps and he goes radio fuckin' rental. He's completely lost the plot recently an' I told him it was a disgrace. Keep that to yoursel' though.' He touched the side of his nose and winked.

The informant tried to keep his face straight but knew that the idiot who was drinking with him would have ended up in hospital if he'd ever called his brother a disgrace. The drink was taking its effect and he decided it was time to start pushing. 'What's that then, Frankie boy? Did he sort someone?'

Drew realised that he was talking in the wrong territory, but he admired the informant and he felt like a mate now, so he would tell him a bit to impress. 'Can't say too much but we were on a job through the west and it went tits up, and lucky I was there to keep us right. That's all I'm sayin'.'

The informant had been around a long time, read the papers and was savvy enough to grasp what Harkins was after. He swallowed the rest of his drink in a oner. This was not what he wanted to be involved in, and the realisation of what these mad fuckers had been up to was enough to make him decide that he was no longer Frank Drew's new best friend. He would make the call then tell Harkins to get on with it without him. He didn't want Billy Drew at his door. 'Got to go, Frankie, but it's been good talking to you. I'll probably see you around – and you always know where to get me if needs be.'

Frank Drew was disappointed that it was all ending so suddenly, especially as he hadn't the price of another drink and was just getting into that groove where he believed he'd have an interesting view on almost any subject. 'Don't suppose you could spare me a bit?' he asked. 'I'll be fine when we get the next job. You've always got it back with interest in the past.'

The informant clapped him on the back and laughed, threw down a twenty on the damp bar top and made his getaway. He'd forgotten to bring the clean mobile he used for contact with Harkins but a phone box was the next best option. He got as far from the pub as possible before opening the door of a rare phone box and trying not to inhale the smell of pish.

Harkins was ordering his third pint when his phone trembled in his pocket. He picked it up, nodded to the barman and walked outside to talk.

'What's up? I'm in the middle of a very nice

session and now I'm standing in the pissing rain.'

'Listen, Mick. We've known each other a long time so I want to make sure you understand. I've just filled young Frankie with lager and he's off at the mouth. All I can tell you is that they pulled a job through the west, Billy lost it completely and someone seems to have got hurt. Whatever it was, the boy hasn't a bean so there was no big score and Billy is out looking for another job at the moment. Now I may not be Sherlock Holmes, but I listen to the news and can put two and two together and all that shite. I want fuck all to do with a double murder, and I particularly don't want mad Billy Drew opening up my head. They're the boys and it's over to you. Too many risks, Mick. I'm enjoying life and don't want to end my days staring at the sky from a skip. To be honest, if you can't get that daft fucker that I've spent money on then you need to retire now. By the way, will I ever get expenses?' He laughed – Harkins had never given him a penny in expenses all the time he'd known him.

Harkins knew there was no point arguing, and in any case the informant was right and it was time for him to step back. He'd enough to say that Billy Drew and his team were legitimate targets now for an operation and he smiled at the thought. 'No problem and understand. Fancy a drink some time?'

The informant laughed down the phone and knew that their long relationship was coming to an end. 'Not while you're after this team. Tell you what though – when you get them wrapped up, do us all a favour and retire. I'll have a glass with you and you can pay for a change.' He put the phone down and breathed a sigh of relief.

Harkins went back to his seat at the bar and started to work on the fresh pint that was waiting for him. He should have had the old buzz, but it wasn't there. He should have been spinning the ideas round his head, what moves to make next, but they weren't coming. He felt flat and realised that even his long relationships with his informants were coming to an end.

He wasn't even supposed to *have* informants since the new system had come in and they'd put an end to developing and owning your own. There had been so much abuse of the system and payments that specialised source-handling units had been set up to take over ownership of informants and bring in tight rules on managing them. Harkins had played along but put up an act that the best ones wouldn't speak to anyone else but him.

He knew that his type was being replaced by the O'Connors of this world, and for the first time in years he felt something he realised was fear. Fear of the future, because he couldn't see it. He had nothing against O'Connor, and Grace Macallan was the first person he'd actually liked in a long time. She and O'Connor were good in a way that he could never be. His way had been to kick doors in and go face-to-face with the villains, but those days were over. The criminals were smarter, more violent and had dropped the old rules of the game.

He sipped his pint and sighed. 'What the fuck am I doing?'

He knew that the job kept him from the full-blown alcoholism that would be his fate once they gave him his pension cheque and a pat on the back.

He sank the rest of the beer and stuck his hand up to the barman. 'A wee goldie to go with the pint this time.'

Macallan walked in then and he waved to the barman again to fix her drink. She pulled a stool in beside him and stretched her back and neck. 'I'm knackered, Mick, so make it a large one. Have you heard anything from your unofficial sources?'

Harkins told her what the informant had reported and she nodded without interrupting. He waited for her reaction. 'Think that'll do for us, and I've done the application for authority to bug him. If we can get the car wired for sound then we can stay well away and watch where he's scouting from the office. We'll keep a team near enough to go in if needs be but far enough away not to spook him. Cheers! Now let's see how good we are. I'm going to arrange with the murder squad to give him a visit; we'll go with what you said about him expecting that.'

Harkins nodded. 'Good. This guy won't give a toss about a pull from the Glasgow team, and he'll be looking for it. The sooner we can get it done the better.' They clinked glasses.

'Consider it done – I'm on it in the morning. By the way, you look like you've had a better day. You okay?'

He swallowed the whisky and gave her a tired smile – only it was forced and just for effect. They both knew it.

'Right as rain. Now tell me about Belfast. I've

heard the stories but you've never mentioned it, even though I've given you the privilege of my friendship.' He cheered up at his own joke and it moved his mind away from the future.

She stared at him for a moment. He'd disarmed her, and for Macallan that was the puzzle that was Harkins – despite his fearsome reputation and all the warnings, he'd been with her from day one. No threats, no crude advances by an older man looking for a scalp to hang on his collection.

She told him as much as she could, and he marvelled at what she described without a shred of self-pity. She trusted him to listen and he realised that she was something good in his life, but if anything the thought made him feel empty again and that the choice he'd made all those years ago wasn't going to pay him a dividend. Friends and family gave you a life of problems, but if you were lucky they gave you something to hang on to when you realised that you were the past. He hoped Grace wouldn't make the same mistake.

Over the course of three rounds she talked about her former life as if Harkins was her confessor, and at times her honesty baffled him – as did her vulnerability, given her talents and strengths. In the end she took Harkins right to the day she'd left the shores of Northern Ireland, the memory sharp, clear and painful.

The Belfast Incident – Leaving Northern Ireland

Grace Macallan pulled the collar up on her coat to protect her face from the cold north-easterly wind that tossed her hair and ruffled the waves on Belfast Lough. The ferry pushed slowly away from its dock and the engines growled up a beat as the ship gathered speed for the trip to the mainland. Her face was pinched and thinner than it had been months before, on the night that Tommy Doyle and Cowboy had met their ends. Her complexion was pale and dark shadows propped up her eyes. She hadn't smiled in a long time, but at least she felt some relief that Northern Ireland was moving into the distance behind her.

No one had come to the docks with her although Bill Kelly had joined her for one final drink the previous night. He'd told her she'd be fine, that she was strong, just a bit beaten up – and so she should be. This had been bad, but she would learn from it, and it would make her stronger. They'd lifted their glasses for the last time.

The ship beat past Carrickfergus as the Irish Sea opened up ahead, but she couldn't prevent herself musing, for the thousandth time, over what had led to her current situation.

When it got out about the statement she'd made against Jackie Crawford, she became marginally less popular than PIRA with the men and women in the force. To make it worse, the commander had parked her behind an administration desk in HQ, just to make sure she could spend her days being cold-shouldered. The senior levels had to praise her publicly for her courage and honesty but privately they were cursing her treachery. There was no such problem for the junior ranks, and they just cursed her openly and, whenever possible, in hearing distance. Bill Kelly, who never ate in the canteen, made a point of joining her whenever he could, but in a way that only made her isolation stand out even more. She could never say that to him though, and knew that he would pay his own price for loyalty to her.

She thought of young Jackie Crawford and how her evidence had corroborated the medical findings and put him away. No one else admitted to seeing a thing that night. The truth was that if she could turn the clock back, she would have seen and done nothing herself. Tommy Doyle would still be dead and she'd have Jack. He was the real hammer blow, and the shock of his last visit had stunned her for weeks after the event. She remembered the call the evening after she'd met the commander and been interviewed by the internal investigation team.

'We have to talk.'

Those words were such a well-used precursor to the message that one half of a relationship is off in a different direction. She'd been so sure of Jack. How naive! That evening had been bad enough but she'd thought she could get through it with his support. The problem was that he wouldn't tell her the why – just that it was over. It had to be connected to the incidents; maybe he didn't want the fallout touching him once their relationship became public.

The strange thing was that she hadn't even been able to get angry that night; she'd just told him to go. She'd never felt lonelier and had called in sick the next day, which she'd spent lying in bed. She'd wondered why women made the same mistake over and over again with guys like Jack Fraser – that was their real curse.

Eventually Macallan had taken Bill Kelly's advice and applied for a transfer to a mainland force.

As the ship punched across the sea the last sight she had of Northern Ireland was a thin grey strip on the horizon.

Macallan's mood calmed – the daily reminders of her position were being left where they belonged. She promised herself that she would never go there again.

She walked to the front of the ship and saw the mainland come into focus, and for the first time in weeks she thought things would get better at some point in the future. She was tired but in good health, and it was time to get her act together again. She was tempted to order a drink at the bar but realised it was time to get back to tea and coffee during the day. She ordered a black tea, smiled for the first time in weeks and thought that whatever the future held it couldn't be worse than the past.

She touched glasses again with Harkins and smiled. He smiled back and was glad that she'd told him her story, because he could spot a fraud a street away. Grace Macallan was flawed but no fraud, and the only problem was that in this game that was a weakness. She would be hurt a few times or make the choice that he did and build a protective shield of cynicism. He hoped she'd just go with getting hurt, as at least it kept you in touch with the human race.

'Right, that's enough of that, Macallan, now I'm going to tell you a proper war story.'

He hailed the barman for the round that was the point of no return and guaranteed a double aspirin breakfast in the morning.

13

Billy Drew got his visit from the murder squad two days later, and he almost felt relieved when they knocked at the door. Colin Jack got the knock at the same time. Macallan didn't mention Frank Drew to the Glasgow detectives and agreed with O'Connor that they'd take the risk and leave him as a possible weak link for later.

Billy Drew had a day in the local CID office not answering questions and he'd rehearsed what they'd say with Colin. He wasn't surprised that Frank hadn't been lifted and presumed that the fact he'd been on a couple of jobs hadn't been picked up by the boys in blue. He was thankful for that and realised how little trust he had in his younger brother. He'd have to ditch him at some point or they'd all go down the swanny.

When he walked out of the station a few hours later, he went straight to the pub he'd arranged to meet Colin in if they were lifted. Jack was halfway through his pint when the door opened and big Billy Drew walked in and nodded. Jack winked at him and smiled. 'How'd it go?'

'Walk in the park – they're not making Glasgow detectives like they used to. One of them offered me a tea! I'm telling you, Colin, Taggart must be spinning in his grave.'

14

Billy Drew always used a stolen car on a job, but for scouting he used his own wheels, which he changed every few months. He knew that even if for some reason he was stopped by a patrol, there wasn't an awful lot they could do him for. Nevertheless, he was aware that no matter how careful he was, it just took a piece of bad luck on his part to give the pigs a break against him.

This time it was just an off-duty and very eager young probationer that clocked Billy Drew parking up an Audi well away from his home, which was what he tended to do. The probationer passed the car number to HQ and it was fired down the pipes to the MCT intelligence section.

The information reached Jack Forbes as his surveillance team were watching the front doors of the Drew brothers and Colin Jack from unoccupied flats. He set up another OP on the Audi once it was located.

Drew was seen on two consecutive days getting into the car and on one of those days picking up Colin Jack at his home, and Macallan decided that there was enough to get Jack Forbes to carry out a night job – installing the electronic beacon on the Audi. It took a big team operation to make sure that the area around the car was safe, and at 3 a.m. on a moonless and very wet night, Forbes' team got into the Audi, leaving the area with the job done just nine minutes later. The bug pulsed every few minutes to tell the team it was working then lapsed into sleep mode; it would activate if there was any movement on the car.

When Forbes got back to HQ he walked into Macallan's office and she gave him a thumbs-up as a technician altered some of the settings on the laptop. The screen glowed with an electronic map showing the exact location of Billy Drew's Audi. Harkins was with her and O'Connor had come out to show support.

Macallan put her hands on Forbes' shoulder. 'It's alive and kicking, Jack, so good job for you and the boys. We're going to let him run for two or three days to see where he goes and when we get him settled at night just leave him be. In any case, every job he's ever pulled was done early evening so we don't want to do twenty-four-hour cover at the moment. Let's all go and get a couple of hours' sleep.'

15

Billy Drew opened his door the next morning and frowned at another miserable, wet day. He swore he would fuck off and get a bit of sun after the next job. His head throbbed morning till night, he was sick of his lot and his guts told him that bringing his brother on board had been a major-league fuck-up.

He looked round the street and watched a couple of smackheads walk past talking shite. He had no time for these wasters, didn't feel sorry for them and regarded them as somewhere below the bottom rung of the criminal ladder.

He zipped up his waterproof and jogged the few hundred yards towards the Audi. He was just going to have a couple of runs past the house he fancied turning over to make sure of the ground and then recce the job after dark. Once they'd got it all done he'd have a look at the casino. He still kept fit so the run to the car got his blood flowing, and he was getting a buzz as the job developed.

Five hundred yards away a surveillance officer sat in a disused office block and made a note in the log of the exact time Billy Drew left his home, what he was wearing and that he was alone. He fired the information to HQ on an encrypted system and down to the rest of the team, spread well away from the area but ready to move.

Drew opened the door of the Audi and jumped in, starting the engine and putting on the heaters almost in one movement. The car was freezing; he made a call to Colin Jack while it heated up and the windows ran off the layer of half-frozen water.

'Listen, I'm having a bit of a run round the place today to see if there's anything behind me. I'll give you a shout about two and drive past your place. Usual drill, wait till I'm past and have a look at the cars behind me to see if anything smells. Call me if you see anything resembling pork.'

The conversation was picked up clearly by the listening device in the car. In the MCT office the listeners were monitoring the car and relaying the information back to the surveillance team, so they were warned that Drew would be using a third eye in the form of Colin Jack to identify any surveillance activity later in the day. There was a general sigh of relief in the office and cars that the equipment was feeding back the necessary to the operational team, and Harkins slapped his hand on the table at the news. 'Not so fuckin' smart after all, Billy,' he said.

Drew pulled away slowly and started what for him was his day's work. He prided himself on taking every precaution, but he had to be right on his toes with the murder squad still digging away, although he knew they would have a pile of suspects in Glasgow to get through while he earned. He couldn't stop thinking about Frank and whether he'd done the right thing bringing him into the team. If he didn't look after him, the boy would do something extra stupid and end up with a blade in his throat. Frank liked to play with the big boys, but he just wasn't equipped.

As big Billy Drew headed into the centre of the city, he would have been a bit upset to know that behind, to the side and in front he had an escort of surveillance cars hundreds of yards distant but following as if they had an eyeball on him.

He spent the early part of the day doing his counter-surveillance moves and relaxed when he never saw the same car twice. He ran into the country and took a couple of long quiet roads then pulled into field entrances to draw anything in. The electronic device did its job and the team following could see exactly what he was doing and where he'd stopped, and they put even more distance between Billy and themselves. On script, he ran past Colin Jack at the appointed time and the team ran an alternative route.

Drew called Jack after the run. 'See anything, Colin?'

Jack coughed into the phone, trying to draw on a cigarette and talk at the same time. 'Fuck all, unless the bizzies are dressing up in Lycra, wearing plastic helmets and using racing bikes. What about you?'

'Nothin', and I've run outside the city so we're fine. I'll have a look at the place later and see what it looks like in daylight. Probably have a walk round the streets there. Speak to you later, and get a hold of Frank but tell him fuck all at the moment. Just make sure he's available when we need him and that he's not sticking a needle in his arm or some shite like that.'

16

Macallan was still in the office and concentrating on the movements of the team when O'Connor walked in and sat opposite her and Harkins, who as always was sipping a stale coffee. 'How's it going, Grace?' he said. 'Any problems?'

She stretched her arms above her head and noticed that for the briefest moment O'Connor's gaze flicked downwards. Normally she would have had a problem with it, but she almost smiled and felt flattered that such a disciplined man had lost control, short as it was. What she didn't know was that Harkins had spotted it as well.

She gave O'Connor a weary smile. 'I don't want to tempt fate, but it's going like a song – the devices in the car are working perfectly. He's definitely looking at a job so we've just got to stay the course. It's going to cost a bomb running this job, but that's the battle you've got to fight with the gods upstairs.'

O'Connor made his usual notes and scratched his forehead with a pen. 'How do you see it going – and chip in with any thoughts, Mick?'

Macallan wanted to pick her words carefully as these jobs could be easily blown off course if they became protracted and expensive; there was always something else that needed done yesterday. She sounded as confident as she could be, and Harkins started to believe that she was at least as good a manipulator as O'Connor.

'The big bonus is that he's scouting, and if we can work out how he's picking his target then we can do it. We have his car beaconed but they'll steal fresh wheels for the job and we might not know what that is so we have to identify the target first and hopefully he'll come to the party. The problem is that we want him for the murders as well and he's not prone to leaving clues. If they just go for a break-in, they might do six months and then be out on the street again. However, Mick reckons that Frankie Drew is where it can go wrong for them. We'll prepare for full searches if we can get them lifted for a job, and who knows after that. We're also liaising with other forces on the historical jobs so maybe if we can get him doing one, we can tie others to him.'

Harkins agreed with Macallan, and O'Connor seemed satisfied, leaving to explain to the DCC why it was money well spent and likely to cost a lot more.

17

Billy Drew parked his car in Morningside Road, an area of the city that reeked of money and still felt like a small town on its own. It was that rare thing in that there was enough wealth in the place to keep a whole array of small, specialised shops in profit, and it did that even with a Tesco brandishing its muscle in its heart.

The surveillance team were warned where the car had stopped, and two female surveillance officers were dropped off to see where he was. He was gone by the time they eyeballed the Audi, so they took up seats in a very nice coffee shop where they could refresh on expenses and hopefully see him returning to the car.

He walked back into view about half an hour later, just as the two officers were enjoying their second overpriced latte. He could have been anywhere in the area but they were close to some of the most expensive bricks and mortar in the city, so Drew's target had to be close.

He drove straight back to his home and waited for the darkness.

Macallan decided that she would go out with the team; she was sure now that Drew was getting ready and they had to find out what his MO was. 'What do you think of the show so far?'

Harkins looked up from his expenses claim. 'I'll tell you when it's done. Somewhere along the line we'll need a bit of luck. You always do, so let's hope the lucky fairies are with us tonight.'

18

Billy Drew heaved himself back into the Audi about the time Macallan was considering calling the operation off for the night. That was always the way of it with surveillance – sitting for hours or days with nothing happening. The trick was to be patient and have faith in the job.

The electronic beacon pulsed and betrayed Billy Drew to the surveillance team, who could afford to stay a bit closer with the cover of darkness. He headed straight to the same casino he'd gone to the previous night with the team keeping him company. They followed him in past the bouncers; it was busy enough to let them watch him with the minimum of effort.

The casino was a handsome art-deco building that laid on a nice service for the punters and stood on any trouble with maximum force. It had a good clientele, and at this time of night was filling with customers looking to break the bank. There was the usual mix of dreamers, loners, gambling addicts and the odd criminal trying to launder a bit of the profits. It was also this late in the evening that the real money started to arrive in the shape of restaurant owners who'd sweated for twelve to fourteen hours trying to keep their customers fed and happy. The majority were ethnic Chinese who just loved to spin the wheel at the end of the day. The casinos went out of their way to encourage them in through the doors, and for the Chinese it was more than the gambling – it was a meeting place for their community, and they would travel long distances after a day's work to chew the fat with their own.

Drew played the tables and the surveillance team watched him place the odd hand but realised he wasn't concentrating on his game. He was doing what they were doing and watching someone else. They passed the information back to the rest of the team, spread well away from the casino and any over-inquisitive bouncer with a dislike for law and order.

Macallan realised that they'd just worked out how Drew picked his targets. He could be sure that most of the Chinese were involved in the restaurant industry, especially if they were late-night arrivals. Look for the better-dressed big spenders and follow them home, then once he had them home, he could do it the other way and watch them leaving for work during the day. Eventually he could work out a pattern of behaviour, judge if they were well heeled, and when their homes would be empty, and if it was going to be a just break-in or a tie-up job. Simple, and it had worked for fifteen years.

She radioed the rest of the team. 'I know it's late, guys, but we have to see what he does next. I want eyes on the car park and I want someone to get a note of the numbers of all the cars there so we can check ownership and addresses.'

No one had a problem and Macallan ordered a car to run up to Morningside where Drew had been seen leaving his car during the day. Mark the spot and see if he went back there again.

Some of the team were starting to struggle to stay awake when the call came in from the footmen inside the casino – Billy Drew was leaving. Macallan called to the eyes on the car park to see if anyone else was there. They confirmed that a middle-aged Chinese male had left just ahead of Drew.

They had it, and the Audi trailed the owner of a chain of successful family restaurants back to his home, which must have pleased Drew because this area was wall-to-wall money and perfect for what he had in mind. Large detached stone piles of real estate with field-sized gardens to the rear. The area could have been outside the city it was so quiet, and no one bothered anyone in this piece of the town.

Macallan radioed Harkins, who was in the squad room, to make sure he'd heard it all.

'Got it,' he replied. 'What's the plan now?'

'Billy's on his way home now so not expecting anything tonight, but we'll leave some of the guys in the area in case Sod's Law comes to visit. We'll get everything in place – he must be thinking of doing the job some time over the next couple of nights. Get off home for some sleep and I'll see you first thing to start planning the op. We'll have it well covered.'

19

Harkins pulled on his coat and left HQ realising that he wasn't pulling the strings any more – and that he was contributing little to the operation. In the good old days they would have just pulled the bad guys in and started twisting a few handfuls of nuts. He knew he represented old ways but reassured himself that the informant was his and had given confirmation on the Drew boys at least.

He opened the door that led out to the street, felt the cold air swarm over him and cupped his hands around the cigarette as he fired it up and sucked in a lungful. The cold crept into the spaces at his neck, clawed its way under his collar as his nose chilled and tears boiled over his eyelids. The days when the cold air would invigorate him were gone, and he stepped into a monochrome world where the wind scorched the skin on his cheeks, cursing as he felt a damp worm creep in through a coin-sized hole in his shoe.

He walked as fast as he could to get to the protection of his flat and wished that the pubs were still open. There were times when he worried he might be an alcoholic – but what would life be like without its numbing friendship, and what was there that he could replace it with?' All he was doing was existing in the bubble of each separate day, where there were no anniversaries or flowers taken home to remind someone that they were loved. He couldn't look forward and was afraid when he looked back and realised what could have been.

He saw the apartment light beckon him. This was the only place now where he could hide from a world that was changing in front of his eyes. The MCT was to be his last big play, but it was just turning into an overdose of reality.

He looked up to his windows on the fourth floor and a dull ache spread from the base of his neck, beating through his shoulders. He stepped onto the road, reaching for his keys and wondering why they were never in the first pocket you tried, before he snapped up straight as a car blasted the horn and hissed past him so close it touched the cloth of his flapping raincoat. He swung his head to the right and watched the red tail lights disappear. The car hadn't been speeding and he hadn't heard a sound until it had brushed past his life. He ran to his front door and leaned against it till his breathing had calmed.

His eyes snapped open. The TV was on but the sound was on mute and he looked at the small table next to his chair, where the remains of his whisky coloured his glass. He glanced at the clock to find it was 4.30 a.m., rubbed his face and walked through to his bedroom.

20

Macallan couldn't sleep and was in the office before the morning cleaners. She was still high from the night before. There was nothing like it – that buzz when a job came together and there was the scent of an arrest. It was the hunt, and there was always that possibility that the target could escape, but she'd make sure she left no way out if Billy Drew gave them the chance.

She started planning the operation to bring down Drew and his team. Something could always go wrong of course, but there were days when the gods smiled down on you and it just happened. It felt like one of those days.

The high had spread through the team and they started to pile in early, even though they'd only have managed two or three hours' sleep. Their biggest fear was missing the show.

The Audi hadn't moved, and Macallan breathed a sigh of relief. She'd feared Drew would take off during the night with only a skeleton surveillance team to try and keep up with him.

O'Connor sat in on the briefing as Macallan outlined her plan to the team. 'We believe that Billy and co are ready for a job, and we think we have the likely target. It's unlikely that it'll happen during the day, but we'll have him covered, and if it follows the pattern, they'll have to pick up a set of stolen wheels – that'll be down to Frank Drew or Colin Jack.'

The door opened and Harkins walked into the briefing. He was late for the first time in his career. Anyone else would have had a dig from O'Connor, but he deserved better than that and Macallan waved him into a seat, wondering at the spark now missing from his eyes. His shoulders seemed less square and he looked weary.

'Mick, I'd like you to make an approach to the owner of the house and, if he's agreeable, get two or three guys who can handle themselves into the place as a reception party. We'll have to get them from the locals, and we don't want any of our surveillance guys involved. What do you think?'

Harkins pulled himself up and got into gear. 'I'll take care of the owner and see what we can do. There's a few bears who work locally and one's an ex-marine who'd be a fair match for Billy Drew.'

There was no sense of drag or tiredness, and as the day moved on the pieces fell into place. A young probationer called Jimmy Lee, whose parents had come from Hong Kong, had jumped at the chance to work with the MCT as liaison, and Harkins smiled at the raw enthusiasm he saw in the boy. He must have had that at some point; he just couldn't remember it now.

Despite their fears that the owner of the house might have been shy about allowing a reception committee into his home, it was quite the reverse. The Chinese community in Scotland was close, and they knew all about the murders in Glasgow. Although the man hadn't been told that it might be the same group involved, he had worked hard to be a success and despised the type of people who would invade someone else's home. He was a widower, his children grown and flown the nest, and over the years he'd served hundreds of his meals to night-shift policemen, meaning he'd lost the traditional suspicion his ancestors had held about government officials, and particularly the police.

The likelihood was that Billy Drew was planning a break-in while the owner was in the casino – but they'd protect him in either case.

21

In the early afternoon Frank Drew drove the car they'd stolen back into the city as the sleet beat down and parked it behind some garages near his flat. Although the two surveillance officers didn't pay attention to the car going in, they saw Drew emerge from the garage area and that was enough to ring the alarm.

When he left his front door about an hour later and headed to the bookies, Macallan asked for the garage area to be checked. Anyone watching would have seen a messed-up alky shuffling round the garages looking for a place to piss – and nothing unusual in that. The surveillance officer took a slug at the can of Carlsberg and memorised the number of the VW. Frank Drew had been told to park it well away from the area, somewhere safe, but he'd fucked up again and Macallan did a quiet 'thank you, God' when the wheels were confirmed as stolen.

'We can't let them get too far from us,' she'd told the surveillance and arrest teams during the operational briefing. 'So once they're in the stolen car we'll go in as close as we can and hope this is the night.'

As Macallan checked the time around 9 p.m., the calls came in from the surveillance officers that Frank Drew had driven off in the stolen car. This was followed by calls that Colin Jack and Billy Drew had been seen getting into it. The surveillance team moved out behind them but kept their distance, and they all willed Frank Drew to drive safely to the reception party.

They followed the stolen car to the dark, peaceful streets of the conservation area known as the Grange and its stone-built, late-Victorian homes. Macallan gave the order to let Drew and his team run in the area and a dozen cars closed off the surrounding streets.

Billy Drew got out of the car and nodded to his brother and Jack. The plan this time was to break in knowing the owner would be away till the early hours.

'I'll watch it for an hour and give you the call to come in,' he told them, before walking across the deserted street and then climbing over a dividing wall at the back of the darkened house. On the other side of the wall he waited for a couple of minutes without making the slightest move, then he slipped into a shrub border and settled down again to watch and listen. His army training and discipline had never left him, and he took care before a job. He waited until his eyes had adjusted to the darkness, then watched and listened for anything that might alert him to a problem or a neighbour's dog taking an interest.

In a darkened bedroom on the second floor of the house the police team waited, their tension rising as they realised the man they wanted was close. Ex-marine Steve John was one of them, and like Billy Drew, he had never forgotten his training. He'd barely moved a muscle since getting in place, though the other officers shifted impatiently in other parts of the house. He whispered into his head mic: 'Target one is in the garden and not moving. No sign of the other two.'

Macallan was in a car half a mile away and had been here before. 'Patience. Just give Billy and his boys time to do their job.'

They did need patience – Billy Drew sat still for fifty minutes before he called Jack to give him the all-clear and tell him to climb over the wall so they could get started.

John watched the dark shapes struggle over the wall as Billy Drew moved out of concealment. He moved down to the ground floor so he could be part of the reception committee, relayed the information, and Macallan gave the order for the arrest teams to move in close. There was no alarm, and as Jack got to work on the window, a dozen officers moved in on three sides of the house, and the street either side of the stolen car was blocked.

Billy Drew went in first and all hell broke loose. Jack

couldn't make sense of it and froze, but Frank Drew had no problems in deciding to get the fuck out of there. Jack looked round, trying to decide whether to go in the window and risk whatever was in the dark and definitely giving Billy a hard time. When he saw the bodies coming at him from all sides, though, he realised it was time to put his hands up. Frank Drew got over the wall like an Olympic jumper and tried to run but was pulled down by a police dog named Captain who ripped into his calf muscle. Billy Drew had tried to put up a fight inside the house, but he'd realised he wasn't as sharp as he used to be because whoever had hit him had known exactly what they were doing – the first blow was a winner, and it wasn't much of a struggle after that.

Macallan ran her hands through her hair and punched the air. The first part of the job was done. She left her team to clear up at the house and headed for the squad room to get the next part of the operation moving.

As she headed back to HQ she was struggling to clear her mind and missed a red light. Then, when she tried to turn left, she just managed to miss a Mercedes who had the right of way. She banged the steering wheel in frustration and decided to take a minute, pull in and take a few deep breaths.

The driver of the Merc cursed. 'Fucking woman driver.' But he had more important business that night and headed on towards Leith to take his next step. He felt on fire and looked forward to the night ahead.

22

O'Connor was with Harkins when the news crackled across the airwaves that the arrests had been made. He smiled at Harkins and slapped the table. 'Nice one. Now if we can get something to tie them to the murders in Glasgow, we're off to a flyer.'

Harkins didn't give a fuck about the executive floor, but this was a good result, although still only a partial one. They would need a break to put them away for a lifer. 'I'd like to have seen the face on Billy Drew when he broke into that house and met Steve Jones. Grace has done a great job; I take my hat off to her.'

O'Connor nodded at that one. She was turning into the lynchpin of the MCT, and he had no problem with that if she could bring the results in. He knew that as head of the team, good results reflected on him first as far as the chief's office and, just as importantly, the press were concerned. If she could nail the murder charges then any lingering doubts in people's minds after Belfast would be just what they were – history.

O'Connor had had doubts about coming back to the force after Germany, where he'd been offered a string of UN jobs that would have had him living in style, but he still had his ambitions about a chief constable's post. It was what he'd always wanted, and he was young enough that if it didn't work out, then he still had time to jump back onto the international merry-go-round.

He glanced at the worn face on Harkins and thought, not for the first time, what it would have been like to have taken his path. O'Connor played safe bets, and his eye had always been on his career above all else. He'd had a good start in life with money behind him, and a decent 2:1 from university. Even when he joined the force he'd been planning the road ahead while the other young cops were enjoying the excitement of the streets and partying on their days off. While they'd been dealing with hangovers, he'd been in the books and applying for anything that would add to the CV. The older guys could spot what he was a mile off and had kept him at a distance, just in case he was too honest when they were slightly adjusting the rules. He was good at everything he did but didn't take risks. That was the problem: there had to be risks taken and that's where guys like Harkins came in.

O'Connor knew that he would never have the legendary status among the troops that Harkins did, but at the end of the day, someone had to sit in his chair and someone had to sit in Mick's. He tried not to dwell on it, but there were times when he would have loved to have been that man and have the old cops trading stories about how he'd gone face-to-face with the bad guys and pissed on their shoes. However, looking across at Harkins again, he reassured himself that there would have been too high a price to pay.

'You look shagged out,' O'Connor said to him. 'You okay?'

Harkins manufactured a laugh. 'All good – counting the days to retirement and just want to see Billy D off to the pokey.'

They both knew that was shite, but there were more important things to think about, and Harkins shifted the conversation back to the job in hand. 'I'm going to get the warrants – we'll get teams organised to search their homes and full forensics. We've told Strathclyde and they'll send someone through, but at the moment they're still going through all the possibles on their side of the country. Trouble with the Weegies is that they think they have *all* the violent psychopaths instead of just most of them.'

O'Connor nodded, then headed back to his office and poured some of his own coffee, having given up on the canteen muck a long time ago. He'd been worried that coming back to the daily grind of a force would have been too much reality, too hard to deal with again, but the world had changed in his time away, and the criminals were getting bigger and better everywhere. The movement of people meant that exotic gangs, which in other times wouldn't have moved out of London, were all across the country. Yardies, Balkan gangs and Triads were competing with the locals, and it would keep Her Majesty's Constabularies in work for a long, hard time. The force had changed, and it just about matched his ambitions, although he was impatient to get where he wanted to go.

His thoughts wandered to Grace Macallan. It was unusual for O'Connor to take too deep an interest in anyone, but she did it for him. It worried him slightly, and he wanted to take time and consider all the options before making a decision that he might regret. He was intrigued by her complications. An attractive woman, with eyes that could laser through metal, and a complete lack of pretence. She was what she was. When he looked at her service history, he felt the same pangs that Harkins generated in him. She had a stunning record, working in one of the most dangerous police environments in the world, and had been face-to-face with men who'd cut your throat for swearing an oath to the Queen. He'd had relationships with women but always outside the job and found it easy to knock back the occasional offer inside the job, which helped stoke the rumours about his sexuality. He was conflicted by Macallan, found her wonderfully attractive but worried she might be a threat down the line.

His desk phone rang – it was Harkins telling him that Billy Drew and his team were ready for interview, and the search teams were on their way to take their places apart.

Macallan walked into the cramped interview room with Harkins and had her first look at the real Billy

Drew. She thought he was impressive, in good shape – his eyes were sharp, clear, and he was calm. She knew this was likely to go nowhere, but she wanted to meet the man and introduced herself. He wasn't impressed.

'Look, I'll give you my name and address even though you already have that, and apart from that fuck all. Just get me locked up and I'll take my chances in court.'

Macallan didn't want to ask questions about the murders because they had nothing to go on, but she at least wanted him to know they were thinking about it. They would plant a seed and let it germinate. She let Harkins take the pleasure of that one.

Harkins looked straight into Drew's eyes. 'We've got Colin and your pissed-up brother. I reckon Colin will hold but what the fuck were you thinking taking Frank on your team? You're getting old, Billy.'

Billy Drew decided he would speak after all. 'Mr Harkins, you might not have noticed but we're both getting old – and you look a bit further down the line than me. Time was you would have planted the evidence and game over, but I guess that's not allowed now. Fuck me, you trail in here with a woman for a boss and try and take the piss. Fuck off back to the bar, Harkins, and drink yourself to death. From what I hear that's what you're doing anyway.'

The two men stared across the table at each other and declared a draw.

Macallan cut through the testosterone filling the room. 'Okay, Billy, we'll be back after we see Colin and Frank. Search teams will turn over your places and then we'll see. There's a chance that the boys from the Glasgow murder squad will want to talk to you again.'

Drew looked at Macallan and didn't like what he saw. He didn't understand her. He understood Harkins but he just didn't like her. She looked too fucking smart to be a cop.

The interviews were a frustrating struggle. Colin Jack played the same game as Billy, and Frank managed to hang on without making any kind of admission. He was on the verge, but fear of his brother and what they faced meant he'd held his nerve.

Late into the night Harkins, O'Connor and Macallan sat down together and tried to find a positive. O'Connor had lost a bit of spring – getting Billy's team for a break-in would be a result but not a headline. It looked like they could tie some other jobs to them on circumstantial, but that was it.

O'Connor tried to lift the mood. 'What do you think, Mick? Is there any chance of an admission to anything?'

'Not a chance – Frank is holding the line. It wouldn't take much to break him, but at the moment there's no lever apart from the stolen car and the break-in. They're even denying the stolen car so we need a break.' It was the same old story with the real villains. You could catch them with their hand wrist deep in the till and they'd deny even being in the shop – it was the game

Macallan's mobile trembled. It was the lead officer

in the forensic team so she apologised to O'Connor, stepped outside and took the call.

Harkins leaned on the table and felt the weight pressing down on his shoulders. Billy Drew had touched an open nerve. 'Years ago I would have wrapped them up, evidence or not. I fucking hate seeing them walk away time after time. They need the shit knocked out of them.'

'Leave it. Those days are gone so leave it and don't talk like that outside this room. What the fuck is wrong with you?'

It was unusual for O'Connor to curse and it added to Harkins' bad mood.

The door opened and Macallan walked in.

'Forensics have been to Frank Drew's house and guess what? He's an old barbecue drum in the back garden. They've recovered part of a balaclava and a boiler suit. He's fucked up. Apparently there are hairs on the mask. We just got that bit of luck, Mick.'

Harkins spoke for all of them. 'Fuck me pink.'

23

Macallan was sitting in her office, pretending to concentrate but praying to a god she didn't believe in for the break they needed, when the Senior Forensic Officer walked in. 'Sit down, please, but let me get Mr O'Connor through.'

O'Connor and Macallan listened to the scientist without interrupting. They didn't need to.

'Basically the part of the balaclava we recovered had human hairs, and we're still running tests, but they're almost certainly Billy Drew's. Now that proves nothing, but there's DNA on the front part and it's from Mr Yip and we believe it's saliva.'

Macallan and O'Connor shared a look then O'Connor picked up the phone to get Harkins in the room as the Senior Forensic Officer continued: 'On part of the boiler suit we've recovered we've sprayed blood patterns and they're from both victims. No doubt about it. Inside the suit we have DNA from

Billy Drew. We think that Frank Drew burned the majority of the kit, but the rain did us a favour and at some stage he probably lost interest in the fire and didn't finish the job.'

Harkins entered the room.

'Sit down, Mick – I want you to hear this.'

The SFO repeated her account then left the room, and it was O'Connor who broke the silence: 'What do you think?'

Harkins was the first to answer. 'I think Billy Drew is fucked. Can I be the first to tell him? I should add: God bless Frank Drew.'

'I think I can go with that. Grace, get the work done, and then let the team know the drinks are on me.'

He looked at Macallan longer than required, and they asked each other questions without saying a word.

24

Billy Drew was seething, but he didn't let it show when Harkins dropped the forensic evidence on him. He was even more pissed off that the only forensic evidence belonged to him. Frank had burned Colin's gear and his own before leaving Billy's stuff for the pigs. He swore that if he got near Frank, he'd forget he was his brother and do the world a favour.

'You'll be a happy man then, Harkins. Probably get a few free Chinkies out of this. Close the door on your way out – I've got fuck all to say to you.'

Harkins relished the moment, wanting to enjoy it while it lasted. 'Wee bit to do yet, Billy. The boys from Glasgow are here and they're going to charge you with the murders ... enjoy.' He moved to leave the room but turned to face Drew again at the door. 'By the way, I may be getting fucking old, but I'll be on the outside while you, my friend, will be eating stewed fucking cabbage for your Christmas din-dins.'

Colin Jack decided that he would try and carve a few years off by making a full statement blaming Billy, claiming that he'd lost the plot and there had never been a plan to harm the victims. Harkins loved that one.

Frank came apart when Harkins went in to tell him the story so far – that in all likelihood his brother would try to kill him. He already knew that though and started to blub like a five-year-old. Harkins wrinkled his nose and looked under the table to see that Frank had pissed himself, and not from laughing.

'You really are a fucking tragedy, Frank. Have you any idea what some of those lifers are going to do to you in the showers?'

Frank blubbed even harder and Harkins took a shot at the open goal.

'You could help yourself by telling us all about it – and while you're at it, all those other tie-ups and break-ins across the country.'

Foolishly, Frank believed him and sold everyone down the river. He'd have shopped his granny if he'd ever met the woman.

Back in the office Harkins shook his head and summed the boy up.

'That boy is so fucking low he could walk under a snake's belly without waking it up.'

25

O'Connor was man of the moment in the Chief's office; he played the story to maximum effect, and his bonus came with the order to front the statements to the press and media. He was born for it and made sure that every reporter who wanted a story from him was welcome. The boys from the Glasgow murder squad were full of praise in public but they knew the MCT had kept information back from them.

O'Connor made sure that Macallan was mentioned in the right places but always with just a touch less stardust than he gave himself. She didn't mind; knew that's how the big boys' world spun. She would probably have done the same thing herself. What O'Connor forgot was that crime reporters spend an awful lot of time, and expenses, cultivating parts of Her Majesty's Constabulary that other people can't reach. Macallan had been in the dirty war over the water, was a class act and on top of all that had links to the tragedy on Ormeau Road. That made her news, and the more talented hacks were as interested in her as they were in O'Connor.

No successful police operation ends without a drink, and Harkins had arranged a takeover of a friendly pub. The Drew brothers and Colin Jack were safely remanded in custody and there had been a nice touch of drama when Billy had tried to attack Frank at court. As far as Harkins was concerned life didn't get any better, and he called his informant to make sure he was okay. 'The boys were safely remanded,' he said.

'What they deserved. It was completely out of order what they did. Now shouldn't I get expenses for once? Don't want you drinking them without me.'

Harkins smiled at that one. 'You'll get the drink, my friend; just wait a bit till I hand in my ticket. Won't be that long because I'm getting past it – I can't keep up with the new generation.'

'You and me both.'

The MCT took an early finish on O'Connor's orders and had retired to the pub to let off steam. The mood was high; O'Connor was as good as his word and had agreed to pay for the first couple of rounds. Macallan watched the orders going over the bar and shook her head, knowing he would likely have to take out a second mortgage to pay for it all. Harkins joined in, ordering a large eighteen-year-old malt.

'It's the privilege of rank, Grace,' he told her, 'and anyway he can afford it.'

She decided he was right and told the barman to

make hers the same. 'He's doing a TV interview as we speak and then he's going to join us.'

They touched glasses and sipped the malt, feeling the soft heat melt on their tongues and dull the edge of their stress. Harkins looked at Macallan and gave her the compliment. 'You did a great job. I don't say that very often, but you deserve it. You've got the team eating out of your hand – they'll do anything for you now.'

They clinked glasses again and threw the remaining malt back in one.

'Thanks. They're a great team and I think we can do good things. JJ does a good job as well, gets us resources and that makes him worth his weight. At some stage he'll lead on a bigger case and have to get his hands dirty, so he deserves our support when it comes.'

Harkins was a natural when it came to reading people; he'd never been trained in non-verbal communication and didn't need to be. He saw the look in Macallan's eyes when she mentioned O'Connor, and not for the first time it worried him. He'd seen the same look in O'Connor's eyes.

'He'll get all the support we can give him because at some stage he'll need us,' Harkins said. 'You know better than anyone that you're just as good or bad as the last job in this game, and the snakes are always just a bite away. I know that you don't like me saying it, but I'll say it again anyway – don't get involved. He won't march you up the aisle and live happily ever after. Cheers.'

He nodded to the barman to fill them up again and put it on O'Connor's bill.

'I know what you mean, and I'm not saying anything will happen, but we're both adults, both single, so surely we're allowed to take a chance, and if we make a mistake then that's life. On top of everything else that happened in Northern Ireland I had an affair, got badly burned and I haven't been involved with anyone since – unless getting pissed with you counts.'

She laughed, realising that the malt was stripping away her natural reserve and the cares of the day. It was time to enjoy the moment.

'I'm talking to you about things that are normally restricted to girl chat. What would your fans think if they knew you were a closet agony aunt?'

Harkins lifted his glass to his lips and realised it was true. He looked sideways at Macallan then joined in the laughter. 'Fuck me, you're right. I'll stick the head on someone later to get my credibility back.'

They slapped the glasses on the bar again and ordered a third round on O'Connor's tab. The noise level was rising; it was the way of squad celebrations that the hard discipline the job required could be left at the door. Everyone knew that someone would make a complete arse of themselves and others would wake up in the wrong bed. That was how it worked, and anyone above sergeant needed to leave after the first couple of hours so they didn't get the chance to fuck up their career. Macallan knew this – but she was going to enjoy those two hours.

She kissed the side of Harkins' head and clapped as one of the guys got up on a table to sing the only song he knew the words to. It was a tradition: he sang 'Mac the Knife' badly and after the first two lines he was pelted with crisp packets, peanuts and anything else the crowd could get their hands on.

O'Connor walked in the door, smiled and shook his head at the same time, wondering at the capacity of cops to fall overboard when the chance came along. He headed for Macallan and Harkins.

'I suppose I'd better get a drink before I'm bankrupt. The TV interview went well. Get a few of the more sober types to come in early, let the rest start around midday and we can get things tidied up. We need to make sure we're ready, because there's a report of a missing prostitute and a concern that it's tied to the previous attacks. Hopefully not, but it would mean we're not going to get much time to pat ourselves on the back. But let's forget that for the night and the team can move on with getting the best hangover my money can buy.'

O'Connor ordered a red wine and Harkins nodded to the barman to pass him the bill so far. He raised the glass to his mouth as the slip came over the bar then looked at the numbers at the foot of the paper. 'Jesus!'

He scanned the list of drinks and spotted the eighteen-year-old malts – and knew that Harkins and Macallan were the culprits. 'I should have known.'

Harkins ordered another round and slapped O'Connor on the back. 'The privilege of rank and, yes, you should have fucking known after all these years in the job. Anyway I'm going to mix with the guys before I get a bad name.'

He left the two of them at the bar, and O'Connor turned to Macallan, happy to have her to himself. 'So what do you think of the show so far?' he asked. 'If you're up for it, why don't we get away from here and I'll buy you a nice meal before we get a line of drunk detectives telling us their theory of life?'

Macallan was on her third drink and knew that if she stayed, her head would regret it in the morning – and one more drink would mean that she wouldn't want to leave anyway.

'Can you afford it after the drinks bill?'

'I'm not sure, but I know it's time to leave the guys to it.'

She put her hand on his forearm. 'Okay, as long as we agree not to talk about police work. I'll get my coat.'

She looked across at Harkins as they left the pub, and he raised his glass to her. He was still staring at the doors that had closed behind them long after they were gone.

Macallan and O'Connor sat in a beautiful sixteenth-century restaurant in the shadow of Edinburgh Castle, where candles flickered and a sense of history bathed the diners as the food was served.

Macallan hadn't felt like this for a long time, and it was good to be away from the job – to remember that there was another world away from the killers and nasties out there in the shadows. O'Connor knew his food and wine so she let him take the lead. The deep red Malbec he'd chosen peppered the back of her tongue, and the soft candlelight made her forget that she was a detective sitting opposite another detective. He began to tell her about his family, and she was surprised by his candour – this was, after all, a man who spent most of his day behind a stiff professional image. Certainly the polar opposite to someone like Harkins, whose message to the world was 'accept me or fuck off'.

He asked her about Belfast and she told him. She wanted to tell him; wanted him to know who she really was. He listened intently and hardly broke eye contact with her. He ordered a second bottle of wine, and for Macallan the other people in the restaurant had disappeared. There was only John O'Connor.

When she described the day she walked onto the ferry that would take her away from Northern Ireland, she was unprepared for the tears that welled up and stung the corners of her eyes. She apologised. He ran his thumb under her left eye and realised how difficult it was to know people – this was another Grace Macallan he was seeing. There were still people in Northern Ireland, some from her old force, who would toast her ruin, and he wondered what they would think of her if they could see what he saw now. He told her she'd done the right thing and realised that saying it meant nothing.

'The truth is that hardly a day passes that I don't wish I'd kept my mouth shut and carried on with my life.'

She straightened up and noticed that his hand was still on her side of the table. She took it and they turned their palms to grip each other. Her face broke into a smile. 'If you tell Mick Harkins I cried, I'll never forgive you.'

'Okay.' He paused for a moment, hesitant. 'Look, we've both had a big day and you must be shattered. What if I order a taxi and see you home?'

She paused and tried to make the right decision but the combination of malt, red wine and human need made it a no-brainer. 'Well, my place is like a shoebox, and I'd guess that you live in some kind of show home. You make me coffee at your place and it's a deal.'

As the taxi rattled over the high-street cobbles John O'Connor leaned over to kiss Macallan and she did nothing to stop him.

She was running up the Ormeau Road and it was dark – very dark. There was no sound, and her feet were dragging; for some reason she couldn't get speed and something was coming for her. Those dark shapes that lived in the Belfast shadows. She tried to call for help, but her voice was a long way off and no one could hear her.

She broke through the surface of the dream gasping for air.

'It's all right, Grace. You're safe and with me,' O'Connor said.

She realised where she was and put her head back on the pillow. The protective comfort of his presence was overwhelming, and she pulled his arm round her like a child before they both drifted back to sleep.

26

They were both woke early but lay without speaking, trying to work out the situation in the reality of the dull morning light. Macallan felt a small knot of panic but this was calmed by the tactile warmth of another human being beside her – the close contact she'd missed so much since Jack Fraser had last held her in Belfast. She knew O'Connor must be turning his own thoughts over in his head. He wasn't someone who normally did humour, but someone had to speak first so she turned and flicked the edge of her hand along his cheek. 'When will we announce the engagement then?'

His smile wasn't quite wide enough and there was no light in the eyes. It wasn't that funny, but he should have come back with a smile at least. Instead he kissed her cheek. 'It was a good night, and I think we both needed that.'

She thought about 'we both needed that' for a

moment. He'd gone back behind his cover and they weren't even out of bed yet. She tried to find the warmth that had wrapped them both up only hours earlier. 'There's no rush – we can go in later.'

But he was already sliding out of bed, and she felt the cold air invade the space where they'd lain together. She leaned up on one elbow and heard Harkins in the back of her thoughts. 'Is that it then, John? One night and thank you, ma'am. Couldn't you have just done that with one of the junior staff? They'd have loved it.'

He pulled a dressing gown round him and tied it tightly. 'Don't be daft. I want to have something with you but there's no rush. I haven't done commitment so far; you must know what I'm like. The truth is that you're the first person in the job I've felt attracted to, and you're something special. You're already becoming a bit of a celebrity with your background so let's not rush. We both have the same problem in sharing with other people – the difference between us is that I know it, and you've still to find out. But what you need to know is that people describe you in much the same way as they describe me. Think about it. Now I'm going to cook us a nice breakfast and just take last night for what it was ... wonderful. This is today, and there'll be another set of problems when we get into the office.'

She thought about it and decided that O'Connor might have a point. He cooked her the perfect breakfast, and they both relaxed, discussing the latest bad news coming from the Middle East. They were on their second coffee when O'Connor got the call. Macallan watched his face harden and knew that his mind was now a million miles away from breakfast with the woman he'd made love to half the night. He put the phone down and pushed his cup to the side as if it was in his way.

'They've found the second prostitute. They think it's linked to Pauline Johansson and they want us to take it on. Problem is that this one is dead so we have some hard days ahead. Can you get a hold of Mick if he's not in hospital getting his stomach pumped and get him into gear? Ask him to rustle up as many of the troops as he can find. No doubt some of them will still be lying with their legs up in the air.'

She found her phone, called Harkins' number and let it ring.

Harkins wasn't in hospital as it turned out. He was completely fine and in bed with Felicity Young, who'd turned out to be a complete revelation. He'd been surprised to see her arriving at the bar – then even more surprised later when she'd pushed in beside him and asked if he wanted a drink. At first he'd panicked, thinking that she wanted to talk about analysis or badminton, and everyone knew that he didn't do boring bastards. Fortunately he'd not had enough alcohol to just insult her there and then, and the realisation that she was interested in him had been a pleasant surprise. Under the businesswoman look was a very attractive and much softer human being – he'd just never noticed it before. She was from another world, but he'd shrugged and decided that if she wanted a bit of rough, well Mick Harkins was just the boy. She'd got what she'd asked for.

When he took the call from Macallan, Harkins knew without being told that O'Connor and the MCT were about to be tested to the limit. He put the phone down and looked at the woman next to him, shaking his head. 'I never would have believed it – Felicity Young and Mick Harkins falling madly in love.'

She laughed and he thought how little people knew about each other. Whoever this was lying next to him was not the woman who'd talked about nothing but analytical theory in all the time he'd known her.

He slapped her backside gently, just to remind her that he was a born-and-bred sexist. 'We've got work to do so why don't you rustle us up some nice bacon sandwiches?'

She explained about her strict vegetarian diet and offered muesli and some fruit.

'Fucking muesli! You realise this could finish us?'

She rubbed his arm. 'I love it when you do that unnecessary swearing thing.'

They got dressed and Harkins gave the muesli a miss. He decided that he'd head for the canteen at HQ and get an artery buster there before going into what would probably be a very hard day – which was just how he liked it.

27

O'Connor looked around the room and saw that a few detectives were suffering from the night before, but hangovers went with the job, and they could handle it. He explained what they'd inherited – or what it looked like they were about to inherit.

Maybe the gods were about to knock them down after their result with Billy Drew. O'Connor had realised when he'd read the details that this would be one of those cases that could end up in a swamp, sucking up resources and reputations in the dark world inhabited by the girls who worked the streets. Different detectives thought in different ways, but for O'Connor a risk to his CV and reputation concentrated his mind.

Helen Stevenson had been a prostitute for years, and was well known to the uniforms. It was the same old story – she'd had a rotten childhood and everything had gone downhill from there. She'd been injecting by the time she was seventeen, and the only way she could pay for the misery was through walking the streets, summer and winter. For all her problems, she was liked by the other girls and the beat cops treated her well. Her looks were long gone; she hadn't had a lot going to start with and struggled now for punters. Her life story wasn't that far removed from Pauline Johansson's.

Somewhere along the line she'd disappeared from her beat for a couple of nights and that was enough to ring alarm bells. She'd been found by a jogger getting his morning air along an East Lothian beach, about ten miles from the city boundary. He'd done his early-morning run there a hundred times and never tired of the quiet and ever-changing scenery. Having overfilled his bladder with an earlier coffee, he had headed into the sand dunes rather than get a bad name for accidental flashing. He had been enjoying the relief when he'd noticed Helen Stevenson's leg pointing at him from the base of a sea buckthorn. He'd no experience of bodies apart from occasionally watching *CSI* and had to suppress the instinct to run in the opposite direction. For a moment he'd thought about ignoring it, but he'd finally calmed himself and pulled back the branches. That's when he'd really panicked and ran like a sprinter to get help.

O'Connor asked Macallan to attend the post-mortem with him. She'd been at enough in Northern Ireland to get used to it, but there was always a knot in her stomach until it was over.

The thousands of tourists who wander the dark

medieval streets of Edinburgh's Old Town would pass the small drab mortuary building and never guess at the activity inside. This was where unexplained death ended up. The air was always cool, with a background noise of power being pumped in to feed the fridges, and glaring lights exposed every dark corner of the human anatomy. It was a place of learning, science and the search for truth.

For Helen Stevenson, there was an even bigger audience than usual: pathologists, mortuary assistants, detectives, forensic officers and the procurator fiscal all came to witness the final indignity of an undignified life. As post-mortems went, it was straightforward as to what had killed her. Like Pauline Johansson there had been massive trauma to the head, and the pathologist made an unscientific observation: 'This boy didn't mind the sight of blood.'

By the end of the process, Helen Stevenson was more exposed than she'd ever been with a punter. She lay open, laid bare in the cruellest of ways, and the eyes in the room stared at what was left of a life that would have passed almost unnoticed but for the meeting with her killer.

The pathologist removed her gloves and walked to a basin to scrub her hands clean as she gave an informal opinion to the assembled audience.

'Not much to tell you apart from what's obvious to the eye. Head injuries likely caused by a heavy blunt instrument. She died very quickly, and the killer would have blood and other material on him or her. I believe it was a man though, as whoever did this had considerable strength. There doesn't appear to be evidence of semen, but of course she was sexually active and I can't say whether the killer had sex with her or not. She was in poor health for a woman her age, she was malnourished and there are signs of intravenous injecting. Once we get the results from the lab I'll be able to tell you a bit more about that, but I'm sure none of that is a surprise. One thing that might be of interest is that she appears to have been suffering from genital herpes. I'm sure you're going to visit some of her customers so I'll leave it to you how you deal with that one.'

O'Connor thanked the pathologist and turned to Macallan. 'Let's get to work then.'

28

Across the city Helen Stevenson's killer pulled on his coat and left his office for the day. He wanted to pick up the evening paper and read about his work in comfort. The news had broken and he felt elated. No panic – instead the media reports had sent a surge of energy through him that had lasted till late afternoon.

He decided to go to the gym, work some of it off before studying the paper again with a drink. He'd let the police scrabble about for a couple of weeks before his next time. He'd accepted that somewhere along the line a mistake would be made or they might get a lucky break, but that was okay – he'd just play the game through and see where it took them all. He knew all he had to do was wait a few weeks and the police would drop their guard again – too busy with all their other problems.

He also knew enough about the police and the public to recognise that the attention span of news junkies was considerably shorter where a prostitute was involved. Missing or abducted children could leave the readers of the *Daily Mail* quivering for weeks, but a junk-wrecked pro was just a casualty of their trade. He was interested to see who would be trying to find him and would follow every news source he could find, and the thought of some of the local plods trying to tie him down brought a smile to his face as he stripped in the changing room.

When he walked into the gym the thirty-something woman was there again and gave him a full smile. He nodded and before they'd both finished their sessions they were on first-name terms. It just couldn't get any better. She was a class act, wanted to get to know him and she would. She was pleasure; he'd enjoy playing with her for the next few weeks – or until he tired of the game.

29

O'Connor had decided they should start with the punters who used the area or anyone who'd known the two girls who'd been assaulted. There were other attacks that looked similar in other parts of the country, but they could end up as a distraction and he wanted to concentrate on what they knew.

The team who'd worked on the attack on Pauline Johansson had covered a lot of ground already and had pulled in a number of her regulars. A big advantage when a prostitute was the victim was that her punters rarely caused the detectives any problems. When they arrived at the door and mentioned the word prostitute, the clients became very helpful indeed. The threat of exposure to wives, girlfriends and employers was usually enough to calm the worst of them. The suggestion that they might have taken a sexually transmitted disease home to 'her indoors' normally convinced them to do their public duty and help the police with their enquiries.

O'Connor thought they'd be lucky to get the answer this way, but the routine stuff had to be done. It would help them build up a picture of both girls, and somewhere along the line, the clues would bubble to the surface. He wanted to concentrate on the working girls themselves, as they had an interest in warning each other if there was a dodgy punter on the go. They would remember cars, unusual characters and anyone who refused to pay or got a bit rough. It happened all the time.

'Grace, I want you to go and see the Johansson girl. I know she's in a bad way, but I want to be sure there's nothing we can get from her. Apparently she's conscious, but she keeps getting distressed and they can't get anywhere with her. Speak to her doctor first.'

Macallan nodded, wondering where she stood with O'Connor. He was all business now, and this was how it should be, but she wondered anyway. She wanted to know more about him but the question was whether he'd let her.

She grabbed her coat and a set of car keys then headed for the intensive care unit.

The wind and rain slapped at the windscreen as Macallan started the engine. She leaned back in the seat and wished she had a cigarette but pushed the thought away. She'd been off them for months now but still had the occasional moment when she wanted to feel the poison being drawn into her lungs – that brief kick of guilt and pleasure. She shook her head. 'No way, Grace, think of the price of those things now,' she told herself, winking at her reflection in the rear-view mirror before she drove off.

30

Pauline Johansson's doctor was irritated by the visit from Macallan. There was nothing new in that – doctors just got annoyed by anything that took them away from their patients. Macallan thought the job they did was priceless, but they did have a tendency to think they were gods among men, which made an awful lot of them the most arrogant bastards she'd ever met – and that was saying something.

The doctor gave her the usual lecture that it was all a waste of time and she shouldn't stress the patient, then Macallan did her bit of telling him she had to try and that it *was* going to happen. It was the same old ritual every time.

She opened the door to the small, warm ICU room where she found a nurse leaning over Johansson and talking quietly to her. Macallan introduced herself and the nurse nodded.

'Go easy, Chief Inspector. Pauline's doing well, but

she's tired, so please keep it short. She can hear you and this girl's a fighter, so you just need to give her time.'

The nurse left and Macallan sat by the bed, studying the bandages covering the damaged half of the young woman's head. One blue eye remained visible and lines of blonde hair splayed across the pillow beside her.

Up until her visit, Pauline Johansson had been a hazy image in Macallan's mind, a shadow walking dark streets waiting for the next creep who would provide the means to buy her drug of choice. What was exposed of the face showed she'd been a beautiful woman, and Macallan was annoyed at herself for forgetting that she was a person – someone who'd been dealt a shit hand and now had to live with half her face permanently disfigured.

Johansson was looking at her without moving, and Macallan explained who she was and why she was there. She told her about herself, that she wanted to help and that she would come to see her as often as possible, but only if she wanted the visit.

'If you can remember anything, Pauline, try and find a way to tell us. We have to find the man who did this in case he hurts someone else.'

She'd decided not to mention Helen Stevenson, as there was every chance they might have known each other. Instinctively, she reached out and squeezed Johansson's hand as lightly as she could, surprised when it twitched a moment later. Had she meant that or was it an involuntary spasm?

'Pauline, can you do that again?' The hand moved once more and Macallan smiled. 'Good girl, Pauline.'

A tear bubbled up in the corner of Pauline's swollen blue eye and trickled across her cheek. The corners of her mouth moved – she was trying to make it all work and forcing the electrical signals to find new routes past the damage in her brain. Some of those circuits were permanently ruined, but Macallan knew from the shattered survivors she'd seen in Belfast that this amazing organ could reorganise and find a way to cope.

The doctor walked into the room and told Macallan her visit was over.

'Can I come back again tomorrow? It's important.'

'I could say no, but I've a feeling that you'd just ignore me so I think we'll cooperate on this one – and it might be good for Pauline as long as we take it easy. She doesn't get a lot of visitors.'

The doctor smiled and Macallan decided to forgive him for being an arse at the start of her visit. She smiled over at Johansson and raised her hand. 'I'll see you tomorrow, Pauline.'

The rain streamed down as she headed back to the car park, and she shivered as the damp soaked into the folds of her clothes, sucking the heat from her body. She pulled open the car door and jumped in, slumping forward in the seat as she thought about Pauline Johansson. 'You poor cow – you poor fucking cow.'

How could anyone do that to another human being? She'd seen too much death, too much damage and too many grieving families. She'd heard all the excuses, all the reasoned academic analyses, but in the end she just didn't understand – and never would. The police just cleaned it all up, got little thanks for doing so and when they got it wrong – well, they were just written off as Keystone Cops. She asked herself the same question every detective asked a hundred times: 'What the fuck am I doing here?'

She drove back to HQ and thought about cigarettes again.

31

When Macallan walked into the incident room, she headed straight for O'Connor, who was sitting with Harkins and going over the statements that were pouring in. This was the problem that affected all teams. The public wanted to help, but the vast majority of information they provided was useless, and could easily distract or mislead them. If there was an advantage with a prostitute murder, it was that there was less sympathy for the victim, which tended to keep it manageable, and not everyone wanted to admit knowing or having had anything to do with prostitutes.

Harkins poured her a coffee without asking. 'How did it go then? A bit of a struggle I guess?'

She took the mug and warmed her hands on it. 'She's still in a bad way, not able to talk but conscious, and I think we might be able to get something going with her. There are only brief hand movements, and she can see, but it might take time. I had a lot of experience in Northern Ireland with badly injured and traumatised witnesses and there's ways to do it. I know we don't have the luxury of time, but it would be worth it. Anything interesting coming in?'

O'Connor looked tired and had a right to be. The pressure was building and there was no rest for the SIO when something like this kicked off.

'The main lines are talking to the street girls and the punters we can find. We're going through CCTV to see what cars were in the area and whether any kerb-crawlers were pulled in by the uniforms. The analysts and researchers are going through the historical cases and possible matches in other forces. Nothing big but we just have to keep going through it until we get a clearer picture. Stick with Pauline regardless of time. She saw the guy, presuming it's the same one. Anything she can give us might help.'

He slugged from a can of juice and Macallan saw the look – that worry that this might be a whodunnit. The nightmare all detectives feared, especially the ambitious ones like O'Connor.

'To top it all, some genius on the beat wrote down what he thought was a punter's registration but got it wrong. Two of our heavyweights have been accusing a completely innocent haematologist of being a dirty little punter. Thank God the man isn't taking it further. These things are sent to try us, Grace.'

He squeezed the bridge of his nose and Macallan was concerned that this was far too early in the game for him to be showing signs of stress. She thought about Harkins' assessment of O'Connor. Was this the test that would make or break him?

About midnight, and around the time Macallan was able to finish and grab some sleep, Pauline Johansson was struggling to climb out of her dream. She was in a dark room and something was in there with her. She knew she was dreaming and tried to struggle towards the light, but it was as if she was trying to climb through mud. She woke sucking in air. The hospital room was the safest place she'd been for a long time – people were caring for her, and she couldn't remember the last time that had happened. Her vision was foggy but she could see the doctor standing next to the bed looking at her, and she wondered why he was wearing a surgical mask.

'How are you, Pauline? I thought I'd just pop in to make sure you were okay. I was a bit concerned I'd not done enough to keep you quiet, but I think I can safely say that although you're not a vegetable, you're not far off.'

The best she could do was moan quietly when she realised who it was. He pushed his face close to hers. She had lost her sense of smell and didn't catch the garlic on his breath. He was pleased at her lack of movement. 'I'll leave you to it, Pauline, and you should think yourself lucky considering what

I'm capable of.' She was screaming without a sound leaving her lips. 'See you later and be good.'

He blew her a kiss as he left the room and closed the door quietly behind him.

Macallan was sitting at her desk the following morning, reading up on the information piling into the system, when the phone rang. She wanted to ignore it so she could catch up on her reading – there was never enough time to do it all – but she dutifully picked up the phone and took the call, which turned out to be from the hospital. The doctor treating Pauline Johansson was concerned about her condition, which had deteriorated – for some reason she had become distressed and upset.

Macallan thanked the doctor and said that she would call in.

32

Pauline Johansson blinked several times when Macallan walked into the room and told the uniform guarding her he could go and fill up on caffeine. Johansson looked corpse pale and there was something in her one exposed eye that Macallan had not seen on her first visit.

She walked over to the bed and put her hand over Johansson's; it felt cold. She smiled down at the shattered face and sat as close to the bed as she could.

'What's up, Pauline? Did you have a bad night? Let's do one blink for yes and two for no.'

One blink.

Macallan tensed but tried not to show it. 'Good girl, Pauline. Do you remember me being here before?'

One blink.

Macallan sat closer. 'Try squeezing my hand.'

There was the briefest pressure on her hand.

'Again, Pauline.'

Brief pressure again.

'You did it, Pauline. You did it.'

Macallan smiled and wondered. 'Has something upset you since I saw you?'

One blink.

'Okay. I'll run through some things and you can show me what it was. Was it me?'

Two blinks.

'Was it someone from the hospital?

Two blinks.

'Someone else.'

One blink.

'Give me a second, Pauline – I just want to talk to the nurse.'

Johansson's hand squeezed tighter this time and her eye widened. Macallan knew what she was seeing. It was fear. A ball of tension squeezed the muscles at the pit of her stomach. She slipped her hand away from Johansson, who moaned.

'I promise it's okay, Pauline – I'll just be outside the room. Keep looking at the window and you'll see me.'

She called to the nurses and asked if anyone else had stopped by besides her.

'To be honest she doesn't seem to have anyone close. It's tragic for such a young woman. There's certainly been no visitors since you were here the last time.' The nurse looked like she cared.

When Macallan walked back into the room, she sat down and took Johansson's hand in hers, felt the squeeze.

'Has someone frightened you since I was here, Pauline?'

One blink.

'Was it a dream?'

Two blinks.

Macallan didn't want to ask the next question. 'Was it a man?'

One blink.

She couldn't delay it any longer. 'Was it the man who attacked you?'

One blink.

'Are you sure, Pauline?'

One blink.

'I'm going to make a call and get someone to stay with you.'

Her hand was squeezed tightly this time.

Macallan called the uniform back, but it hadn't been her guarding Johansson on the night shift, and when Macallan told her what had happened, the policewoman saw something in the chief inspector's eyes that made her glad she wasn't the unfortunate but stupid bastard who'd left his post during the night and allowed this fuck-up to occur.

When she was done with the uniform, Macallan called O'Connor and struggled to keep the emotion from her voice as she told him what had transpired.

'How the fuck could this happen? How could we not cover this situation?'

'Look, Grace, this girl is in a bad way. We need to find out if this actually happened. She's on heavy-duty medication so this might be a hallucination. I'll send a team round to make some enquires – check if anyone saw anything – and we can get the CCTV covered at the same time. In any case, we'll get extra uniforms there 24/7 for as long as it takes. I can't think why he would visit her and not harm her. It makes no sense.'

'It makes sense to him, John, and we'd better hope that the press don't get wind of it.'

She walked back into the room to find the doctor had been in and sedated Johansson. Macallan watched her and wondered. Would it be better for the girl to have died instead of being in this prison?

The additional uniforms arrived as Macallan spoke to the doctor, telling him part of what had happened and asking if it could have been a dream or imagination. The question annoyed the consultant, who was too busy as usual and hadn't slept in a day.

'The answer is obvious, Chief Inspector. Of course she could have imagined it, and of course she could have dreamt it. She's suffering the effects of a terrible attack and she's pumped full of drugs. In addition she's an addict; don't forget she's in withdrawal at the moment, with all that entails. I'm sure I don't need to go into detail. There's terrible stress on her body and mind, and I'm not even sure she'll survive all the complications. So yes to the question. On the other hand, someone could indeed have come into the room, but that's your problem and not mine.'

There was no point in arguing, and he was right. The answer was obvious, but they would sure as fuck have to find out the truth.

One nurse thought she'd seen a doctor she didn't recognise near the ICU but hadn't thought anything of it. The description was worse than vague and the CCTV was inconclusive. It wasn't that unusual to see staff who weren't regulars – it was just part of normal hospital life.

Macallan had the room and Johansson checked in case there was DNA, though they couldn't be sure that her attacker had even been there. Time and again investigators were left with questions from the fevered minds of victims whose memories had been infected by false memories as a result of trauma, and given the attack Johansson had suffered, it wouldn't have been surprising if she *had* imagined it all.

When Johansson came out of her sedation Macallan was called and she decided to try questioning the girl again. There was a chance she could get some answers – it just depended what Johansson could remember. In Northern Ireland, she had seen so many cases of memory loss where the moment of trauma was concerned, but it was always worth a try in case they found one small lead that could take them to the killer's door.

When she walked into the room she saw the corners of Johansson's mouth turn up. 'Hey, Pauline, that looks like a smile. It's not often that people are pleased to see me.'

She clasped the girl's hand and felt her squeeze it. 'You're getting stronger. Do you think I can ask you more questions?'

One blink.

Macallan took it slowly. It was clear Johansson had little recollection of the attack, and she took walked the night backwards to see where the edge of the girl's memory lay.

'Do you remember being on the street before you met this man, Pauline? Go back to leaving the house. Do you remember that?'

One blink.

'Did you have any other punters before that?'

She ran through the possibilities and established there had only been one and that he was a regular. 'Now how do we get his name, Pauline? I'm going to run through the alphabet and stop me when I get the first letter of his name.'

They got there eventually and Macallan was pleased. The punter wasn't on their systems and might be useful once they'd dragged him into a station. She could see that Johansson was tiring and a nurse was starting to give her grief. 'Last thing for tonight. Can you remember what car the man who attacked you was driving?'

Johansson stared back at her. Her thoughts had turned to glue and she wanted to sleep. She could picture the dark street and it was as if she was looking at herself in a film. The film had almost frozen.

Macallan brushed her cheek. 'It's okay, that's enough for tonight. You sleep, and I'll see you soon.'

She began to put her papers away then reminded the uniform that the girl could not be left unguarded, and she was to be called if there was any change.

Johansson felt her eyes dropping then the car drove into the picture in slow motion.

The nurse saw her rapid blinking. 'Chief Inspector.'

'What is it, Pauline? Have you remembered something?'

One blink.

It was the car and they did the alphabet again. It was a Merc in good condition, and Macallan realised that they'd just taken a step towards the bastard's door. She called into the squad room to get them researching Mercs seen at other crimes or in the area and ordered them to revisit the street girls to see if they could add to the description.

Less than two hours later Pauline Johansson's regular punter had his night and his marriage ruined when a pair of detectives arrived to take him away. It was a real problem for him because they couldn't write him off as the attacker – his sole alibi was his wife, and she could only verify when he got home. He was fucked all ways, but he had seen a Merc in the area when he left, though he'd thought nothing of it at the time. He confirmed it was in good nick but there was nothing else he could add, and he forgot to ask how Pauline was, which hacked off the detectives no end. He expected sympathy for helping and having his life pissed on, but he was in the wrong place for that kind of support.

After the punter was released he walked into his nice suburban home and the first thing he saw was a couple of bin bags filled with his clothes. He stared at them for a moment before his wife came out of the kitchen carrying a wine glass that seemed overfilled with red.

'Have a drink before you leave, honey.' She threw the contents of the glass in his face.

'And leave the fucking keys on the way out.'

33

Jacquie Bell left the bar on the south side of Edinburgh and felt quite pleased with herself. She'd flirted with a cocaine supplier who'd given her a nice little story about a top-drawer city councillor who'd just got a bit too close to some equally top-drawer criminal clients trying to push through dodgy planning applications. In many ways it was an old story: he thought he could stick powder up his nose, launder money and remain invisible at the same time.

This was what Bell did; she was made for crime reporting. Her editor loved and hated her at the same time because she produced great stories but monumental problems to go with them. Half the time they were receiving threats from legal representatives or, even more worrying, pissed-off criminals. She loved it though, and when she spoke to the detectives she had in her pocket, she knew they were all working for the same buzz. It was that power thing – knowing what was going on under Joe Public's nose while they wandered around unawares. She always got an extra kick when it was the great and good she was exposing, and in her view it was healthy to uncover hypocrisy among those who looked down on the masses.

She'd come up the hard way and hadn't received any favours to get where she was now. She came from a skint but happy working-class background in the East End of Glasgow. Even as a child she'd wanted out but knew that her old man hadn't the readies for a posh school, so she'd got her head down and worked her way to a decent education. She'd picked up an addiction for news even in her teens – which to most of her contemporaries made her a 'fucking weirdo' – but she was determined and got her first job on a small-time and very local paper, making tea and taking male abuse. She had been a star from the off, though it hadn't made her popular in every quarter, and she'd made it worse by hunting stories when the rest were in drinking mode.

Crime was what she'd wanted – and she'd got it. She had looks and didn't need to try; one of those fortunate creatures who just needed to smile to disable every man within twenty feet of her. Her hair was jet black and accompanied by pale skin that only drew attention to her huge dark eyes. She knew it, used it, and it worked a treat. Detectives, criminals, the big dogs in the city, it didn't matter – they all thought they'd worked their magic on her and that they were special. There was nothing wrong with it; using charm was part of all business, but what mattered was that she also had good instincts and a forensic brain that could see stories forming where others completely missed the point.

They were wasting their time anyway because she was gay, but she kept her private life discreet so she could keep the boys dreaming.

She walked along Edinburgh's George Street and hardly noticed the world around her. She was writing the story in her head, getting the headline right and wondering how the councillor would try to wriggle out of this one. He'd sailed too close too often and it was just his turn. She wanted to get it to bed ASAP and dig into the attacks on the prostitutes. It was becoming a story and she needed to get stuck into it before it left her behind.

The tremble of her mobile brought her back to reality and she scrambled through the debris in the pocket of her wax jacket to extract the phone. A missed call could be a missed story. The cop who called her wasn't high up the food chain, but he worked in the Chief's office and gave her a heads-up when anything a bit interesting was taking shape. He told her there'd been a bit of wailing then a frantic stampede to cover up the fact that a uniform might have allowed Pauline Johansson's attacker into her hospital room.

'You have got to be kidding me.'

The voice came back to her. 'There was doubt that it happened, but it looks very possible now, and the story is that even though she can't talk, she managed to give one of the senior detectives a lead. The point is that the uniform guarding her was chatting up the night shift when it did or didn't happen.'

'What senior detective?'

'Grace Macallan. She's the DCI who transferred from Northern Ireland – under a cloud or as a pillar of integrity, depending on how you look at it.'

'Nice one – and I'll buy you a beer as soon as.'

Bell ended the call, annoyed at herself. She'd been interested in the whole Macallan thing but hadn't got round to it, and now here she was at the centre of the prostitute investigation.

It was time they got acquainted.

Macallan's mobile rang in the middle of Harkins' description of the various sleazeballs they'd pulled in so far.

'I tell you, some of these guys embarrass me, and that's saying something. We've got punters from all walks, and it looks like a few dog collars made good use of the services during the General Assembly of the Church of Scotland.'

'Real life – it beats fiction every time.'

She picked up the phone and Jacquie Bell introduced herself. Macallan recognised the name; she'd heard the reporter described as the best in the business and a devious cow in equal proportions. She asked Harkins to give her a minute; he gave her a nod and headed for the coffee machine.

'I'm sorry but you really need to go through the press office for this, and I think you know that.'

Bell expected this and knew she'd have to come at Macallan from a different angle. She'd done her homework.

'It's not about the attacks, although I'm interested. I spoke to the press office a while ago and wanted to talk to you about your story and how you ended up here. There's a tremendous human-interest angle there, and it would be fascinating, particularly for women. I've just been too busy with other stories, but I have a bit of time now.'

Bell played it easy: don't press too hard and make a little play to Macallan's ego. The woman had been through a tough time and they all need a bit of flattery.

'Look, I'll leave it with you because I know you're up to your eyes, but if you even want to discuss it without a commitment then we could have a drink and see where it goes?'

Coming from the Troubles had made Macallan cautious of strangers, but she realised that since moving from Northern Ireland, her life had been solely about the MCT. She hadn't really thought about it till now, but it wasn't healthy, and this was an opportunity to neck a drink with someone different. Okay she was a crime reporter, but what the hell? She took them both by surprise and agreed. 'Okay, let's do it. God knows I could do with a drink, but the ground rules are that I buy my round.'

Bell smiled down the line. 'A detective buying a drink. What's the world coming to?'

The both laughed and made the arrangements.

Once she'd hung up, Macallan stared out the window and wished again that someone would clean it. The station windows were always splattered with the sediment of the Edinburgh weather. She knew the dangers of meeting reporters, but if she was anything, she was streetwise, and she decided not to mention it to O'Connor for the time being. He had enough on his plate, and they were too tied up in the case to think of what might develop between them. He had been businesslike with her, and in their private moments they'd promised to get together without making a where and when. She knew they were both too busy to plan a romantic evening with candles. At the moment they were living off the nightmare of canteen sandwiches and all the hazards that accompanied them. As for sleep, that was flopping into bed and probably being woken after two hours because one of the teams had arrested a weirdo and wanted guidance. She wondered why it couldn't be like it was on TV, where you just had to shout loudly at a suspect and it was all solved in one to three episodes. Unless you were Danish of course.

She headed home to get changed and decided she should make an effort. If Bell was going to do a story about her then she should really look the part. Since she'd started working with the MCT, she'd dressed in drab colours and had hardly applied a lick of make-up when she went to work. She wanted to feel like a woman again and make an impression rather than trying to act tougher around the boys.

As she dabbed on her seventy-quid perfume, she

promised herself she'd get a life away from the squad. She spoke to her reflection in the mirror.

'If JJ doesn't realise what he's missing, I'll try online dating.'

She did the V sign in the mirror, stuck out her tongue and laughed. She put on the suit she kept for court or meetings with bosses and liked the look. A bit serious but not bad – not bad at all. She realised how excited she was about meeting someone new and shook her head. 'You are one sad bastard, Grace Macallan.'

34

She walked into the smart George Street venue where the bar staff tried not to laugh as they charged their customers a mile over the odds. It was quiet enough and the after-office rush had started to drain away. She looked around for the black hair and fur-collared coat Bell had described as a way to ID her.

Finally Macallan spotted her at the bar and raised her hand. She was impressed. Bell looked more like a news presenter than a crime hack. Her hair was swept straight back off her face, and Macallan had to admit she was a stunner – and it was all natural. Bell could have turned up in dungarees and a top hat and still carried it off. She was nothing like most of the reporters Macallan had met in the past.

They shook hands and exchanged pleasantries, realising that for both of them their first impressions had been right on the money, and to cap it all they both liked malt whisky. Bell insisted on getting the first round and looked at the price list with a frown.

'Hope you've brought a big bag of money if we're doing malt.'

'To be honest, with the investigation and the last few months of my life, I'm not getting to spend what I earn, so in the words of the philosopher, "Fuck it".'

Bell found she liked Macallan, and that surprised her. She really never warmed to anyone beyond her cat. Liking people got in the way of what she did, but Macallan lacked the drabness that seemed to infect so many public officials. Her intelligence was there without being obvious; she didn't try to impress – and why should she? Bell knew where this woman had been, and she wanted to know more about her. The most important thing was that Macallan didn't bore her and that made her a bit unusual.

They avoided business initially and Macallan relaxed in a woman's company; that hadn't happened since Belfast in those days when she'd had friends and dreams that didn't wake her up choking for breath. Those dreams still happened but less often now.

They talked easily and the Talisker added to the relaxed mood. Bell had read up on Macallan and recognised someone who was certainly different from the pack. Bright, surprisingly good company and attractive. It was difficult not to stare at Macallan's eyes, which were the clearest green, and when she smiled they sparked in a way that disarmed her. This was unusual for Bell, who even by her own admission was a control freak when it came to dealing with potential sources for her stories.

Macallan just let it flow, surprising herself in the way she was opening up to the reporter as if she were her oldest friend. They both let their defences down, and by the time they decided to order a third malt, they knew there was a mutual admiration exercise going on and were content to let it happen.

'You're not what I expected. I thought you might be a female version of Ian Paisley, carrying the good book under your arm for God and Ulster.'

Macallan raised her glass. 'Well, I'm glad I didn't live up to that image. It was the same for me though. I was told that you would do anything for a story, but I guess that's your job, so why not?'

Bell put her glass on the bar and tried to ignore the guy leching after her from a few feet away. 'So we can be friends but we can't avoid work. How about I do a bit about you and your journey from Northern Ireland to the mean streets of Edinburgh?'

Before Macallan had left Ulster she would have baulked at that kind of proposal, but things had changed. She saw how the world worked on the mainland, and O'Connor was a good example. If you were on the ladder, you might as well try and climb upwards; as far as she could see, self-promotion was part of the routine, and no one seemed to expect anything else. This was a night of surprising herself, and she did it again.

'You know I had a tough time and there are people I still care about in Northern Ireland, so take it easy if you do it. I'm not asking for favours but let me see the piece before you print it. Obviously you'd be better to run it past the press office first, and I'll speak to my boss just to clear it with him.'

Bell smiled at the comment. 'JJ O'Connor. You better watch that one, Grace – he might get jealous if he sees a rising star too close to him. Great guy but definitely knows where he's going and doesn't miss a bit of self-promotion himself.'

Macallan looked and wondered, realising that Bell obviously knew O'Connor. 'You haven't?'

Bell laughed loudly. 'Christ no. He's definitely not my type, and that's enough information. What about this incident at the hospital? Is it true that the girl who was attacked had a visit? Don't be surprised that I know about it; you can't keep something like that hidden. I'm not going on the record, just interested, and I'll never use anything you don't want me to.'

Macallan had let her guard down but snapped back to business mode.

'Look, Jacquie, we hardly know each other and this has been a good night. I don't want to ruin it, but most of all I don't want to do anything that will harm that girl. She lived a life that no one deserves, and now she's trapped in her own little prison. I want to get the bastard that did this, and I'm going to – and I won't let anything get in the way.'

Bell looked straight into those green eyes and believed every word.

'You know what, I believe you'll do just that. We can be friends, help each other at the same time. I'm sure I can do something for you in return.'

'Okay, let's do the story about me, and off the record

the hospital security issue was a fuck-up. Trouble is we can't be certain it actually happened. I'm sure it did, but there's a chance given the circumstances that she's imagined it.' She paused, then said, 'I do think that whoever hurt Pauline has been working up to this for a while though. We've got attacks in other forces that look similar, but again we just can't tie them together. I'm sure we have a pretty sharp serial offender, but because we can't present clear evidence, the forces are reluctant to go public.'

Bell ran her hands through her hair and considered what this would mean as a story. Normally she would have run with it, but Grace Macallan was different – she would cooperate.

'Thanks for being open with me. I'll do nothing other than run the usual stories about the enquiries and any quotes I can pick up along the way from O'Connor, who'll undoubtedly do a few grim-faced detective conferences to keep us happy.'

Macallan relaxed and decided she was okay with it all. 'I'm back on the job at the crack of dawn so probably best if I go and get some zeds. I'm going back to see Pauline tomorrow and we'll evaluate all the leads we have so far to see if we can narrow it all down. We have something on a car, but I'll come back to you on that later. Let me know when you want to meet up again.' Bell nodded.

'Last thing is that if there's something to give and I think it can help the case then I'll let you have it. This force is paranoid about the press but they play it the wrong way. I think we might need to feed this bastard some publicity, and I know the force won't like that so watch this space. You have to protect me though if we go that route, or I think John O'Connor would have me measured for a traffic warden's uniform.'

It had started to drizzle outside so they decided to share a taxi. It stopped outside Macallan's block of flats and she pulled up her coat collar. 'I didn't realise how much I needed that – and how much I needed a bit of female company. See you soon.'

Bell wondered how someone could have lived through, and achieved, what this woman had and yet be so entirely vulnerable at the same time. Before meeting Grace Macallan, she would have said that it was impossible to be a senior detective and yet display the raw wounds she saw just beneath the surface of Macallan's character, but the inspector had proved her wrong.

She leaned over and kissed Macallan's cheek. 'I could see how much you needed it. By the way, I don't normally kiss police persons goodnight. Definitely see you soon.'

Inside, Macallan got ready for bed and burrowed herself under the sheets, completely exhausted. She ran the night and the taxi ride through her mind a dozen times before falling into sleep.

She was walking through the Markets in Belfast. It was dark, but her footsteps sounded like gunshots and every light in the place came on. Women screamed at her from every window – 'Murdering Special Branch bastard bitch.'

She started to run towards the centre of the city, but the screams of the women seemed to be right behind her. The streets were dark and wet, and she moved on lead-weighted legs. The shadows were everywhere, and as she ran past the old Belfast Gasworks Tommy Doyle stepped out in front of her. She crashed into him and they fell onto the wet pavement. He was laughing and calling her the RUC bitch. His hands were everywhere, and she could feel his teeth bite into her neck.

She sat bolt upright in the bed and gasped in cold air as she looked around the room for Tommy Doyle. She shook her head and calmed her breathing as the fear passed. *Jesus, Grace. You're fine and Tommy's in the big Maze Prison in the sky. You're okay. You're okay now.*

She fell asleep again; she was learning to deal with the dreams.

The last image she saw before she slept was Bell smiling at her.

35

Harkins had discovered his recently acquired influence with senior analyst Felicity Young to be gratifying in more ways than one. He found it hard to believe that it had turned into more than a one-night stand, but if opposites attracted then they were a match made in heaven, and he'd learned in the process that he wasn't as smart as he'd thought he was. He'd always believed he could read people, but that definitely didn't apply to Miss Felicity Young.

Despite their new-found attraction, Harkins had pushed hard at Young and the other analysts and researchers to look for patterns in the attacks or something from the past that might give them a steer. They had the possibility of a Merc in good condition and that was something.

The other certainty was that the killer hadn't just popped out of a Christmas cracker. There had to be signs in the past. It might not have been a full-blown attack but something that had been recorded on the vast array of intelligence systems operating throughout the country. That's what the exceptional analysts could find, and Young was in that range; she thought differently from the rest of the pack and saw the patterns, the flashing light in the morass of reports that gave the detectives the leads.

The old days of instinct and a hard time in the cells were just a memory for the veteran detectives on their way to the knacker's yard. In this day and age, a confession on its own was about as much good as a bottle of malt to the Ayatollah Khomeini, and they would need people like Young to have any hope of a conviction.

36

He'd followed the press coverage closely. He was by nature a careful man, and it made sense to see what the plods were doing. Jacquie Bell gave it good coverage, and a special press briefing had been announced for the next morning.

The timing was perfect as he'd left another whore down by the seaside, and he guessed that an early-morning dog walker would get the surprise of their boring lives. That should make their press conference worth watching. The girl was alive, tied up and should survive to the morning – but it was touch and go given what he'd done to her.

He wanted them to live and suffer, but it was a difficult art, and if he lost one or two then so be it. He hadn't got it right with Johansson, but this one wouldn't be telling tales to anyone. Not without her tongue anyway.

37

Macallan was trying to shower some enthusiasm into her bones when she heard the phone ring. She cursed whatever it was she was about to learn.

Harkins was in the office already and told her the story. 'Another girl found this morning in a disused quarry in West Lothian. The girl is alive but apparently in a mess, and unless I'm mistaken her head injuries mean she's unlikely to recover consciousness. On top of that, he took her tongue this time. The press are going frantic, and I think JJ is probably going to age ten years today with the problems building here. We need to get to this fucker soon before the press turn us into human turnips.'

Macallan sat on her bed, ignoring the fact that she was still dripping wet. 'Jesus, what are we dealing with here? He's playing with us. There's cops every-where covering the street girls and he's managed to do this. How the fuck did we miss him? I'll be there as soon as.'

When she tried to put the phone back in its cradle, it rang again. Bell said good morning and took Macallan completely by surprise.

'Take it you've heard the news, and I know you'll be racing to get into the office, but I need a quick word.'

'Go ahead, Jacquie. It's good to hear you but I wish it was under different circumstances.'

'We'll catch up soon, and I'm looking forward to that, but look, this attack raises the game on this fucking beast. I've got my boss kicking my arse for an angle, and I wanted to speak to you first. I know O'Connor is doing his press conference, but we have to start asking the awkward questions now – that's what we're here for.'

Macallan was easy with that; she wanted this animal cornered more than anyone. She knew the force lived in permanent terror of the headlines, and she just didn't get it. They operated by fear of criticism. Her background was to use the press and manipulate when necessary. She knew the killer was vain and engaged in some sick crusade, but she wanted the tabloids to start making up banner headlines declaring him as just another sick fuck that needed locking up. Maybe, just maybe, it would upset him enough into making a wrong move. It might not work, but she knew that unless she got to him soon, another street girl was living her final days.

'It's okay, and sometimes we need those questions. What can I do for you?'

'Is there anything you know that might be worth highlighting?'

Macallan took a breath and closed her eyes. Once a detective crossed the line with the press, they were in a swamp. Lifelines were few and far between, and in any case, no one from the job was going to throw you a rope unless it was to hang yourself. In this instance, what was important was preventing another girl being attacked and to have any hope of that, they needed to use the press.

'Mention the hospital visit and the fact that we fucked up on that,' she told Jacquie. 'Second thing is that this girl has had her tongue removed. Third thing is that we think the guy is using a Merc.' The line went quiet. 'Jacquie?'

'I'm here. Jesus, this is getting out of hand.'

'You have to protect me, Jacquie, and don't call this number again. I'm going to get a pay-as-you go mobile and will use that to contact you. JJ would crucify me for talking to you, but I think we need to start getting this bastard's attention. He's clever, this one, and will be following it all. Make sure and rub it in that he's a prime-time sicko. That okay with you?'

'You've got it, and needless to say I'll ignore you at the press conference, hard as that might be.'

Macallan half-dried herself and pulled on her clothes. Breakfast would have to wait. The case had caught national attention and the press conference would be a scrum for the hacks both north and south of the border. The police powers hated this because it drew attention and resources away from the image they all wanted to present, which was leafy streets with a friendly bobby there to reassure the natives. This sort of shit made the old ladies of the parish think they were all under threat and the chief constable was a failure.

It was well known to all detectives that the first law of physics meant that shit fell downwards, and O'Connor would have been told loud and clear by the executive floor that this was his problem.

The girl who had been attacked and dumped died before Macallan managed to get to the office. The profile was so similar that it depressed the detectives listening to the hurried briefing from O'Connor before they faced the press scrum banging at the gates of Lothian and Borders Police.

The girl's name was Dawn Mason, although hardly a soul knew who she was. She'd told people her name was Amber and had used that one since her better days working in the saunas. A drug habit and world that didn't care had relegated her to the streets, where she'd be lucky to even find punters considering she'd given up completely on hygiene. What family there might have been had spent their lives pissed on cider and probably wouldn't remember that they'd had a daughter in the first place, unless it meant receiving compensation from her death.

The HQ conference room was packed out, and their whole morning had been taken up preparing for the difficult job of fielding questions that in many cases they couldn't answer.

It pissed off Macallan and the working parts of the

investigation. Instead of following leads, they were bending the knee to a press lynch mob assembling in the heart of their own HQ.

The assistant chief constable entered the room, followed by O'Connor and Macallan, with the force press officer fluttering nearby in case anyone got into difficulty with the questions. The press officer was sure O'Connor could handle it but knew from bitter experience that the ACC was a true thicko who'd carried his bosses' bags for years, selling his soul to gain a rank he didn't deserve.

There was a tension in the room and no one could deny that this was turning into a headline writer's wet dream.

The ACC opened the proceedings and extended his deepest sympathy to the families, ticking all the appropriate boxes so he could get back to worrying about the parking problems in the centre of the city, which had been aggravated by the fucking trams fiasco.

The fact was that he knew next to nothing about the case. He was only there to show the uniform and give that little bit of reassurance to the terrified citizens of the capital that all was well and a friendly bobby was just round the corner.

He did his bit and handed over to O'Connor, who would take the questions that everyone wanted to ask. Macallan tried not to look at O'Connor while he was talking, but she had to give him his due – he was good, calm, assured, looked the part and introduced Macallan as the lead officer on the investigation team. He knew there would be interest in her given her background, but she was more than capable of handling the press.

The reporters lobbed the questions O'Connor had expected, hunting for a bit of gore to feed their hungry readers, and he threw them the Merc and told them they were interested in speaking to the driver. It went as planned, they managed to stay on message, then Macallan took a couple of questions and handled them like a pro.

Bell waited her turn and let the other reporters get their fill before she took her shot. The room was losing its tension and the ACC thought they might soon be able to draw the conference to a close.

Bell lifted her hand to get the attention of the panel and the ACC gave her an impatient nod, wondering what was left to ask.

'Is it true that that the killer managed to get to the first surviving victim in hospital, and is this a terrible failure in that there was no police guard there at the time?'

The ACC couldn't stop the red tinge flooding his face, and O'Connor didn't move a muscle, though he had the luxury of leaving it to the ACC. What not one of them expected was the second question.

'Is it also the case that the latest victim had part of her tongue removed, and what should we be telling the women of this city?'

The ACC blustered his way through an answer and the reporters went into panic mode. This was Hollywood drama, and they were all caught up in it.

Bell didn't really receive an answer, but that didn't matter – they had the scoop and inside line.

The conference was brought to a close by a panic-stricken press officer and when they walked off stage the ACC couldn't hold it any longer. He swung round on O'Connor and made sure that the problem was dumped fairly and squarely on his shoulders.

'How the fuck did that woman get a hold of this? We kept everything tight and some bastard from your team leaks it.'

O'Connor never lost control, and Macallan, who was already having second thoughts about disclosing the information, knew he didn't deserve this, but this was how it always played. She knew that better than anyone.

'There's nothing to say. There was more than my team in the loop, and there were others who knew, including your office … sir.'

He'd paused long enough to show that he regarded the ACC as an over-promoted desk pilot. This was unusual for O'Connor, who knew how to play politics, but Macallan enjoyed watching him stick it to the ACC. O'Connor had won a small victory, but the ACC marked O'Connor's card for future reference before trudging off to the safety of his office.

Macallan put her hand on O'Connor's arm and that was as far as she could go. 'Nice one. Now all you have to do is solve it and you can take his desk off him.'

He gave her a full smile. 'I can't believe I just did that. It's the sort of thing Mick Harkins does every time he wrecks his career prospects.'

They laughed together and realised that, despite the lack of opportunity, something good was happening to them, something they both needed, and it had made them realise just how much was missing in their lives.

O'Connor gathered up his papers and scraped his fingers through his hair. 'When this is over I'm going to take you away somewhere warm and exotic where none of this can touch us.' For a brief second he looked vulnerable and it was as if the boy underneath the man had been exposed for a second.

'Portobello would do me. Anyway, it's not the end of the world. The press always get an inside track at some stage and we've just got to keep control. Want my opinion?'

He nodded and realised she hadn't batted an eyelid at the press conference or the aftermath. She was different from anyone he'd come across in his service, formed from the tragedy of the Troubles. She'd spent years in a place where intrigue, manipulation and disruption were the norm.

'Use this against the killer. Speak to the profilers and shrinks and come up with a line that hurts this man. Leak it that we think he's maybe a paedo or been sexually abused by his mother, but let's get at him. Christ, it might even be true. I've a feeling this one is vain so we can hurt him.'

'Okay, get them together and let's see where we can take this.'

She left the room and O'Connor wondered who exactly was being manipulated.

38

He sat in the semi-darkness of his bedroom watching the news coverage of the press conference. He squeezed and released a rubber ball, changing hands every few minutes. This was an exercise he worked on every day and showed how thorough he was about his body. Most guys would go to the gym and that was it, but not him. Walking rather than driving, press-ups in the quiet moments in the office or at home squeezing the ball. Most people forgot about their wrists, but not him – squeezing the ball repeatedly gave him a vice-like grip, and he loved that moment when he was introduced to someone and gave them a handshake. He liked it when there was a wince and he could feel the other person's hand crumple.

When it came to women, it worked a treat. It could impress the pick-ups, and with the sluts he could watch for the pain in their eyes when he squeezed part of them, and the extra work with the ball would become all the more worthwhile.

The assistant chief looked like what he was – a safe bureaucrat, who, he was sure, had clambered up the back steps of the force, avoiding real criminals like a wasting disease. He lifted his crystal glass and sipped his cold New Zealand white. O'Connor interested him though – he wasn't the normal type of plod, and in some ways he reminded him of himself. He looked good, knew how to dress and his education was clearly top drawer. He handled the press like a Tony Blair clone, and if this was the man who was after him then his mission might be shorter than he'd first thought. He expected to be caught at some stage – knew enough about crime and punishment to realise that you could commit one perfect crime or near perfect and get away with it. This didn't work with a series of crimes, and eventually there would be a reckoning, but as long as he could make the last move then he'd settle for that. His mission was to teach and punish all at the same time.

He looked around the room and sighed. The furniture was expensive and everything was the best, but part of the reason he'd started his mission was that none of these material trappings gave him any real pleasure. The women he picked up gave him an initial rush when they fell for his line, but the physical result was empty and sometimes humiliating. Visiting the street whores at least gave him an extra thrill, and running the police ragged was a challenge. He'd accepted that if the prison gates beckoned then he'd finish himself rather than decompose behind the walls of a stinking cell.

The questions the press were asking bored him, and the truth was that the public wanted pictures of open wounds and blood. The pretence that horrific pictures of violence could not be published in order to protect the public made him sneer, and the hypocrisy choked him. They wanted what he wanted; the papers titillated them – kept them in a permanent state of excitement, gasping for the full Technicolor honesty of what had actually happened.

He sat up and sipped his wine again. The thought stayed with him and excited him. The tongue had been a nice touch and should pile pressure on the police. The girl had struggled a bit but that had just added to the enjoyment. He wondered if he should take photographs or another trophy the next time – it could be a final flourish with some coloured brush-strokes to finish his project.

Macallan was introduced and answered a couple of routine questions. He studied her, and if O'Connor interested him then she did a bit more than that. A career that could have come from the pages of a thriller, and she'd come through the terrorist campaigns in Northern Ireland with distinction. The fact that she'd given evidence against a colleague made her an individual who was prepared to stand against the pack; the thought thrilled him and he really hoped they would meet. If he had O'Connor and Macallan after him then he probably should think about his endgame. It would be interesting to talk to O'Connor and Macallan as friends, share their thoughts and fears.

The questions from Bell livened up the proceedings, and of course it wasn't news to him, but he enjoyed the ACC's flustered attempt at a response. They were all partly responsible for what he was doing, and he decided to move things on before they got to him. One way or the other, he would meet O'Connor and Macallan before the last throw of the dice.

39

Nearly two weeks after the press conference a fox trotted along the edge of a field – a black silhouette in the light of a full moon. He'd picked up a scent but drew up at the noise that he couldn't know was a car door closing. He waited until the rumbling noise of the car's engine had faded towards the bright lights of Glasgow then moved cautiously towards the smell of blood again until he found the girl's body crumpled in the corner of the field. About ten yards from the girl he stopped, sniffed the air and tried to decide whether the groaning should make him run or wait. He realised this was a badly injured animal so he would wait and move in slowly. The girl died quietly after about half an hour and the fox shuffled warily towards the body.

As he pulled onto the M8 and headed back towards Edinburgh, the killer pushed his foot down on the accelerator, but not so heavily as to attract the attention of the traffic boys. If he was going to make a mistake, it wasn't going to be that basic. The Merc's engine had real power and he loved the feel of the car, the way it enclosed him in luxury and shone among all the dull family wagons he overtook on the motorway.

A boy racer pulled past him and he looked at the two chavs sitting in the front. Pimply skin, half a brain between them and a couple of baseball hats made them what they were. They roared past the Merc, no doubt feeling a sense of triumph at leaving the luxury wheels behind. He smiled, letting them have their fun. What else did they have in their miserable little lives? They'd probably be lucky to survive into their forties.

He was buzzing from fixing the girl in the field and he would have loved to see O'Connor's face in the morning when Glasgow CID called to say they'd one through on their patch. He knew how difficult this made it for the police, and their territoriality would no doubt come into play. The boys from Glasgow would think the Edinburgh squad weren't up to the job and so it would go on. Meanwhile, shifting the centre of attention would mean he'd have the chance to complete a few more visits before his endgame. He'd made sure to leave the girl where she'd be found quickly, and it was obvious the field was a popular walking route in daylight.

He booked into a decent hotel in Edinburgh rather than going straight back home, where he might leave contamination from the girl. He would pay cash, leave a false name and clean up in the hotel before getting rid of his clothes. He liked hotels and all the secrets they held.

As the high wore off he would tire quickly and need to sleep. He'd done a bit of cocaine in the past, but like everything else it eventually bored him. This was better: the intense high it gave him and the added benefit that he could run and rerun the images through his mind when he was finished. Though even this would begin to bore him some time soon so he would have to plan a grand finale to make sure no one forgot who he was.

40

The retired teacher walked along the path, calling to his old spaniel and wondering how he could have had a dog for so long that still ignored his every command. He loved her though, and she'd been his lifesaver after the death of his wife.

The air was crisp and he never tired of the woodland, rarely missing his morning trek. Two or three hours out with the dog made the rest of the day easy and the future less frightening.

He stopped and wiped his nose, cursing her again. She was barking non-stop and that meant a rabbit, fox or rat.

He eventually found her at the side of the field.

'For the love o' God will you give it up?'

He laughed at the words he relayed to the dog almost every day, kneeled down stiffly and rubbed her wet back.

'Come on, girl. We'll head back. No rats or rabbits for you today.'

He glanced up through the fence and saw the heap lying just the other side. He stood up and pushed past the branches of a young rowan to get a better look, saw what was left of the girl's face and threw up on the crime scene.

41

Harkins shook his head. 'Fuck – now we have a problem. We'll have teams of Weegies telling us that we don't know what we're doing because we're not from Glasgow. Brilliant – that's all we need. They're not going to forget that we fucked them over the Billy Drew case.'

Harkins looked across at Macallan; they both wanted to give O'Connor some good news, but there was none to give. Macallan spoke but only told O'Connor what he knew already.

'It has all the marks of the same killer. The girl was a street pro, and the level of violence looks like our boy. There's a chance it's not him, but for the time being we've got to count her in.'

'Anything to report before I meet our friends from the west?'

'Felicity came up with this one.' Harkins put a report in front of O'Connor. 'And we've started looking at the main suspects. We're going to visit Jonathon Barclay today. He's got a bit going for him, has a Merc, but I suppose the fact that one of the highest paid advocates in the land has a Merc isn't going to send him away for life. Having said that, his history is interesting and there's a story with this guy. I've gone nose to nose with him a couple of times when you were both swanning about in different parts of the world and I was keeping Lothian and Borders safe.' He hesitated, smiled and put on a pretend serious face then added, 'With the greatest respect.'

They all smiled, but it was strained – the investigation was taking its toll on their sense of humour.

'We haven't come across him for a few years, apart from ripping us apart in court, and there's no doubt he's a police hater. Some advocates play at it in court and leave it behind after the verdict. Some of our best friends and supporters are in the Faculty of Advocates. Not this guy. He was born shouting that we fit people up and have the intellectual capacity of earthworms. He just won't play ball with us and clearly he must have some childhood memory of walking in on his mother getting her make-up smudged by the local constable. I just made that up by the way but you never know. Whatever happened, this guy is the enemy, and all the best villains go to him for advice. He delights in that, and it's his weakness. He thinks he's fireproof, but he's almost sailed into our field of vision a couple of times. We know he's done a bit of coke, but who hasn't, and there would have been too many problems in trying to fix him for fifty quid's worth of powder. The main thing is that on a couple of cases where pros had been attacked, he turned up as a punter. I was involved on one of them, and to be fair there was never an allegation that he hurt the girls, but he did like to humiliate. Some of the pros described him as a nasty bastard, but that's as far as we could get it.'

O'Connor interrupted. 'What do you think, Mick – is it a waste of time?'

'I think you never know but most of the creeps we process over the years show signs and patterns of behaviour. I've had run-ins with him, and he holds me up as all that's bad with the police, so I think the DCI will have to be the good cop and I'll stay bad.'

'Sounds like a good plan. Go get him but keep me informed because the first thing he'll do is make a complaint, and we need it like the proverbial hole. Do it right or don't do it at all – and please don't assault him.'

Harkins scratched his chin, which he'd forgotten to shave that morning because Young had asked him to stay in bed for another ten minutes.

Macallan took Harkins by the arm. 'I'll make sure he behaves.' She steered him out of the door and looked back at O'Connor. 'The rest of the suspects look like they have alibis so I hope he's interesting.'

O'Connor wondered again about Grace Macallan. Most detectives would dread the job of going to see a high-profile, police-hating advocate who would give them as hard a time as possible. Not her – she was relishing it. What was it about this woman? And, he wondered, was it possible to fall in love with someone like her?

Harkins had been correct in his assessment of the Glasgow detectives. If O'Connor hadn't known better, he'd have sworn they had part-time jobs as Taggart impersonators. They just wouldn't listen, and it was the old east–west divide – the eternal chip on their shoulder that a city half the size of Glasgow was the capital, held the parliament, the seat of law and one of the Queen's holiday homes in Scotland. Eventually he reminded them who was the ranking officer in the room and that seemed to calm them down for a bit.

Once they were back on a level playing field, they all remembered they were involved in more than polishing their egos, and O'Connor explained just how big the problem was.

'Look, guys, what we have is someone who's off on a run. The shrinks tell us that this guy expects to be caught and is filling his boots while he can. The problem is that we think he's also highly intelligent, and at this moment in time he's dictating the story. He knows we're all over the streets in Edinburgh and anyone looking at a pro is pulled in. He could well start to travel and our researchers and analysts think he may have been attacking woman all over the UK for some time. These attacks were never linked because, to be honest, they were serious assaults on prostitutes and that doesn't grab our attention. Now you'd think some of the girls would have provided a few clues, but he went for the junkies who were on the street out of their skulls, so what we have is patchy, and we'll just have to wait and see. I know you're going to ask about the girl with part of her tongue missing. Again we're not sure but the suggestion is that she managed to get off some sort of insult that hit the spot with him and that was his response. Who knows?'

The air had cleared rapidly. O'Connor knew that Glasgow produced some of the best detectives in the UK, never mind Scotland, but like their motherland they had to get their grievances off their chest every so often, hence their initial sparring. They dealt with more gangsters than one city needed but kept forgetting it didn't grant them a God-given right to lead on everything. He wondered how that would pan out if or when a unified Scottish force came to pass.

The senior Glasgow detective George Dillon explained what they had so far and admitted it wasn't much. The issue was that there might be a problem identifying the latest victim. The feeling from the other girls on the street was that she had just arrived from Eastern Europe. A couple of them thought her name was Anna, and that was about it.

'Her pimps are believed to be Albanian bad guys, and if it's who we think then we've got more chance of winning the lottery than getting a word out of them. We've sent a message to Interpol with photographs but don't hold your breath on that one.'

The girl was in too much of a mess to put out a photograph to the press, but that was the least of their worries. At the end of the day, Strathclyde agreed to set up a team looking at the Glasgow murder, and they would include liaison officers from Edinburgh. Glasgow would also put a liaison officer in the Edinburgh squad and they would be linked by the HOLMES computer system.

O'Connor told them about Jonathon Barclay but only to try and put something positive on the table. The Glasgow detectives had gone very quiet but at least realised that O'Connor was not the chinless halfwit they'd expected.

The meeting ended with handshakes and, if anything, O'Connor felt having these guys on side wouldn't be such a bad thing. There was no doubt in his mind that if the culprit was on Glasgow's patch, they'd go the distance to get him and that was all he could ask.

42

Macallan and Harkins pulled up outside the grand pile of stone that was the home of Jonathon Barclay QC. It was one of the biggest and best houses in the Grange area of Edinburgh, not that far from the house where Billy Drew's career had been disrupted and turned towards a few years inside – quiet, beautifully designed and built in an age when as much thought and craft was put into the outside as the inside of the homes for Edinburgh's finest – or sometimes most corrupt. Old-world charm just didn't do it justice.

Macallan sucked her teeth and tried not to get bitter that a man who'd defended some of the worst characters society could produce should be rewarded with this display of wealth. The house dominated even in the Grange, but then it reflected its owner, who dominated his own part of the Edinburgh landscape.

'There's just no justice in this world, Chief Inspector.'

Macallan agreed but didn't say it. 'Come on, let's get in there and try not to pocket any of the silverware.'

Diana Barclay had been married to Jonathon Barclay too long, but she was where she was. She sipped her Earl Grey tea and stared at the front page of the *Scotsman*. She wasn't really reading it, just vaguely staring at the headlines, because her mind was elsewhere, rerunning the same thought she had almost every day. She lived in a home that the vast majority of souls in the city could only dream of, and yet it gave her no joy. For years she'd spent money on the house, thinking that each new acquisition would suddenly turn the key and open up the door to her happiness.

She had married Jonathon Barclay when he was a young, very ambitious advocate and she was a young, rather unambitious lawyer. When she'd seen him working the court in his gown and wig, she'd been impressed, even though his family was a few rungs down the social ladder from her own well-connected tribe. He was going to be successful – that was a fact, and she'd wanted all the trappings, but she definitely hadn't wanted to work for them herself. She came from the best stock and he'd seen her as the perfect other half for his drive for the top. Neither of them had ever really considered love as crucial to the relationship, although they spoke the word occasionally, just for effect.

She sipped her tea and her heart sank once again at the awful truth that their whole relationship had only been a vehicle for their ambitions. The home that impressed almost everyone who passed through its door was devoid of the fond memories that can inhabit even the humblest place. They'd produced a son then a daughter who'd been given everything that money could buy but were starved for warmth and affection.

He'd become involved with other women at an early stage of the marriage, and she'd been well aware of it, but at that time it hadn't made any difference to her. She'd never taken another man, and she regretted that choice now. The discovery that he used prostitutes had been the one that hurt. Affairs were one thing, but associating with women who Diana Barclay regarded as vermin was quite another matter.

The doorbell startled her; she didn't get many visitors in the morning. She checked herself in the mirror and saw an immaculate, middle-aged woman who would soon be old. She made sure that nothing was out of place and pulled the heavy oak door open.

Harkins held up his warrant card to her. She'd often wondered how she would react if the local constabulary came calling, but she felt calm and smiled in a way that she reserved for staff. First impressions were everything to Diana Barclay and if Harkins hadn't flashed a warrant card, she would have taken him for a door-to-door salesman. The woman was something different though, and she recognised strength of character when she saw it, which meant she disliked Grace Macallan before they'd exchanged a word. She made a habit of disliking talent in women.

She was polite, ignored Macallan and spoke to

Harkins, who explained that they were involved in a routine investigation and wanted to speak to her husband.

'I take it by routine you mean the attacks on those street girls. Please come in.'

Macallan was trying to work Diana Barclay out and why she'd immediately associated their call with the attacks. She didn't seem the least bit surprised to see them – as if she knew exactly why they were there. In most cases, there would have been questions – and anger that detectives could arrive at the home of people who didn't see themselves as living under the same constraints as the rest of the taxpaying public. She decided to force her way into the conversation, and Harkins, reading the situation, let her.

'I'm sorry to trouble you, Mrs Barclay, it *is* about those girls, and it's your husband we need to talk to. But you seem to have expected us – can I ask why?'

Barclay regarded Macallan for a moment and tried to give her a look that transmitted her contempt. She may have had a loveless marriage, but living in the same house as a man who delighted in attacking the police had rubbed off on her. She'd heard Harkins introduce Macallan as a chief inspector but couldn't resist a childish swipe.

'Well, Constable, I did watch the press conference, my husband drives a Mercedes and he visits prostitutes. I expect that's why you've come to my door. But he's involved in a case in Glasgow and won't be back here until tomorrow. He's been there for a few days so I suppose that's another reason you might want to see him, given the latest incident. I'm a trained lawyer myself so I know how these things work.'

Macallan smiled at the cheap dig at her rank but decided to let it go. The woman was trying for a reaction and she was definitely not handing it to her on a plate. She would let her play the lady of the manor for the time being.

'Okay, we'll leave our numbers, and perhaps you can get him to call us as soon as he's back in town. Given that you know what we're investigating, I should say there's nothing other than what you've mentioned that brought us to your door. It's routine from that point of view, and we have to go through the motions. Normally we wouldn't have said anything to you before seeing your husband but, given that you do know what it's about, would you be able to confirm where he was on the dates that the attacks took place?'

Harkins looked at Barclay and wondered what got her up in the morning. She was dressed to the eyeballs, sat just on the edge of the seat with her ankles crossed and her hands clasped as if she was the fucking Queen, giving the servants their instructions for the day. Still, it cheered him up that Jonathon Barclay had her to put up with; it was no wonder he paid pros for a bit of company as far as Harkins was concerned.

'Again, given that I know how this works, I might as well be frank. I share this house with my husband, and if I invited you to look around, which I am certainly not going to do, then you would realise that we live in separate rooms. We speak in the morning and we occasionally even attend the odd function together for appearances' sake, but that is as intimate as our lives are. I have my life, he has his, and as to where he might be on any particular night or day, unless we were at one of those rare functions together then I have absolutely no idea.'

Macallan decided to give it a slight push. 'Is there anyone else in the family who could help? I believe you have a son and daughter?'

Barclay flinched but recovered quickly and her mouth tightened. Harkins and Macallan saw a woman wound up very, very tight and wondered what the story was. They realised that her response meant this was going to be a tough one, and no doubt Jonathon Barclay QC was going to be banging the door down at HQ when he found out about their visit.

'My son lives in town; my daughter lives and works in New York. I speak to my daughter on the phone every week but she has little or no contact with her father. My son comes to the house, but he's not close to his father either so I don't see how they could help you.'

Macallan decided to leave it there and think this one through. They thanked her without warmth and left, then sat in the car and thought before starting the engine.

Harkins broke the silence. 'Jesus, the long winter nights must have flown by in that fuckin' place.'

Macallan nodded 'Well, he'll be one pissed-off QC when he finds out what was discussed in there today. Clear the desks of our other stuff, I want to get clued up on this one before we meet Mr Barclay.'

43

Macallan walked out of HQ just after nine and realised this was an early finish. Her legs were heavy,
and the only word she could think of to describe
how she felt was 'knackered'. She decided to defy
her body and walk back to the flat. She had hardly
seen the inside of the gym for weeks and realised that
Northern Ireland wasn't the only place in the world
where life could be hard. All this shit, and yet she felt
she was in the right place.

She walked through the darkening Georgian
streets and realised she was falling in love with a man
and a town. This city reeked of its past. The skyline
silhouettes looked like something from imagination
rather than reality, and the Old Town was filled with
legends and ghosts. What more could a woman want?
She thought how strange it was that more people had
died violently in Edinburgh than in Belfast yet their
reputations were quite different.

Her phone rattled in her pocket and she guessed it was Harkins, gasping for a drink and a gloat about Diana Barclay. She saw 'JJ' on the screen and paused – she was too tired for another problem or development; sure he was phoning to say some other tragedy had taken place and why didn't they all just cut their wrists.

'John, please not bad news.'

'Christ, is that what a call from me means? I'm so tired I can't think and wondered if you fancied a meal from the man who's neglected you?'

'I'm intrigued, so speak, but it's under caution.'

'Okay, I fancy you, and you have slept with me, so I think there's something there. How's that so far?'

'That's not that interesting, but let's hear the rest – and it better be good.' She was smiling despite her exhaustion.

'Okay, I'd like to sleep with you again, but the problem is that we're detectives – both neurotic, both working on a case that'll probably see us back in uniform, and both knackered and up at six to start all over again. What I was going to suggest is quite unconventional, but what if I come to your place because it's close, I bring a bottle of wine and then we go to sleep like an old married couple, because to be honest, Chief Inspector, I want to cuddle in and crash out. That's probably the worst offer you've ever had, but it's my best at the moment. By the way, I'll probably have a bad dream imagining myself in a uniform when it all goes wrong. You know I'm a poseur.'

'Okay. You'll take your socks off though or the deal's off.'

Any other time they would both have avoided this. Both retreated into their shells when things were hard, and that's how they liked it, but tonight – tonight they both needed something different.

When she opened the door and he dangled the wine before her, she could smell the tiredness on him. It wasn't bad; this was the guy who was a walking advert for male grooming after all, but there was a musk instead of fifty-quid cologne and it felt like intimacy. Of course she needed a bit of a wash herself but that made the moment all the better.

'Come in. I'm just glad you're here.'

They drank the wine, talked all over the place and hid from the day job. She found another bottle, and they were slightly relaxed by the time midnight rolled around. They kissed, went to bed and dropped like stones into sleep without making love.

They didn't have to.

She was in the Crown Bar in Belfast. Some people say it's the most beautiful pub in the world and it had to be a contender. Macallan loved it, but she'd had to put on a ton and a half of make-up and part disguise in case a Provo had her identified and there was an ASU on the way. She didn't want to die in a pub in front of all those witnesses. When she died she wanted to be alone.

She ordered a pint of Guinness – but what else would you order in the Crown? Tommy Doyle walked in the door but it was the young Tommy, fit and strong.

'Fancy a pint, Grace?' he asked. 'There's no hard feelings you being SB an' all. The war's over for both of us so time

to drink a Guinness and get on with what's left. You didn't kill me – I killed myself. Truth is that the boys will sing about me for years so I'm not complaining. I was terrified of the peace, tired, ill and hadn't a fuckin' clue what I was going to do. Keeping the war going was all I had. Anyway, cheers!' He sipped the pint and walked out of the door.

She lifted her head off the pillow and O'Connor moaned, pulling her into him.

44

O'Connor straightened up in his chair and the slump in the shoulders lifted as Macallan recounted their visit to Jonathon Barclay's home. As always he made notes, but this time it wasn't for effect – he was interested.

'Okay, I can't believe he's the killer but stranger things have happened so who knows? Whatever happens we're going to get flak, and I'm just surprised he's not got a complaint into the rubber-heel squad already. Just do it by the book and make sure you don't take any new course of action against him without running it past me. What do you intend to do next?'

Macallan had thought it through and knew O'Connor was right – this would have to be by the book, but if he refused to cooperate then they'd have to rattle his cage.

'You know what the problem is, and I think we can

all guess what'll happen. If his CV is correct then he'll tell us as little as possible, and if all we have is that he uses pros and drives a Merc, then it's going nowhere, but the wife's reaction was something else. She just shouldn't have acted in the way she did, so I'd like to try her again if he refuses to cooperate. In the meantime, I've got the analysts and researchers on it to see if there's anything that we know about him that can be linked to any of the other cases. For example, he's high profile and a bit of a star in the legal world, so if he appears anywhere else in the country, it tends to be mentioned somewhere in open sources. If we can show that he was in the area at the same time as one of the attacks then it might give us a start. At the moment we do nothing and wait to see if he'll get in touch with us. We don't have enough to bring him in so no doubt he'll pick the venue if he agrees at all.'

O'Connor nodded towards Harkins to see if he had something to add.

'He'll be in touch all right and it'll be hard. I told you I've had my run-ins with him. I did get under his skin so maybe that's something we can exploit, but I think we should go back to the street girls and see if any of them know him. It's a long shot given most of them are doped up to the eyeballs half the time, but occasionally they get it right. He's one hundred per cent Mr Suave right down to the grey temples. The information we had before was that he uses high-class escorts but occasionally he likes to pick them up off the street. I was always amazed that the papers didn't run something, but they know as well as we do that he would be one hell of an enemy. Other than that I think we should get on this now, then if it comes to nothing, it comes to nothing, but the quicker we know the better. We either do the business on him or clear him out of the system. The last thing is I want to remind you that I'm no longer a sexist now I'm one half of a couple, but this guy will be interested in Grace, and I've a feeling that whatever happens, he'll at least keep the communication going.'

Macallan smiled at the admission. 'Christ, when did you stop being a sexist? It's amazing what a senior analyst can do for you.'

O'Connor was about to close it but Macallan hadn't finished. 'I just think that we shouldn't forget that, whatever happens, this guy seems to treat women badly even if he's not the killer. He sounds like a pure bastard so we owe him nothing. He belongs to the cream of Edinburgh society and is a pillar of the legal establishment. I think if we get anything at all to hurt him then we should use it.'

O'Connor shifted in his seat and saw that this was a genuine plea, but he was enough of a strategist to know that the wrong move against Jonathon Barclay could cost both them and the force. Barclay would take great delight in giving the police service a kicking, especially if he could play the victim at the same time.

'I get it, Grace, but there are all sorts of problems with this one, and we all need to talk to each other to get the best result. Look at it this way: if he's the killer, it's going to be a nightmare trying to prove it.

He's defended dozens of murder cases and knows exactly how we'll run the investigation and what we'll be looking for. On the plus side, he's human and this number of crimes means he would have to have made mistakes somewhere along the line.'

Harkins stood up; he needed a tobacco hit. 'Amen to that.' Young had been putting pressure on him to give up the fags and he was doing his best. He knew well enough what the years of smoking and alcohol abuse must have done to him, but it was hard going. The big surprise to him was that he even wanted to try, and for the first time he could remember, he was looking forward to something worthwhile. The big worry was that he wanted this to last and he wasn't used to looking forward to good things in his life.

O'Connor decided that it would be smart to brief the ACC before hassling Barclay. He didn't particularly want to, but he knew it would be used against him if the shit hit the fan and he'd kept it to himself. The ACC was just waiting for his chance to club him, and this investigation was probably going to give him all the chances he needed.

Macallan went to the canteen, not for the wet sludge they advertised as coffee but to run it all through her head. She kept thinking about Jacquie Bell but couldn't work out why. The one thing she did know was that she didn't want to lose touch with her. In Northern Ireland they'd used leaks to the press as just another way to get things done, and where necessary hurt people who needed to be hurt. More than one political career had come to a grinding halt after their nocturnal habits had been dropped to a friendly reporter. She thought that Bell might appreciate an inside brief on Mr Barclay, depending on what they could dig up.

Back in her flat Macallan picked up the phone twice and put it down again as she struggled with the idea of giving Bell more inside information. There was something else bothering her, but it was indistinct and she couldn't work out what the problem was.

'Fuck it.' She picked up the pay-as-you-go phone she'd bought, called Bell's number and closed her eyes, still trying to work out whether being involved with her was a good idea or just creating one more problem in her life.

When Bell answered, the sound of her voice soothed and confused Macallan all at the same time. They made small talk, and Bell sounded genuinely pleased to hear from Macallan, but they both knew there was more to the call.

'Look, I've had a shit day, and I'm positive you have too, given what you're up to, so how about a fine red wine at my expense? I can still catch the off-licence so you can either come here or I'll jump a fast black and come to you. Sound good?'

'That sounds perfect and here's the deal – you get the wine and the taxi and that'll give me time to have a shower and open a packet of something and stick it in the micro.'

'I'm on my way.'

45

Macallan wrapped the towelling robe round her, rubbed her wet hair and thought about having real time with John O'Connor. Time to really get to know each other – not the 24/7 obsession they currently had with a sick bastard who liked to torture women.

Not tonight though.

She felt a stab of guilt because the person coming to her door was Jacquie Bell, and there was a nervous orchestra playing in her belly. She looked in the mirror and fretted over the dark circles under the eyes, deciding it must be the harsh light above the bathroom mirror playing tricks.

'What the fuck are you like, Grace?' She pulled a grotesque face and was smiling back at her reflection when the knock at the door startled her. She wasn't ready, and the plan had been to at least make herself look less knackered than she did. She sighed. 'No time for the Polyfilla then. I hope the sight of you doesn't frighten the poor woman.'

She pulled open the door and found Bell with a bottle of wine in each hand. Macallan thought how similar the scene was to her visit from JJ, and the guilt orchestra kicked off in her stomach again.

'I'm sorry I'm not ready; I didn't think you'd get here so quickly.'

She felt like a schoolgirl, and Bell sensed it and seized the moment. She put the wine on the hall table and pulled Macallan towards her.

Macallan was shocked by the suddenness of it all but gave in to her instincts and let her feelings run free. The next couple of hours were a dream, and at one point she shed tears, but not from guilt or fear, just the pleasure of giving in to her own desires. She'd lived a life of control, even when she'd been involved with her lover in Northern Ireland, and the Troubles, plus her own strict Presbyterian upbringing, had left her afraid of herself and what she might really want in life.

They lay quietly while Macallan tried to work out what it all meant, but for the moment she felt warm, satisfied and didn't want to move. Bell had dozed for a few minutes and there was just a hint of a very low-level snore. Macallan smiled and pushed the hair off her forehead, and Bell woke, smiling at Macallan as she pulled herself up onto one elbow.

'Don't worry. We don't have to be in love or get married or anything – and for God's sake, don't feel guilty! I know they don't have lesbians in Northern

Ireland but you'll be okay. I think you're just a bit confused and maybe this'll help to clear it up in your head.'

'It was amazing; it's just that I've never been with a woman before.'

Bell wasn't surprised, and she laughed and kissed Macallan lightly. 'I kind of guessed that, but I'm more worried about that wine going off so I'll go and get glasses and bring it back to bed.'

Bell had no hang-ups. Macallan watched her walk naked to the kitchen and decided this wasn't the night to worry about her sexuality, although she was now trying to get to grips with the term bisexual. 'Jesus, what would my mother, Ian Paisley and the PSNI think of me now?'

Bell came back to bed with very large glasses of red wine and for the next half hour they talked and giggled like teenagers before they each fell into a deep and dreamless sleep.

46

Bell struggled to open her eyes but the smell of toast and coffee brewing kicked her off as she padded through to the kitchen.

'Christ, you're up early. It's only six thirty. Are you always so domestic?'

She walked over to Macallan and gave her a bear hug. 'Thanks for last night by the way. It was what we both needed so let's leave it at that and feed me some breakfast. Normally I just have a fag and coffee, but if you want to be Mum then that's good for me.'

After Bell had ignored Macallan's protestations and smoked her first cigarette of the day, she pulled on her jacket and made her goodbyes. There was no embarrassing guilt, no false promises, and Macallan realised that this was someone worth knowing. Bell hugged her at the door and held her face in her hands.

'It was a good thing last night, so like I said, we can just leave it like that. But if you want me anytime, just call – there are no strings. I'm not the type to get involved anyway, so hopefully whoever the lucky man is, they'll realise you're a prize. Anything you need on the murders, just let me know.'

Macallan asked her to come back into the kitchen, poured her another coffee and told her what they knew about Jonathon Barclay. Bell pulled out another cigarette, though Macallan insisted on opening a window and letting the cold morning air take care of the fumes.

'Jesus. He's a fucking gold-plated lawman and bastard of the first order. We've had the stories for years that he played away and liked the odd hooker, but the guy is very well connected and very careful. He also has some seriously bad people who owe him favours, so all in all he's a very bad enemy. I'll do a bit of quiet digging and if he becomes a real suspect maybe we can run something in the paper to try and stimulate interest.'

Macallan had already thought it through. 'Why don't you run something like it's understood that a number of significant suspects are being investigated, including a prominent lawyer and a police officer? The last one is true by the way, but we've almost ruled him out. We always turn up a cop or two when hookers are involved. It never fails. I'll keep you informed but I've got a feeling for this one.'

Bell threw the last of the coffee down her throat and made for the door. 'Have to run, but let me know how it develops. I've a story to do on a local coun-cillor with a drink problem. It won't get me a literary award, but it'll keep me in red wine and fags for a bit.'

Macallan felt fresh and alive and there was no guilt, at least for now. In fact, she felt like something had been freed up in her, but what surprised her was that she couldn't wait to see JJ again, and she was more certain than ever about wanting to spend time with him.

The dark memories of Northern Ireland were beginning to fade. There would still be dreams, but they were passing, and she started to remember that there had been good things there too. She thought about her friend Bill Kelly. She'd only spoken to him twice since leaving Belfast and on both occasions it had been him who'd called. He'd been her greatest support there and she'd almost cut him off. It was time to make amends.

She lifted the phone and knew that calling him this early wouldn't be a problem, unless he was out doing his morning run. The phone rang too long and she was about to hang up when Kelly answered – but she could hear there was something wrong in his voice.

'Bill, it's Grace. Sorry I've not been in touch, you know how it is.' She said it all too quickly.

She told him that she was fine; that she was sorry for ignoring him and that her life was getting back on track. The response was not from the Bill Kelly she knew; the voice on the other end of the phone was fragile and wavering.

'Bill, is everything okay with you?'

'Grace, I'm just happy to hear you – and don't

worry about not being in touch. You needed to get this place out of your system, and I knew that better than anyone. I'm glad that you're getting a new life – hopefully with people in it. Unfortunately I've discovered that I'm human and not immortal. The Provos couldn't get me but Hodgkin's lymphoma can. Looks like my career is over.'

He explained it all, calm as he always was and without a trace of self-pity, but then that's why she cared so much about the man. She couldn't stop the tears as she struggled with the implications of what he was telling her. He stressed that she shouldn't worry – he had no regrets and the investment in his family had paid off: they'd become what he'd hoped for and so had Grace Macallan.

She struggled to speak and told him that she would come to Northern Ireland to see him as soon as she could get time away from the investigation.

'I've been following it and it sounds like a tough one. I remember you saying that you would never come back to Northern Ireland, but I knew you'd have to lay the ghosts to rest at some point. This place is improving out of all recognition and you can take a pint of Guinness almost anywhere now. I say almost because a lot of those nutters who were released under the Good Friday Agreement have to live somewhere.'

They said their goodbyes and promised a weekly call – and that she would come back to Northern Ireland.

47

Macallan picked up the phone. On the other end, Jonathon Barclay identified himself in a calm, polite tone, which caught her off guard. No aggression, no complaint, all he wanted was to make an appointment to meet Macallan. She signalled to Harkins, pointing at the phone and mouthing, 'It's him.'

'Would you like to bring a lawyer along with you?'

Again the answer threw her – this wasn't going to script. He didn't want anyone with him and was happy to attend a police station. She made the appointment, put the phone down and Harkins walked towards her desk.

'Are you sure you're describing the right guy to me? Unless I'm much mistaken, that was a perfect gentleman who just volunteered to come in of his own accord. Given Jacquie Bell's story this morning about a lawyer being a suspect, I thought he would be seriously pissed off.'

Harkins looked as puzzled as Macallan. 'Not possible in this world, Grace. Just not fucking possible where he's concerned. The bastard must have some horrible plan. No other explanation.'

Jonathon Barclay pulled up near St Leonard's station and stared at the red-brick building that looked like a million others dotted on modern industrial estates around the country. Still, not as bad as some of the cesspits he'd had to visit his clients in when he was a much younger and permanently struggling lawyer.

The older he got, the more he reflected on those days, when he defended anyone who could bring in a few notes. It was usually the housebreakers, assault and robbery merchants and the general clientele that gummed up the Sheriff Courts almost every day of the year. He'd hated them, but he was a good lawyer and therefore a good actor. They'd all thought he was their best friend. He was the guy who answered any call, and it had never mattered what despicable act they'd committed as long as the bills or legal aid had been paid on time. Within ten minutes of briefing Barclay, he'd convinced them that they'd been fitted up by Lothian and Borders or whatever force had lifted his clients. He'd entered their world of self-delusion, and he'd enjoyed accusing police witnesses of everything but starting the Second World War, relishing the tremendous power he had as a defence lawyer to say whatever he liked to whomever he wanted.

He'd matured with his clients, and when he'd

eventually entered the Faculty of Advocates, he'd walked into the world he was destined for – the big stage, complete with theatrical wigs and gowns. He'd managed to win a couple of stonewall cases against all the odds, and his power to mesmerise juries meant they forgot the actual evidence. He had the gift good criminals paid top dollar for, and the real bad men started to hire him as their personal brief.

In many ways, he saw himself in the most talented criminals. They may not have had the benefit of his education, but it took balls and nerve to get to the top of the organised crime league. In any other life they'd have been a success, and he often thought that they must have something special carved into their DNA – or was it a flaw? They didn't feel pain or emotions when it came to business. If someone got in their way, they just removed the problem or fell to their rivals. Real dog eat dog.

Barclay's problem was that he preferred the company of these men, and sometimes women, to his own circle of friends or colleagues. He didn't see it happening – the thrill of drinking the best champagne with men who were prepared to kill their rivals blinded him to a simple fact. They were outside the law and he was with them. He forgot that they were predators – had to be; they studied him for weak spots, and normally after the third drink it was easy. The women who lived in their world were like a drug to Barclay. He couldn't hide it, and some of the women who hung on the arms of the top men made him tremble with embarrassment and excitement. He wanted to experience these creatures that would do anything with anyone as long as they could flash the cash. He'd been told that police investigators often had the same problem with women who were criminals or associated with criminals, and now he understood why. It was the forbidden fruit, the things you're told not to touch as a child – everything that we're told is bad for us but would take if no one was looking.

A well-connected drug trafficker who had walked from court courtesy of Barclay had spotted the look in his eyes and given him what he wanted. He ran some top-of-the-range escorts and had instructed one he used himself to seal the deal. She had been well briefed to make sure Barclay got whatever he desired and was made to feel special. All she'd had to do was convince him he was irresistible then leave it to human weakness and the power of self-delusion. By the end of the night, she'd managed to get a drunken Barclay to take her to a five-star hotel and, as a bonus for her employer, helped him to his first snort of cocaine.

The next morning he'd been full of self-loathing, and like any other addict he was hooked, but it was the women he craved rather than the coke. He'd decided there and then not to touch the nose candy again, but it made no difference to the man who'd supplied the girl and the contents of her handbag. He fell down on the cocaine – but to be fair, only rarely – and that was fine with his supplier. They wanted him clear-headed when they needed him, and under control.

In the years that followed, he found he could only get the high he needed by being with women who sold their bodies and souls for cash. The gangsters never asked him to do anything other than defend the indefensible, and that was okay for him. His problem was that despite all the outward signs of success he felt empty, a failure, but he was locked into a road with no turn-offs. To the outside world he was something else: a big player and a feared courtroom specialist. It was the place he was made for, and even his critics admired his ability if not his charm.

He walked to the counter in St Leonard's and told the clerk that he was there for an appointment with DCI Macallan. The whole situation worried him. Normally a call like this would have kicked off a storm, but his instincts told him there was a real threat to him and it was near. Smart men knew when to fight and when to simply hold their ground. This was not a time for taking on the local constabulary. Not yet anyway.

Macallan was in the control room watching the monitor at the front of the building. 'Not bad, Mick, not bad at all, but just a bit too smooth a dresser. His hair looks like something out of a male fashion shoot.'

'Not my type, Chief Inspector.'

When Macallan walked into the interview room, Barclay stood up and offered her his hand. 'Chief Inspector, it's a pleasure to meet you.'

Harkins walked in behind her and though Barclay's face hardly changed, Macallan did notice the slightest of movements there. He'd demonstrated enough control to show her he knew how to act depending on the occasion. Whether he hated Harkins or fancied the pants off him, he had suppressed the emotion, but something had clicked, though that wasn't surprising – Mick tended to have a strong effect on people.

'And Mr Harkins,' Barclay added. 'I thought maybe you'd be retired by now and writing your memoirs.'

It was impossible to know if he was taking the piss. 'Mr Barclay,' Harkins acknowledged him. 'It's been a while. Think the last time was that murder on the Calton Hill – your client walked away from it, despite the overwhelming evidence against him.'

Barclay smiled and relaxed. This kind of banter was fine by him. 'I think he was found not guilty by a jury of his peers, therefore innocent and justice done.'

Macallan gave Harkins enough of a look to bring their fencing to an end.

'Let's get to it, Mr Barclay, and of course you are only here as a possible witness. Cards on the table, we know that you've associated with prostitutes in the past, including escorts and street girls. We know you drive a Mercedes, and we just want to ask you a few routine questions at the moment. It may be that you can give us enough to let us leave you in peace.'

Barclay smiled and Macallan wondered how often he'd practised it in the mirror. In another life, she might have been impressed but not this time.

He threw his first spanner in the works. 'I'll answer anything I can to help with these terrible crimes. Go ahead, Chief Inspector – I'm all yours.'

Macallan's skin crawled. It was everything and nothing. He talked, admitted using prostitutes and refused nothing. He knew that like so many others he could not account for where he was at the time of the attacks in Edinburgh and Glasgow, though he admitted being in Glasgow on the day, acting for a client. He was open about his relationship with his wife and that she would not be able to say that he was in or out on a particular evening.

Macallan didn't mention the attacks in other cities beyond the one in Glasgow, keeping that in reserve until the researchers and analysts had done their job. She decided that the interview was going to end up a draw and thought perhaps they should try to dig up a bit more before speaking to Barclay again.

She threw in the last set of questions. 'Mr Barclay, I know you might not know any of these women by their proper names, but I can show you a photograph of one of the girls who survived an attack here in Edinburgh.' She pushed a photograph of Pauline Johansson across the table. And for the second time in the interview something pulsed briefly across his expression before it was gone, but Harkins and Macallan had caught it, and his answer surprised them again – none of it was going to script.

'I do know this girl and so the answer is yes, I've used her services but I can't remember when that was. Probably weeks or months ago but I can't think where.'

Macallan realised they had moved into a place they had no plan for and what followed would have to be off the cuff. Barclay's reaction to Johansson's photograph had puzzled Macallan though. It was as if some awful truth had hit him between the eyes. What did it mean? She decided to ask two more questions. 'I want to show you a photograph of the girl who was killed in Glasgow. It's not been published as very little is known about her at the minute.'

She pushed the photo across the table. 'Do you know her?'

Jonathon Barclay stared at the photograph then looked up at Macallan. Something had changed in his bearing. His shoulders had fallen, but he could dig deep, and he kept his composure. Macallan almost admired the way he was handling it all and realised she knew the answer to her question before he spoke. It was there in his eyes.

'I know this is going to sound terrible, but yes, I know this girl as well. I should say though that it would be entirely possible for a man who uses the services of these girls to have been with both of them and not be the culprit.'

Macallan knew that if they'd been in court, he would have been the first to sneer at that answer.

'Again, I think it was weeks ago, and I picked her up off the street.'

Macallan asked her last question: 'Are you the man who attacked these women?'

'No, and I don't really want to say any more today.'

Macallan sat back and looked Barclay straight in the eye, and he broke first, looking down into his hands. Macallan closed the interview then spoke to Harkins in another office. 'I think we should cut it there for the moment. What do you think?'

'Fine with me. I don't know if I can come to terms with what's been said. We could soon have enough to detain this guy. I'm sure I'm dreaming. Why the fuck is he admitting to knowing the girls?' Harkins shook his head. 'Anyway the only thing we need to do is ask if he'll let us have a look at the car, and if he refuses there's not much we can do at the moment, but I think JJ will want it grabbed ASAP.' He shook his head again. 'I just don't get what I'm hearing.'

Harkins looked like someone had stolen his wallet.

'You okay, Mick? You look a bit frazzled. Thought you'd have been happy seeing old Beelzebub coming apart in there.'

Harkins didn't smile and didn't try. 'I just can't get my head around it; this is not the way he plays it.'

They walked back into the interview room and discovered Barclay had just about recovered any lost composure.

'Okay, that's all for now,' Macallan told him. 'You've been very helpful. Clearly we'll want to see you again, and if there's anything you want to ask then go ahead. Before I forget, is there any possibility we could have a look at your car? You know you can refuse but we always ask.'

That was when the game changed direction for the third time in the space of the interview. 'I'm sorry, and obviously your colleagues haven't told you, but my car was stolen last night. It's still not been found as far as I'm aware.'

She couldn't hold it back. 'You have to be pulling my leg. That's the oldest one in the book.'

Barclay sat back in his seat; he'd known the effect this would have.

'I know how it looks but I can assure you that the car was stolen. Do you think I'd have been stupid enough to use my own car anyway if I was the man you're looking for? I've seen the publicity like everyone else.'

Macallan took control. Barclay's answers had made him their prime suspect, and they needed to get a plan of action put together before he could take care of any remaining evidence. Though she personally didn't think he was the killer, there was no way they could ignore the line of investigation, and once Barclay had been escorted out, she rang O'Connor to arrange a meeting.

Barclay walked to his taxi. The truth was beginning to crush him, and normally he would have known what to do next, but not this time. The car being stolen looked bad, and if he'd been an everyday lowlife they would have tossed him into a cell already.

Pieces of his past floated through his imagination; like a new life forming, the sum of his parts would join and meld into something that frightened him.

He opened his eyes and realised he was nearly home. He'd never cared about the house other than as a commodity that reinforced his image, but he wanted it to be home now. He felt like a soldier facing battle, suddenly discovering a god he'd never believed in, and he was afraid that there was no one in the world who could or would give their shoulder to him.

The problem was that he didn't know why he was afraid.

48

Macallan and Harkins sat in O'Connor's office, and he listened without interruption until she finished her account.

'What do you think?' he asked her. 'And I'm fine with gut feelings.'

Macallan knew the dangers of being distracted by what seemed to be the natural line of investigation. So often in murder enquiries what seemed obvious turned out to be completely wrong. Coincidences happened, and innocent people got caught up in the hunt.

'I think he has to be worth putting a team on full time, though it may all just be coincidence. He didn't need to tell us a thing, and I wish I could understand why he admitted to knowing the girls, but then maybe it's because he *is* the culprit and he knows we'll get him eventually. Regardless, I think we need to move fast, because if it is him and there's any evidence left, he'll be getting rid of it – though it's more likely it's already a pile of ash. I've no doubt the car will be torched, but I've got a marker on the PNC when it's found.'

O'Connor looked out of the window and wished he was out in the field rather than sitting in his office. He'd never thought that way, and a picture dropped into his mind. He was with Macallan and somewhere a million miles from his office. He smiled and got down to business.

'Great work. Get all this to the analysts, create full profiles of all the cases and I think once that's done get an interview strategy drawn up as soon as. In the meantime, it seems to me that the only chance we have to secure evidence is getting DNA from clothing, presuming that the car's a non-starter.'

Macallan's phone went off and interrupted them. It was a message that Pauline Johansson wanted to see her.

49

Macallan hadn't seen Johansson for nearly a week and the improvement in her was remarkable. Time and again during the Troubles she'd witnessed miracles in the way people had survived the most appalling injuries. A senior doctor had once told her that it was the will to live as much as medical intervention that made the difference in recovery. Johansson would be scarred for life but there was a spark in her eyes, and her colour looked more like that of a healthy young woman.

Macallan smiled and it was genuine. Johansson returned the smile although it was lopsided, and despite the damage there was hope in her expression. For the first time in years she was off heroin, and her body was feeding on something other than the odd chocolate bar and can of oversweetened juice. It occurred to Macallan that maybe something half good might come out of all this carnage. If she hadn't been attacked, she'd have been dead within another few years – and that was if she was lucky.

'How are you, Pauline? Looking good and putting on weight I think – no bad thing.'

Johansson squeezed her hand; there was strength there now – a recovery of sorts. Macallan decided at that moment that she would speak to Johansson's parents, even plead with them if that's what it took to get them back in her life.

'Okay, let's do some work. Have you remembered something? If you have, let's use the blink system. Okay?

One blink.

Pauline Johansson had remembered something. As the days had passed and her strength had returned, she'd wrestled with the pieces of memory like they were from a freshly opened jigsaw box. Her problem was that a lot of the pieces were missing for ever. Some remained though, and would flick across her mind's eye like a subliminal message.

Eventually there was one that recurred and flashed without form, but she knew it meant something. She wanted the man who'd attacked her to suffer – to feel as frightened as she had been for too long, so she tried hard to pull it to the surface.

She'd woken the previous morning and there it was, like a grainy old movie. The man had form but no face, just a vague demon tormenting her. But she'd remembered that, as she lay on the ground half-conscious, the demon had stopped beating her and removed her cardigan before beginning the torture anew.

It took a full hour but Macallan eventually got the story and sat back, considering. The killer was collecting trophies. It wasn't something that had been picked up as a pattern in the cases, but it could be crucial in putting him away – if they could find them. If it really was Barclay then he would have to be crazy to keep these things. It was one for the shrinks.

She called the office and asked Young to look at the other cases and establish if there was any possibility of items being taken from the victims. She knew that the Glasgow victim hadn't been wearing underwear, but it had been presumed this was more to do with getting her job done than anything else.

She wrapped her arms around Johansson and promised to come back soon, then decided to visit Johansson's parents, who'd moved to Portobello in an effort to escape their own story.

Macallan told them all about the trial their daughter was enduring and how her old life was gone for ever. She told them that their daughter was someone who'd endured a deficit of love since the day she'd taken her first hit, that she deserved to be loved and that it was unlikely she would ever find that love from a man, given the efforts of her attacker.

The parents had sat straight backed and unresponsive, but Mrs Johansson broke first and then the dam opened. Mr Johansson slumped at the sight of his broken wife and put his face into his hands.

They'd been loving parents but had lived for years as if Johansson was dead – and in a way she had been. It had been a necessary pretence to save them from breaking apart themselves. In order to safeguard the memories they had of their daughter before her introduction to heroin, they had buried their love of her.

Macallan sat quietly and let them release their years of pain. Mrs Johansson asked first when they could see her, and her husband simply nodded at the question before putting his arm around his wife.

Macallan told them she'd call as soon as she'd spoken to their daughter then left the Johansson home, managing to wait till she was outside to let the tears fall. She promised herself that she would find the man who'd shattered Pauline Johansson's body and that she would not forget that young woman.

Life had robbed the Johanssons, and Macallan would do everything she could to help the family recover. Too often the system picked up shattered families, extracted the required information or compelled an appearance at court and then left them messed up for life. Macallan wouldn't let it happen to this family – they'd suffered enough.

50

Young sat down at the table in O'Connor's office with Harkins and Macallan. Although they'd already been told, Macallan ran over the information she'd gained from Johansson one more time, stressing what a breakthrough it could be for them. O'Connor knew exactly what it meant – that there was always the danger of a leak so they might have to act on this quicker than they would have preferred.

When Macallan was done, Young announced that they'd finished their research into the lead.

'We've looked at as many of the cases as possible. We have to presume that in the case of the Glasgow murder, her lack of underwear was due to it being taken rather than being an intentional act by the girl. Apart from that we can't see anything missing in the other attacks. However, the early cases we think are connected to the current crimes were serious assaults rather than murders, and the women were heroin addicts with very poor recall. I believe that as there are no previous reports of missing clothing from the victims that he's just started to take trophies. This might seem strange – not what we would normally expect – but there have been other cases where the pattern of behaviour changes or develops, and I think that's what's happening here. It's as if all of this is part of a plan leading to a conclusion rather than it being random acts of violence. It's calculated, not obsessive compulsive behaviour, and the profilers agree.'

She stopped and waited for O'Connor to comment. He ran hypotheses through his head but there was no answer coming.

'Anyone any ideas on what this means?' he asked. 'I really don't know but I agree with Felicity that this is carefully planned and heading towards some sort of climax. If he's just started taking items then it's not a compulsion and he has a reason. He must know that there's a risk in keeping them so why take them now when he's had all the luck so far?'

Macallan looked at O'Connor and saw the strain around his eyes. This case was all bad; they were dealing with something they simply didn't understand. They weren't even close.

'If Felicity is right then this guy is something different, given what he's done in the past. I'm beginning to think he's playing a game with us and probably not concerned about being caught. In fact, I think that maybe he's factored that in. Someone as intelligent as this one must know that he'll make mistakes somewhere along the line.'

O'Connor felt the tremors in his stomach and knew that he had to make a decision – and take some risks.

'We have a number of problems to deal with. This man can and probably will strike again, and given that we have a suspect we'll be hung out to dry if we don't act and it turns out to be him. Nothing seems to be making sense in relation to how Barclay is acting – he's definitely not playing to the script, although we probably shouldn't expect predictable behaviour if he's our culprit. There's the risk that the killer is keeping the missing clothes, and if it leaks, which it will, then again we'll be hung out for not acting against the prime suspect. Grace, I want you to get over to the fiscal's office and apply for a warrant to search his house. I can't believe he'd be stupid enough to keep these things there, but we can't risk doing nothing, especially as the car is probably lying torched somewhere.'

As they left the meeting the news came in from the uniforms that Barclay's Mercedes had been found completely burned out on the outskirts of Glasgow. O'Connor laughed without any humour. 'Well, he played that one dead centre.'

Macallan took the news with a growing sense that although they had a suspect, they were essentially in the middle of nowhere.

She went straight to the procurator fiscal to explain what they had and was surprised at how easily he complied with the request for a warrant to search Barclay's home. The fiscal had locked horns with Barclay in court on a number of occasions, and although he didn't admit it, he tended to come off worst in their verbal battles. In fact, Barclay had humiliated him on one occasion and set the fiscal's career back a few years. That one burned inside him still, and he could hardly contain his joy that Barclay might be about to fall. He encouraged Macallan to move with all due haste.

'If there's a chance of recovering evidence then we can't afford to wait, Chief Inspector. Please keep me informed, and let me know when you decide to detain him.'

The fiscal got hold of a friendly sheriff, and the warrant was put in Macallan's hands.

She called Harkins to get a team together for the search.

'I want trained search teams to do this, not just whoever's sitting around. I want every inch of that house searched and anything that he might have been wearing recently taken for examination.'

Minutes after Macallan left the fiscal's office, he picked up the phone and called Bell. 'Hi, Jacquie. Got something that might tickle your fancy. Have you come across Grace Macallan from the MCT? She's one of the lead officers on these prostitute attacks.'

Bell smiled at how small the world was. 'As a matter of fact I have. What's up?'

The fiscal told her the whole story and she scribbled as he talked. She regarded him as a severe pain in the arse but a very useful source of information, so fair game. He had the hots for her, so she strung him along in the name of keeping the public informed, and, more importantly, keeping her editor happy.

'Thanks for that,' she told him. 'It'll be my turn for the drinks. Need to run.'

She didn't wait for him to say goodbye and called her editor. She told him the story and he liked it. 'What do you need?' he asked.

'Get me a photographer and make it urgent. Get him to head towards the Grange and call me when he's there.'

'It's done.'

51

Jonathon Barclay wasn't home, but his wife was and she stayed remarkably calm when Macallan arrived with search-team officers and detectives. Macallan would have preferred to have Jonathon Barclay there, but they couldn't delay the search. She decided to let the team get on with it while she sat with Diana Barclay.

'Is there anything you want to ask me, Mrs Barclay?'

She stared at Macallan and considered the question. 'I think I said all I needed to say at our previous meeting. I won't give any statement; I don't have to, as the person you are obviously interested in is my husband.'

Harkins came into the room, signalled to Macallan and she excused herself. There was not a flicker of a reaction from Diana Barclay.

'Jacquie Bell and a photographer are outside the fucking house. How in the name of Christ did she get onto this so quickly? JJ and the executive are going to want someone's guts for this.'

In any other place Macallan would have had a couple of gorillas chase them off, but her relationship with Bell complicated her options. 'I'll go and speak to her,' she told Harkins. 'Stay with it here.'

She crunched over the pebbled drive with no idea what she was going to say. When she saw Bell, they both smiled. Bell told the photographer to fuck off and have a quick fag, and he trudged away, muttering like a schoolboy who'd had his sweets stolen.

'Jacquie, much as I like you, this is going to cause havoc back at HQ,' Macallan told her. 'I don't know how you did it, but please help me on this and I'll give you the story later.'

Bell lit a cigarette and coughed. 'This is a good story and all we're going to do is take a couple of photographs. I'll do a few lines without poisoning the case for you.'

'Please, Jacquie,' she begged. 'I'll call you tonight and give you all that we have, but let us do our job. We don't need any flak from the executive – if they look too hard, they might think it was me that set this up as I applied for the warrant.'

Bell relented and motioned to her photographer to head back to his van.

'Okay, you've got it,' she said quietly. 'Give me a call tonight or come round. I'm not going to do anything to hurt you. When this is all finished I still want that story about your journey from the Troubles to the dark streets and deeds of Edinburgh.'

She started to walk away from Macallan, then turned and waved when she reached the car – playing to their audience. 'Look – I'm fucking off.'

Macallan supressed a smile and headed back the way she'd come.

When she re-entered the house, she could have sworn that Diana Barclay had not moved a muscle. She sat down and tried again. 'Mrs Barclay, I won't use anything you say here but can I ask you what you think about this: that clearly, at least in our eyes, your husband is a suspect in this case?'

Macallan's gut told her Diana Barclay was holding back, which wasn't too surprising given that her husband's affairs were about to be thrown under a very intense spotlight. Whatever followed wouldn't be pleasant.

'Don't answer that.'

Jonathon Barclay had arrived and Macallan could have sworn he looked like he expected to be arrested. There was no fight in the man, no complaint, and he sat down on the other end of the settee occupied by his wife. The gulf between them was obvious and there was no exchange or reassurance, just the cold and wasted years that had turned them into strangers.

It surprised the search teams how fastidious Barclay was about buying clothes. They were the best in quality, but he tended to buy regularly and get rid of them once the new gloss had gone. No favourites – for him it was always about looking perfect. They took most of what was in the wardrobes and left what were clearly his court clothes. There was no sign of any trophies from victims.

Macallan cautioned Barclay but decided to leave him be until they had more evidence, if that was possible. She left with barely a word spoken, Barclay following her to the door, and she watched him stand frozen in the doorway until the last of the police team had left the grounds. She left in the last car and their eyes were locked until Macallan's car made the turn onto the street.

'What the fuck are we missing here?' she wondered.

The driver looked at her but didn't have an answer.

No one did except the killer.

Barclay walked back into the sitting room, decided he had to say something, and then regretted it as soon as he opened his mouth. 'Look, we'll get through this.'

His wife lifted her eyes from the floor and shook her head slowly, trying to form a response without anger. Jacquie Bell had already produced an article claiming that a lawyer was under investigation, so the seeds of disgrace were sown and germinating. She wanted the words to cut deep into the falsehood that was her husband's life.

'I've known you for a long time, Jonathon, even though I've spent a good part of that time hating you, and I know how you operate. You were like a rabbit in the headlights when those police officers raked through our life. The Jonathon Barclay I know would have fought them tooth and nail – they'd have been lucky to get in the door unless something was very wrong. Is something very wrong, Jonathon? And answer me this – did you know any of the girls?'

He looked at the back of his hands.

'I just don't understand your behaviour – and then there's the car being stolen. You can see how that looks to them.'

Divorce or death would have at least secured the sympathy of friends but this would turn her into a social leper with nowhere to go and a future that held nothing but loneliness.

Barclay drew a breath, feeling trapped. There wasn't enough respect between them to make an explanation possible. What had been left of their relationship was gone, the final humiliation delivered by Grace Macallan and the police team, but he decided to try nonetheless.

'I know how these things develop a life of their own,' he said. 'I'm not loved by the police, and there's an officer on the case who I've had to deal with a number of times. They're already leaking to the press, and I've no doubt what I'm going to tell you will eventually find its way into the papers. I know at least two of the girls, but it has to be coincidence – there's no other explanation.'

His wife felt cold and calm, and if nothing else she thought she could at least make his downfall as complete as possible.

'The fact that you associate with whores isn't new to me, but at least I was able to lead what passes for a life. This has brought me to the edge of the same cesspit you inhabit. You sit there and tell me that there's no other explanation? Well, I'm afraid there is.'

He nodded, too tired to plead with her, but she wanted to open up the wounds just a bit more and continued. 'There are lots of people who will enjoy picking over your bones. God will they love it – all those people you've trampled over the years because you thought you were bulletproof. How does it feel, Jonathon?'

She was desperate to shed tears but there was too much hatred brewing to allow her that luxury, and all he could do was sit there and listen as she continued tearing into him.

52

When Macallan got back to HQ she told Harkins she needed some food and left the building. She walked to the nearest public phone, called Bell and told her what had happened at the house. Another few lines of bad publicity would pile the pressure on Barclay, and as far as Macallan was concerned that was okay.

'That's all good, Grace, keep me in the loop. Drink tonight?'

'Can't. I'm up to my eyes and can hardly keep awake as it is. Wouldn't want to seem bored if we meet up.'

That was an excuse, and they both knew it, but Bell just smiled at the small lie. 'Well, just enjoy whatever it is that you're up to – or whoever it is that you're up to.'

Macallan wanted to be with JJ; it was just a case of whether she could prise him away from the office.

53

The clothing taken from the Barclay's home was sealed carefully, labelled and sent to the forensic laboratory for examination, but it would take days to complete the examination properly, and the tension in the office was difficult to deal with. If there was nothing on the clothes then they might be left with detaining Barclay and trying to get an admission – but that was unlikely from a QC who knew all the tricks of the trade and then some. The analysts and detectives would push on with all the lines of investigation they had, but for O'Connor, Macallan and Harkins it was almost impossible to concentrate on anything other than Barclay.

After her phone call to Bell, Macallan had gone back to visit Johansson to see if she might be able to recall the face of the man who had attacked her, but she had no memory, and Macallan didn't want to show her a photograph of Barclay or mention him until they had more evidence.

Before she'd left, she'd told Johansson about the visit she'd made to her parents, but now she was home, she was overwhelmed by doubt about whether she'd done the right thing. What would they think of their daughter now – how she'd come to that hospital bed from a life of heroin dependency? Would they be able to give her the support she needed?

Macallan let herself wrestle with those thoughts for a few moments before she swallowed some coffee, called the office and asked if anything had come back from the lab yet. Harkins sounded as frustrated as she was when he told her there was no news, and she thought there might be something else up with him, but she didn't have time to get him to open up about it right now. Maybe they were all just a bit punch-drunk from the investigation and it was simply the sixteen-hour days starting to take their toll. She pushed the thought away.

'I'm beginning to think it's back to the drawing board,' Harkins said. 'If it's not Barclay then we've got nothing else, and as far as I know, our Glasgow colleagues have got fuck all but sore knuckles from dragging their paws along the ground.'

Macallan laughed and tried to sound upbeat even though she didn't feel it herself. 'Chin up, we'll get there.'

But doubts were crawling through all their minds, gnawing away at them like ulcers in the pit of their stomachs, and after she hung up, Macallan let her head fall back, breathing deeply. She needed a break – some kind of distraction – and felt weary down to the soles of her feet. She wanted to soak in a bath with her eyes closed and nothing in her imagination, just music playing in the background.

She phoned O'Connor and invited him for a drink. 'I know you don't want to leave the office until we get an answer, but we all need a break. Come round and I'll cook you something that goes with any kind of booze.'

He was too tired to argue and knew that his batteries were low and that he wasn't thinking straight. A cooked meal with Grace Macallan was an offer he couldn't refuse in the circumstances, and he thought it might help move the knot of worry that was strangling him from the inside.

When he walked through the door of Macallan's flat an hour later, they stared at each other as if they hadn't met in a long time.

'God, we both look like shit!' she said. 'Is this what life is supposed to be about?'

The blunt truth made him smile for the first time in days. 'Why don't you say what you mean? I really don't think that's any way to speak to a senior officer.'

They both laughed and began to relax. O'Connor thought again how much this woman was getting to him and how little he actually knew about her. He promised himself he'd spend the rest of his life finding out.

'Well, if that's no way to speak to a senior officer then this next thing will really put my career down the toilet. That noise you hear in the background is the bath running, and you're invited to join me. Now you can either report me for sexual harassment or get your kit off and jump in.'

He scratched his chin in feigned doubt and then nodded. 'Okay, just this once ... but the next time this happens I *will* file a complaint.'

She took him by the hand and led him towards the bathroom where the steam hung in the air like the edge of a dream.

54

O'Connor was chairing a meeting with the murder squad when the call came through from the lab. Everyone in the room stiffened, trying to gauge what was being said, but he gave nothing away, just nodded at the voice on the other end of the line. When he put the phone down though, his face turned dark and set.

Macallan sank back in her chair guessing bad news – that the clothing was clean and they were back to a blank drawing board. She wondered why she'd expected anything else, but they were all starting to live on hope rather than expectation.

O'Connor apologised to the squad for cutting the meeting short and asked Macallan and Harkins to follow him to his office.

When he sat down at his desk, they saw his face was pulled tight with strain. He looked up at them. 'They've found blood on a jacket that's been DNA'd then matched to Pauline Johansson and DNA on a pair of trousers matched to Anna.'

The temperature in the room seemed to drop, and they sat quietly for a moment, trying to absorb what no one had really believed was possible.

Harkins, however, always knew how to break the ice. 'Well, I'll be fucked,' he said.

Macallan shook her head; she still didn't believe it. 'There's no doubt?'

'No doubt at all. We have him for at least two of the cases. He's away for the rest of his life providing he doesn't rustle up some legal magic. I know we've done it by the book so far but it has to be the same from here on in – we can't afford any mistakes.'

O'Connor picked up the phone and asked Young to come in so he could brief her on the development. She rarely showed emotion in the office, but she was as excited as they all were by what this meant, and she had her own contribution to make.

'I was going to brief you all at the meeting that we've dug up something. Maybe not a breakthrough on its own but it'll help the chain of evidence, given what we've just learned.' She pushed her glasses up the bridge of her nose and flicked to the second page of the report she had on her lap. 'Through researching open sources we've been able to establish that Barclay was dealing with a defence case in Glasgow High Court when Anna was killed. He was attending a legal conference in Manchester six months ago when a prostitute was left brain damaged from an attack, and he was in London nearly a year ago when another street girl was attacked and lucky to survive. The issue with that one was that she was fresh in from the Balkans, and after giving a poor initial statement she disappeared. The Met think her pimps got rid of her. Apparently they're not too keen on police involvement.'

O'Connor nodded, his face still a reflection of his inner turmoil as he tried to work out the scenarios and traps that might be lying in wait for them. The rule of thumb was that something had to go wrong – it was the nature of the game, and you had to be prepared to handle the crisis when it tapped you on the shoulder.

'That's good work, Felicity – it adds to what we've got and the other forces will want to follow up, but as long as we can secure two of the cases then even if we lose some of the others, well we'll take that. Get all this put together as soon as. And, Grace, I want you to put together an interview strategy so we can work on him once he's been detained, then you and I will do the interview itself. You okay with that, Mick? I'm sure you'd love to be there, but it has to be done this way. If there's a fuck-up, then it's my fuck-up, and I'll take responsibility.'

Harkins nodded, looking pale and tense. 'No problem. I'm fine with that.'

'Are you okay?'

'I'm fine, sir. It's just been a hard haul this one, but don't worry, I'll be there for the celebration once we get him settled into a concrete room.'

O'Connor clapped his hands together and came to life. 'Okay, let's get cracking. I want him picked up tomorrow morning at six. Get the surveillance team to watch him round the clock, and make sure he's somewhere we can knock on his door.'

A few minutes later, Macallan was walking away from the station and wondering why she was doing what she was about to do. She checked round and slipped into the phone booth, feeling guilt weighing down on her as she picked up the receiver.

'Hi, Jacquie, are you free to speak?' she asked when Bell picked up.

'Anytime for you. What's up?'

Macallan explained the situation and told her Barclay was right in the middle of the frame with nowhere to go. Bell whistled and promised to keep quiet until they'd taken him in. She would then publish fuller details the following day in an exclusive.

After she ended the call, Macallan decided to take a break from the office for half an hour because she knew it would be a long night getting the script ready for the morning shift. The bulk of the interview strategy would be decided by an experienced DS who was a trained interview advisor, but she wanted to be sure she was happy with it before facing Barclay across the table.

She walked into a coffee chain and ordered a simple white coffee, avoiding the lure of the elixirs that contained enough calories to keep the Scottish rugby team going for a day. She wanted Barclay's humiliation to be complete, and Bell would make that happen, but as she sipped her coffee, she couldn't escape the nagging feeling in her gut that despite the damning evidence they'd found, something about the whole situation felt very, very wrong.

55

Barclay lay fully dressed on his bed. It was still dark, and the fat spots of rain tapping his window added to the thick black depression that filled every corner of his imagination. Sleep had all but deserted him for days on end; he felt exhausted and at times he was delirious through the endless hours awake. All he could see was his future shattered like a mirror, and nothing was certain now, if it ever had been.

Although he'd never been a religious man, he felt that he was about to be punished for a life built on exploiting the weakness and frailty of others. He'd defended the men who deserved punishment, paid ravaged addicts to satisfy his base needs while he enjoyed their degradation, and his family meant no more to him than the expensive trappings in his house; they were lifeless shells who'd received all the privileges he could provide yet left him with no feeling of pride or contentment.

He rose from the damp sheets, regretting the nightcap that had become the best part of a bottle. The whisky helped him to drop him off but there was no peace to be found in that sleep, and he would wake again within an hour, exhausted and trembling.

He searched for answers constantly, a way out of the trap that had swallowed him whole, but his demons were all around the gates and he knew there was no escape this time. He was having to come to terms with the truth, and it was shocking – there wasn't a single human being who could shelter and reassure him. Professionally, he was admired, hated and respected as an outstanding advocate, but no one would want him with the baggage he now carried round his neck like a leper. He couldn't even call on the criminals who owed him their freedom because they already knew too much about him, and there would be nothing in it for them. What could they do anyway apart from sneer at the humiliation of a legal star who'd proved he was far more corrupt than the worst of them?

When he heard the car wheels crunching the stone chips outside he felt relieved – anything was better than this endless self-torture. Whatever the future held, at least it would be real, not the swirling doubts and fears of his imagination.

He checked himself in the mirror, surprised that on the surface at least he looked presentable, although his shaving had been less than successful and the alcohol had taken its toll on his skin. Apart from the slackness under his eyes, he would do.

He heard his wife answer the door. If anything, she was probably sleeping less than he was, but the thought gave him no comfort.

He walked downstairs with his coat over his arm. He was light-headed – the scene was surreal, and it was as if he was sitting comfortably, watching a drama through the gaze of one of the actors. He blinked several times, his eyes dry and irritated by the combination of insomnia and alcohol, to see Macallan and O'Connor dripping wet and standing next to his wife. They stared at him. O'Connor was saying something, and although the voices were muffled, he didn't really care. He knew why they were there, and he was ready. In any case, he knew the words off by heart and could spend a day in court explaining this procedure to a bored jury. He was under arrest.

He felt his hands being pushed behind his back as the handcuffs were snapped into place. Macallan was saying something to his wife, but he still couldn't separate the words into a meaningful form. His legs worked on their own, but when he walked out of the door, the rain splashed his face and the cold water cleared his mind.

A hand pushed the top of his head down and he was helped into the back of the police car. He winced at the dull pain that had started to grip the skin where the handcuffs were biting into his wrists and then stared out the window. There were blue lights tracing the dark morning air, and as he looked towards his neighbour's house, he saw lights starting to click on – witnesses to his downfall getting in on the show.

As the car moved off he looked back towards his front door and watched as his wife pulled it closed and the light within was extinguished. He knew that whatever was in front of him, it was unlikely that he'd ever walk through the entrance of his home again. His wife was beyond forgiveness (and why should she forgive him?), and that house would be her prison as much as whatever cell they would put him in.

He settled back into his seat, a uniform either side of him, and his thoughts started to clear, the adrenalin pushing his exhaustion to the side, at least for a time. They all stared ahead as the city drifted past in streams of light, watching the odd lonely soul tramping to an early-morning job that probably paid no more than the minimum wage. He never saw the city at this time; he rarely started his day until ten, and he wondered if that was a privilege he would ever have again?

56

The car swung through the gates into the station yard, ploughing through a pond of water where the concrete surface had been waiting to be repaired for years. Barclay was helped out of the car and he was led inside, his shoulders aching from the handcuffs dragging his arms out of position. A heavy steel door closed behind him, the noise startling him, and his heart thumped against his ribcage. He was sure the uniforms must have heard it.

He was eventually pushed into a plain grey room and he was thankful that at least it was warm. The uniforms unclasped his handcuffs and he rubbed the red flesh as relief flooded through his shoulders and arms. There was nothing in the room but a table, chairs and a tape recorder.

His lawyer showed up, put his hand on Barclay's shoulder and sat quietly beside him. Barclay almost recoiled; he knew the man despised him – he was only there for the money and the drama he could recount to his friends at the golf club.

A few moments later, the door opened and Macallan and O'Connor walked in. With difficulty Barclay held himself back from his lifelong ritual of standing and shaking someone's hand when in one of these places. He looked at O'Connor, but he'd already worked out that the man had presence and intelligence a few levels above the normal police evolutionary chain. Having done his homework, he also knew that O'Connor had education and money behind him, so trying to impress him with a lawyer's bag of tricks would probably be a waste of time.

He turned his attention to Macallan as O'Connor ran through the formalities and caution. Her background had intrigued him, and he wished they could have met before all this had happened. She was an unusual package, not beautiful yet wonderfully attractive, with luminous green eyes that must have seen all that was dark in the human spirit during her time in Northern Ireland. He'd read about the trial where she'd given evidence against another police officer and understood the price she must have paid to take that course. Traitors never came out well in a war zone.

Whatever happened he knew he was faced with a formidable team and that he would have to be careful with any comment, although he intended to say as little as possible. Nothing different than the advice he'd given to almost every client he had ever defended. It wasn't this process he feared – he knew he could survive it, but his past was now going to be poured into the gutter for the mob to examine in fine detail, and he knew the press would be out there with their wallets open, trying to track down the women he'd paid to abuse and forget. The red tops would have a field day with their headlines, there was so much to expose, and he wondered which maggots would soon crawl into the light and gnaw at the facade that had been the public face of Jonathon Barclay QC.

'Is there anything you'd like to say, Mr Barclay, before we proceed?' O'Connor asked him.

He had regained his composure, knowing that he would have to deal with this one way or another. The lawyer accompanying him stayed quiet; he would stay out of the drama unless his client asked for his assistance. He was only there as a witness for Barclay, and there was nothing he could teach the great advocate beside him.

'No thank you, Superintendent, but as you would expect, I don't intend to make any statement other than to say that I have nothing to do with the crimes you are about to put to me.'

He sat back and waited for the list of questions that would form the interview. O'Connor handed over to Macallan, and he watched and admired her cool professional delivery, imagining her in another setting.

'Mr Barclay, you are aware that we have been investigating a number of crimes including murder, attempted murder and serious assaults against a number of young women in different parts of the country. These investigations showed, as you have admitted, that you have personal knowledge of some of these women. In addition, a warrant was granted to search your home, and a number of items of clothing were taken and examined. As a result of these forensic examinations, we have identified DNA from Pauline Johansson and the girl known only as Anna who was murdered in Glasgow. I am going to charge you with attempting to murder Pauline Johansson and murdering the woman known as Anna.' She paused for a moment. 'Other charges are likely to follow.'

Her words landed under his heart like a hard set of knuckles and pushed the breath out of his lungs in a short uncontrollable gasp. Macallan continued to speak but he lost track of the words. His heart started to pump a flood of adrenaline round his system, and his breathing rasped through his teeth as he tried to control the shock. His thoughts had fragmented again, and he struggled to make sense of what had just been said. He'd expected a long tortuous series of questions then release to face public humiliation, but for his morals rather than what had just crashed into his life. The pieces started to coalesce and the jigsaw locked into place with a picture of the reality that would leave him damned. But somehow the truth of what was happening calmed him, his breathing slowed and his mind returned to the words that Macallan read without emotion as she formally charged him with murder and attempted murder, and told him that investigations were continuing into other crimes.

He sat back in his chair, looked round at his lawyer who had turned very pale and noticed that his writing hand was trembling. He leaned forward and put his arms on the table.

'I have nothing to say at this time, Chief Inspector.'

Macallan walked to the door and called for a couple of uniforms. As they came into the room, Barclay stood up, feeling a strange sense of relief. What he faced was awful – he was trapped with few options – but at least his tortured worries and imaginations could be put aside.

'Is there something you want to say, Mr Barclay?' Macallan asked, and he found himself smiling for the first time in days.

'I'm just getting a very bad joke. Unfortunately I can't share it with you.'

They left the room and the uniform walked him along the cold tiled corridor to the cell area, the echo of his footsteps rattling around the dull white walls. He hated these places; they were always so chilly and drab. Most criminals agreed that they preferred being in prison to lying in police cells, and he could see why.

He stood before the charge bar as a seriously overweight sergeant ran through the formalities of detaining a man for murder. He knew the police would delight in this one – watching the fall of an A-list QC would make their day.

Endless forms followed, and as his belt and shoe-laces were taken, his dignity dropped away a piece at a time. He knew that as with all murder suspects he would be given no privacy in case he tried to top himself, and the thought of sitting with a couple of uniforms revolted him.

Every part of his person was searched before he was moved into a side room to have his fingerprints and DNA taken. He started to shake with the cold air, which stank of the despair that seemed to hang over every police cell block.

'Why do these places always stink of bleach?' He asked the question without thinking and to no one in particular.

The sergeant studied him for a few seconds, enjoying every moment, before he replied, 'You don't want to know.'

He was then taken into his cell, and he reeled at the thought of the trap that had snapped closed on his life. He sat on the stained mattress with his head in his hands, trying to gather his thoughts and work out how he'd have to respond when he faced the judgement of his fellow citizens.

'Would you like some tea or coffee?'

He looked up, startled by Macallan's voice. He hadn't even realised that she was in the cell. His stomach ached with the stress of hunger and the alcohol that had inflamed his insides.

'Yes, thanks,' he replied. 'I could do with that. Don't suppose you could put a brandy in it?'

She ran her fingers through her hair and he realised that she looked as exhausted as he felt, but at least she could go home to find some kind of peace. When would he ever find peace again?

'I'll fix the coffee, and if you need anything in the way of clothes or a visit let me know. The cell staff should be able to get a hold of me anytime.'

'I appreciate that. I'll let you know what I need. Unfortunately I can't think of anyone that will want to visit me. I've a feeling that whatever friends I might have had will be hard to find in the coming days. The lawyer who sat in the interview will take care of any needs I have. I've given him instructions. Poor man was out of his comfort zone in there but charges the earth so I'm sure he'll manage.'

Macallan took in the once handsome face that seemed to have collapsed under the weight of his reality and almost felt sorry for him, though that feeling passed as soon as she remembered Pauline Johansson's face.

She closed the cell door behind her and he lay back on the mattress, trying to ignore the uniform who'd entered and sat down without a word, studying a red top with some story about a footballer and a model on the front page. He closed his eyes and shivered again.

Ten minutes later and Macallan was on the phone to Bell, who was drinking coffee and in the middle of her second cigarette of the day. Macallan gave her as much as she dared, and Bell grinned at what might come her way if she played this one right before she pulled her jacket on and headed for the office.

57

Barclay appeared at court the following day and was remanded in custody. The press were going into hyperdrive, but Bell had already run a story on the cases that mentioned details about the lives of some of the girls who had been attacked – and it was more than she could have found out without inside help from Lothian and Borders Police.

O'Connor walked into the squad room and threw the paper down on the table. 'If I find out that any of this was passed from this team then whoever it was had better resign before I get to them.'

He slammed the door of his office shut behind him and stared out of the window across the rugby pitches that were the backdrop to the Lothian and Borders HQ. Macallan tapped the door and walked in.

'You okay?' she asked.

He looked round and shook his head. He'd lost it in front of the team, and he knew he'd just made a big mistake. The squad lived on the credibility of the people who led them, and if you lost it in front of the troops, they lost it on the ground.

'I've just had all the grief I can handle from the ACC, who took delight in blaming me for the leaks. This force has leaked like a fucking sieve for years, and suddenly I get in it the neck? I just wanted this case to run as tight as possible – no fuck-ups and straight down the line.'

'It doesn't happen that way – you know that. The stuff that's in the papers isn't that bad and won't prejudice the case. Look, we got the bastard, so let's just ease off a bit and put it in perspective. Lasagne and some happy juice at my place? What do you think?'

His shoulders eased off and he smiled. 'You know the way to my heart, Grace.'

She turned and walked out of the room, guilt gnawing deep in her gut. There was something else though: she kept seeing Barclay's face in the cells. There'd been something in his expression that troubled her, but what was it?

That feeling again – it was just instinct, but she knew instinct was there for a reason. There were too many other things to do though, so she filed it away and forgot about it for the time being.

58

The court sparked with the energy and excitement of watching a killer who'd inhabited people's nightmares – it was the most basic form of voyeurism, being close to something or someone terrible yet in complete safety – a zoo where the citizens could stare at a dangerous predator from only a few feet away. It wasn't that far removed from the days of public executions, where a holiday mood had been the order of the day and the accused would have dropped just yards from the same court.

The trial had captured the public imagination and the tabloids were loving it. The revelations about Jonathon Barclay were sensational – yet another pillar of the establishment had been shown to be the stuff of nightmares – and they gripped the public squarely by the throat. MPs' expenses were one thing, but this was the real deal – a criminal defender exposed as a brutal killer. Even if he was found not guilty, his life was now a legend, and what people didn't know about him they would just make up, such was the media frenzy. And if the verdict went against him then he would take his place in Edinburgh's dark history and compete with Deacon Brodie, who'd stirred the imagination of Robert Louis Stevenson to such a state he'd created the legend of Jekyll and Hyde.

Whatever Barclay's fate, it was clear there was nowhere for him to go – the only options he had were guilty and a life inside, or not guilty and disgrace, so either way he was ruined.

Barclay fought hard and got the best out of his legal team – but he was facing rock-solid evidence, and though his defence tried to discredit the forensics, the lab staff had worked the samples with absolute care and the jury was convinced. After all, most of them watched modern detective programmes where DNA equalled guilt. DNA was the silver bullet, and as Barclay watched the jury's reaction to the lab technician presenting the evidence, he knew he was well and truly fucked.

Whatever was said, the burned-out car looked damning, and his knowledge of the victims was too much for the jury to ignore. He took the stand, and his performance was immaculate, but he couldn't deny the evidence stacked against him. Macallan and O'Connor had been immovable on the stand and delivered their testimony with few problems, so when his lawyer had tried to suggest they might have planted the evidence, it had sent a clear message to the jury that the defence was struggling.

In the end, Barclay looked beaten and walked back to the dock like a man who knew the jury's mind. It was enough – someone had to pay and there was a good candidate standing trial.

In his summing up, Barclay's lawyer struggled manfully to present a reasonable case for a not guilty but his frustration showed, and it was clear Barclay was losing – and losing badly. The detectives had expected him to pull a legal miracle out of the hat, but to their surprise, it hadn't come.

Macallan leaned over to O'Connor. 'Can you believe this?'

'He's a coward. He's getting what he deserves. The judge is just about to brief the jury and send them out so let's go get some lunch.'

O'Connor's shortcomings had just about been exposed during the investigation, but they'd had their break and he was all polish again, firmly back in favour on the executive floor.

They left the court together and walked down the Royal Mile. The sky was a pulsing blue, a cool sea air being pushed over the damp cobbled street and up into their faces. It was a good feeling, and although the investigation had left them sapped of energy, they would be able to put it behind them once the verdict was returned – at least in part. Dealing with unnatural death marked the soul, and those feelings drifted around the subconscious mind forever, occasionally breaking through with a reminder of what might lie in wait for an unsuspecting victim or an unprepared detective.

They pushed into the warm, beery atmosphere of a High Street pub and found a space at the bar.

'They'll give us a call if the jury's coming back in, but we should have plenty of time for lunch and to start planning our trip away.'

Macallan sat back in her chair; he'd taken her completely by surprise. 'Superintendent, what are you suggesting?'

'What I'm suggesting, Chief Inspector, is a week – that's one whole week – in a nice little place on the west coast of France near Royan. All paid for – all you have to do is bring a toothbrush.'

She reached over the table and took his hand.

'Grace.' He didn't know what to say next. She shook her head and squeezed his hand tight as he brushed his free thumb across the wet trail on her cheek.

'It's just that when I left Belfast, I honestly never thought I'd feel this way again, or that a decent man like you would want to be with me. So much has happened to me, and I thought I'd never leave the Troubles behind, but I'm here with you now and that's all that matters.' She wiped her eyes and gave him a watery smile. 'I'll be fine – sometimes we girls need a wee cry – now let's eat,' she said, grabbing a menu.

He nodded and began to study his menu as if there was much of a choice between steak pie and fish and chips.

'One thing I need to mention – it was supposed to be in confidence – but Felicity Young came to see me, and I'm not quite sure how to handle it so tell me if you have any thoughts. I know you get on really well with Mick Harkins. In fact, I can't remember him taking to anyone the way he's taken to you – especially someone who outranks him.'

Macallan sat back. She still hadn't found time to trap Harkins in a bar and get to the bottom of what was bothering him, so she kept quiet and let O'Connor continue.

'Apparently everything was great after they got together, and we all saw the change in Mick. He'd cut down on the sauce and stopped visiting the fast fooders every night. Miracles can happen it seems, and he even said to me at one stage that he was looking forward to retirement, which was not the Mick Harkins of old. Anyway, at some point during the investigation, he seems to have nosedived and Felicity thinks he's back on the edge. Apparently he's necking the whisky again as if the world's supply is coming to an end, and she's worried sick he's ready to walk out on the relationship. I can speak to him, but I know him well enough to know he won't share it with me. I'll have a go because he deserves that, but if there's anything you can do without breaking my confidence with Felicity then feel free.'

The nagging feeling that had been chewing the edges of Macallan's subconscious was back, and she was annoyed that she'd been too busy to listen to the alarm bells that had been ringing for her where Harkins was concerned. Being a DCI was about more than grabbing the headlines – sometimes it was playing nursemaid to a team of tough but damaged human beings – and Harkins had deserved better from her.

'Christ, I did sense something,' she admitted to O'Connor, 'but I thought I'd let it be until we got this thing put to bed. We've not had the regular pub nights we had when we were both sad singles, and I assumed Felicity was filling the hole in his life. I could kick myself because he was so good to me, and I care about him, but he's more messed up than the rest of us put together and I should've been paying more attention.'

O'Connor sighed. 'His yearly appraisal's due so let's see if anything comes out of that first. He's long overdue a week's leave so I'm going to insist that he takes it now before the next mess falls on the squad. If we mention any of the modern interventions like a counsellor then he'll probably throw me out of the nearest window. Anyhow, we'll take the next few days wrapping this up then we'll head to France, and I'll arrange that Mick goes off when we come back. If we're no further forward after that then you can take him to the pub and work your womanly magic, but hopefully the break is all he needs.'

They stayed off the booze – that could wait till after the trial – and walked back to a coffee shop near the court, chewing the fat like a teenage couple and enjoying every moment of each other's history, the small stories that meant little on their own but helped to build a deep relationship. O'Connor's phone went off in the late afternoon, prompting a nod to Macallan and they headed back to the court, hurrying across the old Lawnmarket where many a villain had kicked his last in front of a baying Edinburgh mob.

59

Barclay was composed and it appeared as if he'd resigned himself to the result, but he looked good again, healthy – certainly not the shattered wreck that O'Connor and Macallan had charged with murder in a cold, dark interview room.

The jury, on the other hand, looked tired; the details they'd listened to had introduced them to a new world, and the pictures of shattered bodies and faces had shown them the reality of serious crime. Not the dramatised TV detective story where you could switch off, have your hot chocolate and then go to bed – these pictures showed people who were really dead or wasted for life, and the truth of what this meant had shocked them all.

When Barclay heard they'd found him guilty of all charges, he didn't move a muscle, and Macallan had to hand it to him – he had style. She thought he was the kind of man who would have chosen the death penalty for himself if it were possible, because what he faced in the indignity of the awful, mind-crushing routine of prison was probably going to be his own personal version of perdition. The judge rattled off his thoughts about the fall of a fellow advocate, and although it was in the finest lawyerly form, it was almost predictable: 'a prominent legal figure brought to this'.

Macallan didn't hear much more; her mind was spinning with everything they would still have to do to wrap the case up, but when the life sentence was passed, her eyes drifted back to Barclay, who turned to her and smiled just before he was led away.

It startled her, and O'Connor noticed, leaning over to tease her. 'I think he fancies you. Don't think there's a future there for you though,' he said.

Macallan didn't smile – it wasn't that funny anyway. She decided that at some stage, depending on appeals, she would see Barclay again, try to get him to talk and see if he could throw some light on any outstanding cases.

O'Connor put his hand on her shoulder and saw her mind was asking questions again, but this wasn't the time for it. 'Come on, let's get the last of the paperwork done, then try and have a go at normal life and interaction if you know what I mean.'

She met his eyes and shrugged. 'You're right. Lead the way.'

Barclay was marched out to the wagon and took his seat in the tiny holding space as the van moved off towards HMP Saughton. He heard shouts of abuse from some lynch-mob nutters, clenched his fists and tried to keep from shaking. He'd handled it well, so his main aim now was not to come apart and give the mob anything more to sneer at. During his time in remand he'd thought about suicide, but if he was going to do it then it would be done right – it wouldn't be some failed attempt that could be misinterpreted as a cry for help.

He would try not to think too much about the future until he understood what that meant. Other prominent people had gone inside and survived after all.

He leaned back, closed his eyes and wondered who would come and visit him. Not many from his own world, he guessed. There were plenty professional enemies who'd rejoice at his downfall, but what friends he had were already doing a passing impression of the Apostle Peter, and the future loomed like a grey mist inhabited by predators. Although he'd defended the worst of men, he was a wealthy lawyer, and for some inside that would be enough to make his life hell.

He shivered uncontrollably when he faced the truth that he was a physically weak man who had never been in a fist fight in his life, and the thought of what those men in prison could do to him made him groan out loud.

60

They'd hardly moved from the ancient house they'd rented in the tiny village of Médis, a hidden secret a few miles inland from Royan on the windblown coast of France. It was as close to heaven as two career detectives could get. There was nothing in the village but a baker who brought genius to his art, and despite it being late in the year, there was warm sunshine, although the Atlantic air cooled them at the same time. It couldn't last – the job was scratched into their DNA – but for now it seemed as if they belonged to some other world.

A few days into their trip, they drove up the coast to La Rochelle, parked near the old port and managed to grab a table in a restaurant with a beautiful view of the harbour and the Bay of Biscay beyond. They worked their way through a small mountain of shell-fish, hardly needing to talk, laughing and gorging themselves like children. This was time to recharge their batteries – there was certainly no room for restraint, and they'd become intimate enough to drop formal table etiquette for the time being.

They didn't want the day to end and knew that there would never be another one like it. Times like these were precious, unique, and they'd both seen enough of the dark side of the world to know that life was mostly about getting by, so if you could grab a few good moments along the way, then that was a result.

Macallan could tell that O'Connor had been holding something back from her, and like all these situations it would take time for him to share. What was it with men, she wondered, thinking they could hide themselves from their women? But she would wait and let them enjoy the day, because whatever it was would be related to their real lives, and that could wait for now.

In the end, he opened up a bit quicker than she had anticipated – probably helped along by their second bottle of wine.

'I've been sounded out about a job at Interpol HQ in Lyon.'

It was short enough and direct enough. She lifted her elbows off the table and straightened her back, giving him enough of a non-verbal to tell him she was surprised. She hadn't anticipated this after their time together – foolishly she'd hoped for something else and rebooted her brain to reality.

'Christ, you caught me out with that one! So we can go into the details as we go along, but why? And does that mean this was just a short, meaningless break for you?'

She tried to keep her voice matter of fact, but it was difficult to hide the edge in it. She'd naively thought they were learning to share and trust. Was he just another ego in trousers taking advantage?

'Look, you've got it wrong. I should have told you this was in the wind, but I had to work a few things out myself. Up to the day I met you I was a confirmed loner, and that was enough for me.' O'Connor dabbed the side of his mouth with a napkin and ignored what was left on the plate.

'Okay, tell me the story and let's have all of it. I'm tough but I'm only human, and I don't need any more shit in my life. You knew when I came to the force that I'd left enough baggage behind me to keep an agony aunt going for life.'

O'Connor leaned back in the chair and suddenly looked weary again. Reality was a thousand miles away but they'd have to head back there in a few days.

'It's the collateral damage from the investigation plus some job politics. Okay, we got Barclay, but the ACC just can't stand me and he's determined to stop my career in its tracks. He blames me for the incident that might or might not have happened at the hospital – and the leaks to the press. I don't know if I can be arsed with fighting it, and after working abroad, I realised our force is incestuous to its core.'

She felt her anger rising. Another brilliant man more obsessed with his own ego than getting on with life.

'Don't you get it, John? It's nothing to do with the leaks or the hospital. You know that as well as I do. Of course the force is incestuous, and so is just about every other organisation you can name. You're everything he's not – that's his problem. He's gone as far as he can, is looking at walking the dog and counting his pension, but you have a bit to go yet. He wants what you have but can't buy the time back, so you're to blame in his tiny mind. It happens in every walk of life, but I'm only telling you what you know. If you can't rise above that then you're not the man I thought you were. You're vain and invest too much in getting to the top, but you deserve to be there because you have a talent for it. The ACC couldn't lick the soles of your highly polished shoes. But it's your call, and I can't help you on that one. If you want to go to Interpol then good luck with it.'

She became even angrier when a smile spread across his face. A red patch crept up her neck and he remembered the adage 'red for fight, white for flight'. Macallan was definitely ready for a fight.

'For God's sake, I wasn't about to fuck off to sunny France and forget I ever knew you! I thought you were a hotshot detective? I'd want you to come as well. Okay, it might not be right away, but you speak French and how many Brits can say that? With your background you could walk into any job you applied for. You've become a bit of a celebrity, or didn't you know that?'

He'd caught her off guard again – she hadn't

313

thought that she might be part of his plan. It didn't matter though – the plan was wrong.

'Look, I'm sorry, and if I was included then I'm flattered. But it makes no difference. I've not been long enough in Edinburgh to move already, and I've only just started to get a night's sleep without dreaming about an ASU picking me up and bashing my head in. That's because of you, John, but I don't think you get what you've done for me.'

She crossed her arms, reminding O'Connor of a young girl having a tantrum. She'd amazed him every day he'd known her, and the more he knew, the more amazed he became – this woman who'd slept for years with a gun beside her pillow but was sitting in front of him now suppressing the tears he knew were close to surfacing. She was so vulnerable at times, and he loved that about her. She was real, no pretence – complex but simple, hard but soft, and all his if he wanted her. At first, the thought of giving up his independence for all the baggage she carried had frightened him, but the one thing he knew for certain now was that life with Grace Macallan would always be interesting – and it was a life he truly wanted.

He bunched her hands in his and kissed them. In any other situation it would have felt wrong and she would have put it down to alcohol, but she saw that he meant it.

He looked up and smiled again.

'You're right, and maybe I just needed you to say that. I'm a man, for God's sake – I need a kick up the backside from time to time – so let's see how it goes, and maybe in the future we can think about a posting abroad when it suits us both.'

'Okay, it's a deal, but for the moment I'm happy where I am and we have a job to do with the squad. There's plenty of time, and career-wise we can achieve good things together, so let's just keep enjoying each other and see how it all develops.'

O'Connor had booked a hotel in La Rochelle and some time after midnight they flopped into bed and fell asleep instantly. Walking back to the hotel, trying hard to keep steady, Macallan had felt contented and now she dreamt about good things again – John O'Connor definitely included.

61

While O'Connor and Macallan slept off the booze in each other's arms, a dark shadow stepped into a car, started the engine and the Mercedes moved off towards Leith to hunt. The man driving the car crawled through the quiet streets, concerned that it might be too late now, but he was ready if the chance was there – it was time to move into the endgame.

He gripped the wheel and the bones of his knuckles showed through the skin as he hunted without success. In his frustration, he hit the dashboard with the side of his clenched fist and cursed aloud, feeling saliva spurt from the side of his mouth.

And then he saw her. She wasn't far ahead, and he felt a rush of excitement at what was to come. Stopping the car for a moment, he breathed steadily and calmed himself as he watched the woman, who had to be desperate to be on the go at this time of the morning.

She'd spotted him already and moved towards the edge of the kerb, happy there was a punter about that would get her the next bag of powder. She sniffed wetly and tossed her cigarette end into the gutter.

He looked into his mirror. He was fine again, and he had to be. It was all coming to a head, and he wanted to end it in a glorious flourish. He'd done a good job so far, and the finale had to be right or it would all have been wasted.

He smiled at his reflection and ran a hand over his sleeked-down hair, thinking again how good he looked, how much better than the rest he was and how he was just about to prove it.

62

O'Connor was trying to focus in the bathroom mirror, but it was hard – his head was thumping like an Orange walk drumbeat. He steered the razor across his face and swore he could hear it screech across his dehydrated skin. It had been a wonderful day, and he accepted the pain but wondered what they'd drunk later in the evening. All he could remember was that they'd done some kind of bar crawl – and the rest was a blank. They trained them hard in Northern Ireland in all aspects of the job, and he decided that he was never again going to try and go drink for drink with someone who had served there for as long as Macallan had.

He wiped his face and sipped his tepid coffee before heading to the kitchen area for some much-needed hydration. Macallan was lying face down on the bed and still sleeping – or was she just suffering with her eyes closed? It didn't matter – she looked wonderful, and in that moment he wished he had the talent to draw her.

He took his water out to the balcony and watched white scraps of cloud bouncing across the sky on a sea-chilled wind. The sunshine they'd enjoyed had been a freak weather front, but now low winter pressure was back in charge, and he could see lines of rain pushing north-east across the bay.

Beside him, O'Connor's phone hummed across the table as if it had a life of its own. He felt a lead weight in his stomach and thought about ignoring it, though he knew that was impossible. The job was a drug. They'd been off it for a few days but it was just as potent as a junkie's gear, and eventually being without it would eat them up from the inside out.

He picked the phone up just as Macallan lifted her head off the pillow, the same lead weight in her gut. She shifted up onto an elbow so she could watch his face, but the adrenalin was already rushing through her body and she knew the holiday was over.

O'Connor had turned pale, and she wondered why she wasn't surprised. He put down the phone, as she flicked the switch on the kettle, and then scribbled some notes. She fixed the coffee and waited while he did his thinking, and she was just pouring it into two cups when he came inside and sat down on the edge of the bed.

'An Edinburgh prostitute was taken last night and beaten to death, and there's similarities to the Barclay case,' he told her. 'Jesus Christ, what does that mean? A copycat or what?'

319

The words opened up the pending files she'd put away in the back of her mind. 'Let's get packed,' she said.

But as they did so, she chewed her lip, the mist swirling again in the back of her mind. There had been loose ends in the Barclay case – that nagging feeling that something was wrong – and she knew she should have said more – even if no one had listened.

True, they'd landed a big scalp, but they were about to be punished for it. She just knew it.

63

They didn't bother dropping off their luggage and headed straight to HQ, Macallan calling Harkins as O'Connor drove them from the airport.

'We'll be back in half an hour. Can you be prepared to brief us when we get in? If there's anyone else from the analysts or the science lab required then get them there. Are there any developments?'

Harkins voice was flat and she wondered again what was wrong with him.

'Everyone's working flat out but there's nothing new at the moment. The girl was local and you can guess the CV. She was a junkie with a habit that would have killed a horse if it was stupid enough to stick that crap in its bloodstream.'

'What do you think?'

'I think we need to do the job and see where it goes.'

She pulled the phone away from her ear and wondered where the legendary bastard that had been

Mick Harkins had gone. O'Connor looked round and asked her the question without talking. She stared straight ahead – France was a long way behind them. 'No developments.'

The briefing left them with more questions than answers, and O'Connor started to feel that their short holiday was something he'd dreamed. Here they were again scraping up a mess, trying to make sense of the death of a young woman called Mary Waddell, who had no one to care about her besides her junked-up boyfriend – and he only cared about what she could earn or steal from the punters.

Harkins had attended the post-mortem but all they could confirm was that the girl had been in poor health before her death, and according to the pathologist would probably have been dead within a year without the help of the killer. He told them that the pathologist did say that the violence and pattern of the assault were almost identical to the other victims, but that was as far as she'd go. There would be more to come, but it would take time to finish the tests and tissue samples.

Harkins sat back, waiting for O'Connor.

'Okay, Mick, is that it? Any theories on what we're dealing with here? I don't think there are that many options, so we might as well get to the elephant in the room.'

Harkins should have had an opinion but said nothing, so Macallan broke the silence. 'Well, it's a copycat nutter who's as bad as the original – or it's the boy for the other victims, which means that Jonathon

Barclay is yet another casualty of the big bad police. But it can't be the latter because the forensic evidence against him was solid. We didn't fit him up and the forensics clinched it.'

She looked at Harkins for any reaction, but he didn't move a muscle. Macallan didn't believe what she'd said; her subconscious was racing through everything she knew, trying to find a question mark, somewhere to stop and confront the doubt.

The phone buzzed on O'Connor's desk and his face twisted as he took the call. He dropped it back on the cradle a minute later and shook his head.

'No rest for the wicked an' all that. The ACC wants to see me – and it sounds like he's had better days. Crack on and I'll see you when I get back. If he doesn't transfer me to the traffic department, that is.'

O'Connor left the room and Macallan poured coffee into two paper cups, handing one to Harkins. 'You okay?' she asked him. 'You don't look like the demon detective I once knew. Anything I can do? A couple of drinks along the road when we get finished?'

'I'm okay, but thanks for taking an interest. Think I'm just done and can't do this any more. I'm putting my ticket in and collecting my pension at long last.'

'Jesus, Mick! I thought you were enjoying the job again. Is it something to do with Felicity or what? I don't want you to go. We probably need you now more than ever.'

'It's over with Felicity – she was always too good for me anyway.'

He tried a half-smile but it didn't reach his eyes,

and Macallan realised that something was broken inside Harkins. But if he didn't want to share then it wasn't going to happen.

'What about that drink then? That always did us both good when you were my nursemaid.'

'It's okay, you've more than enough to do with this job, so we can see how it goes. I'll be here for a few days yet then I'm off.'

Macallan felt helpless. 'Talk to me, Mick. We're friends.'

'What do you want me to say? It's time to go, and that's all it is. You've sorted a huge part of this squad now, and you'll do fine without me. I have to get on.'

She gave up but it all felt bad. 'Okay, but while JJ is out of the office, tell me what you really think about this.'

He was halfway out of his seat but dropped wearily back into the chair, where he scratched the stubble on his chin and stared at the floor. 'I think that we've been played from the start and all the talent in this squad couldn't see it. I know you weren't happy with the smell of the Barclay case, but you didn't follow your nose and that was a mistake. We were just too anxious to get the headline capture. You're better than that, and given what happened in Northern Ireland, you've already proved you don't follow the pack unless it's going in the right direction. Follow the leads, Grace. This guy is asking us to find the truth. Fuck knows what it's about, but he's not far away and just wants to get something finished.'

She wasn't sure it was the right move but she put her arm round his neck and squeezed him, noticing how frail he felt. He didn't resist, but when she released him, he left the room without saying another word, and she just stared after him and shook her head. How would she cope without Mick?

Macallan started reading through the evidence to get a feel for the job. She would wait for O'Connor before making a move, but what she saw was a mirror image of the other cases, and she found she couldn't concentrate on the evidence with Harkins' voice rattling round her mind. What she needed to do was go back to the start of the other crimes and work the whole case again.

She called Felicity Young, who arrived a few minutes later with coffee in one hand and a pile of paper in the other. She looked strained but Macallan decided to avoid the subject of Harkins unless she wanted to mention it.

'I don't have to tell you this latest case is a problem, however it turns out, but I want to talk to you off the record before Mr O'Connor comes back. He's going to be under tremendous pressure and might be forced to take a line that he doesn't necessarily want to follow. As regards the previous case, is there anything we didn't follow up because of the arrest or because there just wasn't time?'

Felicity Young heaved a sigh and started to polish her glasses, which she always did when she was stressed. She was much prettier and younger looking without them.

'There's always something but HOLMES doesn't let us get away with much so we really have to focus on answering the outstanding questions in the system. But there are always details of a person's life that can be checked. You can always go further and deeper into the lives of the accused – and the victims or crucial witnesses for that matter. In a way, it's endless, and with an unsolved case you could be following up evidence for years, as we've done in the past.'

Macallan decided to push: 'Okay, I know that, but I want you to think about Barclay and let me know if there's anything we have that still needs to be checked or re-examined for that matter.'

'Will this be authorised by Mr O'Connor?' The analyst pushed the glasses back onto her nose.

Macallan blinked and tried to look routine, though there was nothing routine in her thinking.

'It might be but I have to talk to him first. What if he doesn't give his authority and I still want it done?'

Felicity removed her glasses again and polished them even more frantically. 'I'll see what I can do. I'll do it myself but I might need some help.'

'Thanks. Think about it, and I'll get back to you after I speak to the boss.'

When O'Connor arrived back in his office, he looked drained and his shoulders were slack. A few more grey hairs seemed to have taken up residence at his temples. He dropped into his seat and looked across the Edinburgh skyline as the copper sun began to set and darkness started to creep through the streets and alleys in the old city. Macallan decided not to tell him that he looked like shit because she was sure he knew that already.

'The ACC has just given me a kicking, and needless to say this latest development has put his blood pressure through the roof.'

'Fuck him. We've talked about this.' Her lips were a tight line; she was in no mood for executive bullshit.

He looked up from the desk 'That's not the problem, at least not at this point.' She knew by his face that she wasn't going to like where this was going.

'He said that the rubber-heel squad have been conducting an internal investigation into the leaks and analysing the phone traffic from various officers. Apparently you've been in contact with Jacquie Bell on a few occasions.'

They stared at each other and the pause was long enough for Macallan to decide that she could lie, though he might spot it. There was no time for another option and it wasn't the moment for full disclosure about her and Jacquie's relationship. O'Connor had enough problems.

'Please tell me you didn't go behind my back. Not you.'

'I was in contact with her. She wants to do a story about me, so we had a couple of drinks. I gave her some trivia, but she has other sources. And isn't it an open secret that this force has been leaking like a tramp's shoes for years?'

She was angry and she wanted him to know it. 'I worked in Northern Ireland, and we used the press as a tool to suit us. We all do it, and don't forget that when it comes to self-promotion, you've nothing to learn from me.'

He looked beaten and she felt sick. One kicking was enough for him in a day. 'What are they going to do?'

'Well, there are only a few calls recorded, and you can get away with that. There are better suspects than you, and actually they think it's me. I won't mention anything that's been said here so you can carry on.'

Macallan thanked God quietly that she'd bought a pay-as-you-go mobile or used public phones to contact Bell. 'Are we okay, John?' she asked him. 'That's all that matters to me.'

'I'm not sure. I thought you were different and now I get this kicked in my face. Let's just get on with the job for now.'

He'd turned cold and stiff. The protective wall had gone back up around John O'Connor and Macallan felt her heart sink. 'Okay, if that's how it is,' she said. 'Last thing: can I go over the evidence again in the Barclay files in case we missed something?'

'No, and this is from the top. Follow the evidence on this case. You have more than enough to do, and the official line is that this has to be a copycat.'

'John, this could come back to haunt us so at least let me try.'

O'Connor looked like a man who'd been drained of emotion, and Macallan realised that both Harkins and O'Connor had left the team in different ways and they were all working to their own agendas now. It could only lead to disaster and she heard Harkins' words again warning her about becoming involved with O'Connor.

She walked away from his office and called Young to start reviewing the Barclay evidence.

64

The investigation was drawing blanks. Mary Waddell had been nineteen years old when she was murdered, and most of those years had been a waste – abused as an infant, and from there to the gutter she'd died in, she'd been a fairly untalented petty criminal. Reading her life story was enough to depress the most cynical detective and Macallan swore that she was going to be the last for this killer.

She gave up trying to find sense in anything Waddell's boyfriend had said and read the rest of the file. The investigation team had managed to find what passed for a family, and Macallan struggled to contain her anger at the mother who'd managed to shed tears even though she hadn't seen or cared where her daughter had been for the last five years of her life. Waddell's mother had been a prostitute in her own time, and although she hadn't yet hit fifty was ravaged by the effects of drink and depression.

Macallan was convinced it was the same killer they were dealing with, but O'Connor was sticking to the party line that it was a copycat. The media, and particularly Jacquie Bell, were pressing buttons and annoying Lothian and Borders top floor, and they were taking it out on O'Connor. He was cold or, at best, detached with her, and the news that Harkins had put his ticket in seemed to have driven him further into his shell.

There were few secrets in murder squads, and the effect on morale was almost instantaneous and poisonous. The team loyalties fractured and most went with Macallan, which made her position even more difficult. O'Connor smelt it in the air and Harkins seemed to be past caring and worked on automatic. He did the bare minimum, left after eight hours and stopped handing out advice or bollocking the junior detectives. None of it made any sense.

65

Young had worked the Barclay material on top of the endless workload she had in hand with the Waddell case. She knew that the squad had gone toxic, so she was careful not to alert O'Connor to what she was doing for Macallan, although he seemed to spend his time brooding in his office now rather than trying to track down the killer.

She came to Macallan's flat so they could talk openly and Macallan poured her some wine, letting the exhausted analyst relax and get used to her surroundings. She knew that, by helping her, Young had put her career on the line, and the force would be unforgiving if it all went wrong. She'd come to like the analyst, who was much warmer than her office image portrayed, and didn't want to see her in trouble.

'Okay, what have we got – or not got as the case may be?' Grace lifted her glass to the analyst.

Young took an unladylike slug of her Merlot then

polished her glasses. 'Something and maybe nothing, but that'll be for you to find out.'

Macallan nodded and tried not to show the impatience she was feeling.

'There's no point in going through the physical evidence used at court as that was all checked and double-checked by various officers, scientists and SOCOs. Given the proposition that Barclay might not be the killer, or at least not the killer of all the victims, I researched all sources on his day-to-day life. Whether it was a newspaper clipping on a case or a speech at a dinner ... everything.'

Macallan topped up her wine, waiting to be disappointed or intrigued.

'There was nothing I could find other than what we already knew – that he was in various cities at the same time the attacks took place.'

Macallan nodded and realised that her hand was trembling. She took another hit of the wine.

'However, I've found something missed in the original examination. To be fair it was easily done, and I was lucky to catch it myself. I was looking through one of Barclay's pocket notebooks and at one page I placed it face down to get a drink. I'd pressed it down hard, and when I turned it over I noticed that a page had been removed – very carefully.'

'Could it just have been torn out to leave a note for someone?' Macallan felt it coming, they'd missed something and she'd always known it.

'Definitely not. The page had been almost surgically removed from the book. The notebook is no more than a scribble pad – it's not like a diary so we can't say it was definitely on such and such a day, but we could probably tie it down a bit from the entries before and after.'

Macallan knew in her gut that it had meaning. The killer was waiting at the end of the clue; they just had to make sense of it. 'Do you have it here?'

Young drew the small black notebook from her briefcase and handed it to Macallan, who handled it as if it was laced with toxins. She pulled open the marked pages and held it up to the light.

'Well, well. Whoever it was either forgot about indented writing or took the risk because removing more pages would be too obvious. I'm going to get this to the lab and I'll get back to you as soon as I get the result.'

She bagged the notebook, but as she dropped it into her case an alarm went off in her mind. 'If this is something then why not just bin the notebook before we got it?' Young said nothing, knowing Macallan was just thinking aloud. 'Unless it was done after arrest – but how could that be?' She stared at a blank wall.

'Who examined the notebook?' she asked Young.

The analyst rubbed the lenses of her glasses again. 'Mick Harkins examined it,' she admitted. 'It was Mick.'

66

Macallan headed for HQ feeling like she had a time bomb in her briefcase but wasn't sure just where and when it would go off – and, more importantly, who would end up as collateral damage?

As Macallan was driving into the car park at the south side of Lothian and Borders HQ, Harkins filled in a four-line form, handed it in to the pensions office and became a retired officer in less time than it took him to eat his lunch. O'Connor didn't even know that he'd gone, and the only person he made a point of telling was the office cleaner, who'd been there for even more years than him. The squad detectives who were there watched him leave the office without a backward glance. They'd overheard it all, and as soon as he closed the doors behind him the theories started to catch fire. Most thought it was to do with the breakdown at the top and blamed O'Connor.

Harkins stepped out into the yard and looked over at the rows of marked cars and vans liveried with the Lothian and Borders crest. He walked across the car park to the barrier as the winter darkness pushed its cover over the city, pulling his collar up as he walked through the gates and headed away from his career and everything that had made him who he was. As he walked along Stockbridge he lit a damp cigarette, coughed painfully and decided that at least he could drink what he liked and not worry about getting into the office in the morning.

He wandered round the supermarket trying to avoid the other shoppers who looked like they might have a life. The young girl at the checkout seemed to be giving him too much eye contact, and it made him feel uncomfortable. What did she see, and was that pity in her stare? It didn't help that he had to pay for the small bag of goods with handfuls of change, and he could feel the annoyance coming from the punters in the queue behind him.

He relaxed as he escaped back into the dark street, boiling with rush-hour traffic and tired citizens escaping the working day, and fixed his gaze on the ground ahead of his pounding feet. All he wanted was to be safely inside his flat and let tomorrow be another problem.

Harkins saw the apartment building lights beckon him and stared up at the unlit windows of his fourth-floor flat. It was empty but safe, and he was going to drink and drink hard – he was on his own, and he could do whatever he wanted. Doubles, trebles, or mixing it, it was all fine, and he got stuck in. He'd loved his time with Felicity but maybe it was all just as well and she was better off without him. He didn't know, and for a while he ached to hold her and – who knows? He was Mick Harkins so fuck it all.

Three-quarters of the way down, the bottle started to work its magic and he began to relax, remembering the days when he'd meant something . . .

He woke up in the chair as if an electric charge had been pumped through his body, struggling to clear his head as he watched Jeremy Paxman giving someone a hard time on *Newsnight*. For some reason the sound was turned down, but it didn't really matter – he couldn't stand the bastard.

In the morning, which was nearer afternoon, Harkins opened the door feeling as if he hadn't slept in a month – which was close to the truth if he subtracted drink-induced comas. He realised that he could collect his lump sum and do whatever the fuck he liked with it – money wasn't a problem, so he headed for the bookies and then on to the boozer.

67

O'Connor was sitting in his office and decided that he couldn't spend the rest of his life turning the same thoughts over in his head. He was intelligent enough to know that his period of isolation was driving the squad towards total failure on the Waddell case and anything else they might touch. He had to take action and regain control of it all.

The sleet hit the windows like machine-gun fire and he stared across the city skyline as dark smoking clouds hurried towards the North Sea. He'd been hurt by Macallan, but much of what she'd said was true, and he knew that he was just wallowing in self-pity. It was time to get back on the job, and he needed Macallan whether they had a relationship or not.

He walked out of his office and said he needed Harkins and Macallan. It took all his self-control to stay calm when he was told that Harkins was gone.

'Get me Chief Inspector Macallan now!'

Macallan was in the lab when the message reached her that O'Connor was on the prowl. The results of the indented writing weren't quite ready, and she asked that they be delivered to Felicity Young in a sealed envelope. She couldn't tell O'Connor about the notebook in case it was nothing and took him over the edge.

She took a deep breath before she walked into his office because she had no idea what was coming next – and certainly didn't expect to hear that Harkins had left.

O'Connor was surprised that she hadn't known and felt foolish for imagining it was some conspiracy cooked up to make things even worse for him.

'Have you any idea what happened to Mick?' he asked Macallan, doing his best to look as if he was back in control.

She hoped he wouldn't pick up her discomfort, but she had to see if they could make sense of the indentations before she mentioned anything about the notebook. A problem with a squad officer – and particularly Mick Harkins – was the last thing O'Connor needed to admit to the ACC.

'I'll try and get a hold of him at some point to see if there's anything we can do, but I suspect he'll be hard to reach if he doesn't want to be found.' She tried to act matter-of-fact, but they were both struggling to hide the non-verbals.

At the very least O'Connor seemed to be thawing towards her and that gave her some feeling of relief.

'I'm sorry I've been a bit out of it, but whatever happens let's get back on the case, although I know you've been working flat out. How are we doing, and is there anything we need to concentrate on at the moment?'

She gave him all she had apart from the notebook; she had no idea how she would tell him if it turned out there was a trail to follow from the notes.

'I still think we need to look back at Barclay in case he's the wrong guy.' She waited for O'Connor's response, unsure how he'd take the implication.

The superintendent flinched but didn't lose control; however, it was confirmation enough that she had to be careful.

'We've been through this. We go for a copycat. Barclay didn't put up a fight and the forensics from his clothing was 100 per cent. If things change we can go back but that's our focus. Are you with me on this? If not, I need to get someone who is.'

And that was it. Those cold words changed it all and condemned what they'd had to another time and place. He was telling her in no uncertain terms that she could be replaced if she didn't play ball. There would be no discussion or sharing of ideas. She set her face and listened to her own thoughts rather than what he was saying. *Fuck you, Mr O'Connor. I'll drag this bastard in myself and lay him out on your desk.*

He was playing his game so she would play hers. She'd trained and fought in Northern Ireland against

340

an enemy that gave no quarter and hunted Branch officers like dogs. She was more than equipped to deal with this.

She smiled and rose from her chair. 'I'm on it, sir, and will keep you informed.' The word 'sir' was enough confirmation that they had a problem. She kept her control, her expression cold and hard, but it was just a mask to cover her anguish. Once again she'd been let down by a man she'd trusted and loved. She promised herself it was a mistake she'd never repeat.

She closed the door and walked back to her desk, only to find a text from Young asking for another meet.

68

Macallan brought sandwiches and coffee into her lounge as Young spread a stack of photocopies out on the floor, one of which was the page of indented writing. Macallan stared at it for a couple of minutes without comprehension then let Young have her moment.

The analyst's face was drawn, her expression anxious as she said, 'From the previous and following pages I was able to relate the notes to other information in his diaries, which gives us a pretty accurate indication of the dates involved. The problem is that what was written wasn't what I expected.'

Macallan felt her stomach knot. 'What is it? Tell me.'

'It's Mick's name and phone number. On its own that could have a reasonable explanation – he could've been calling on behalf of a client or something like that – but why on earth would they want to get rid of it?'

'I don't get it; none of this makes sense.'

Young was exhausted, but it was clear she wanted to work out what had happened to Harkins more than anyone and Macallan thought there was no better time to ask the question.

'You were close to Mick at the time. I don't want to pry, but what do you think?'

Young looked beaten and there were lines under her eyes that were new, and for life. 'Everything was good with Mick, and he really made an effort. He's not the ogre that some people think, and he can be quite gentle in his own way, but he puts on this show in public.'

Macallan nodded. 'I know that, and I was so happy when you two got together. Mick was the man who kept me sane when I arrived here.'

'Looking back, when the case started, he thought Barclay was just a suspect who'd be cleared eventually, and he was just going to enjoy watching him getting a hard time. It was like some private joke,' Young continued. 'But when the forensic evidence was found at the house, it was as if he'd been told he had a terminal illness. It was downhill from there – he was like a stranger. I know he's in some sort of trouble, but until this thing with the notes, I thought it was something personal. Now I don't know.'

Young looked down at the floor, at a loss for anything else to say.

Another few pieces drifted into place and Macallan saw the direction the arrows were going.

'Work what you've told me into a statement,' she told Young, 'but don't give it to anyone else at the moment.'

69

When Macallan walked into the custody area the following morning, the chill air wrapped round her shoulders and she wished she was back in France with some sun on her face. The trail was heading to a place she didn't want to go, but she wasn't prepared to leave it to anyone else.

The custody sergeant's career had always placed him well away from the front line, although he'd convinced his family and friends that no criminal was safe while he was about, and the visit from Macallan made him feel part of something bigger. It would make a good story, him helping out the murder squad who were struggling with the Waddell case, and he gave Macallan the information she needed immediately.

In the privacy of her office, Macallan ran her finger over Barclay's custody record and there it was – Harkins had visited Barclay in his cell after the arrest and interview. So there *was* a connection that had been kept under wraps. But why? She needed to tell O'Connor – but only when she knew the whole truth.

She walked to the car park and called Diana Barclay. 'I wonder if I could come and see you? I need to tie up some loose ends.'

The silence was long and heavy. 'I suppose I've been expecting a call from you. When?'

'Now.'

70

Diana Barclay walked to her window to wait for Macallan. The heavy make-up she wore couldn't completely disguise the exhaustion that drooped the corners of her eyes. Her face was drawn tight with strain, and she struggled to contain the sense of panic that occasionally threatened to choke her.

Even the remnants of what passed for her life were at risk now. Jonathon Barclay had been a high earner and the only breadwinner, but overnight that had come to an end. The possibility that she could lose her home was bad enough, but what terrified her was where she might end up. What friends they had weren't calling, and she felt completely abandoned.

She'd thought about calling her daughter, but there was no point – she would only see what had happened as confirmation that she'd done the right thing in putting emotional and physical distance between herself and her father.

She bit hard into the top of her forefinger and squeezed her eyes shut, trying to block out her train of thought. In these moments, she remembered the hours she'd spent in airports and train stations, staring at the arrivals, the arms thrown around lovers, wives, children – displays of affection she could only dream about – wishing for a different life.

She looked up as the nose of Macallan's car pulled into the drive and knew that she couldn't hold on to what she knew any longer. It had gone too far for that.

Macallan closed her eyes briefly as she pulled to a stop outside the Barclays' home. Her head was a mess and she needed help. She had no idea what the fuck this all meant, but she did know that Diana Barclay could tell her more than she had. She'd always known that – she just had to figure out how to open her up – and this time, Macallan decided, she wouldn't leave until she'd made it happen.

Inside, they sat down opposite each other, and Diana Barclay insisted on preparing tea. She'd managed to compose herself, but Macallan's expression was troubling her. She felt like the detective was trying to stare into the depths of her soul and raking through her most secret places.

'How can I help you, Chief Inspector?' She'd dropped the piss-taking, addressing Macallan by her proper rank. The hard defences were gone.

'By telling the truth,' Macallan replied. 'This has gone far enough. I was going to say you know that your husband is innocent, but of course that would be a poor choice of words in his case.'

Diana Barclay's back stiffened, and her dislike of Macallan turned into fear of what she knew. She'd always been regarded as a hard, unemotional woman but that had been in another life, when she'd had control. All the protective layers of class and privilege had now been stripped away, and she was facing a woman who had tested her own courage and integrity against the worst examples of humankind. Macallan's eyes glittered with anger as she watched the woman fold in front of her, and for the first time in her life, Diana Barclay wanted to plead for help – to ask for forgiveness from this detective in the futile hope that she would understand.

'You have to help us, Mrs Barclay,' Macallan pressed her. 'There's no more time. I know some of it but not all so tell me why I'm sitting here and what it is I need to know. And just so you know exactly what's at stake if you don't, I want to show you what happens to the girls that are being attacked.'

She shoved the photograph of the latest victim across the table at the woman.

Diana Barclay couldn't drag her eyes from the horror: the legs sprawled at a ridiculous angle, the gaping mouth frozen in the moment of death as the girl sucked blood into her flooded lungs. She choked down the sob, but it was pointless, and Macallan let her take it in. She deserved to see it.

Barclay's shoulders shook with the release of emotion and eventually the tension in her chest eased.

She remembered who she was and, worst of all, who she might become, so she looked up and apologised to Macallan, who didn't see the point in answering. All she wanted was the truth.

'You have to understand, Chief Inspector, that whatever you may think of me, at least consider the effect of what I am about to tell you on what remains of my life.'

Macallan still didn't see the point in answering.

'I've known about my husband's weaknesses almost since the beginning of our marriage. Our relationship was never about strong physical passion; it was more to do with producing two children, and after that it became an occasional event, usually when he'd had too much to drink.'

Macallan wanted to tell her to cut out the history lesson, but she knew this was all part of the deal. The truth was on its way.

'He had a strong drive, and I didn't, so the fact that he became involved with other women, mostly lawyers, didn't really trouble me at all. As long as he was discreet then I was happy to lead my life in the way I wanted. I thought I had what I wanted.'

She delicately touched the side of her eyes with an expensive handkerchief and Macallan began to feel pity for her. She realised just how lonely this woman was and that it would only get worse.

'When I found out that he was using prostitutes, that was quite another thing. I found a card among his papers one day, and to cut a long story short it turned out to be for an escort agency. He tried to deny it at first, and he may be a brilliant lawyer but I've always been able to tell when he's lying. Eventually he admitted that his affairs at work bored him and the risks he took with prostitutes were what gave him satisfaction. Does this make any sense to you, Chief Inspector – though I suppose you've seen so much more than I have?'

'I gave up trying to make sense of what people do a long time ago, Mrs Barclay, especially when it comes to men.'

They both smiled weakly.

'We argued and eventually he convinced me that he'd stopped seeing these women, and quite naively I believed him – or it was more that I wanted to believe him. It was fine for a while ... and then that's when it happened.'

Macallan tried to keep eye contact without revealing her own tension. It was as if Diana Barclay was opening a grubby bag that contained something awful, but it was still out of sight, so she couldn't guess what it was – only smell it.

'Can you imagine someone like me sitting in front of a doctor I've known for years and being told I had a sexually transmitted disease?' The question didn't need an answer. 'He brought disease into my home – and passed it to me.'

She sobbed again and Macallan let out a long breath – then said the wrong thing.

'I'm sorry, Mrs Barclay.'

Barclay's eyes flared for the first time. 'No you're not! You're here for the truth, and I'm giving it to you. You will be sorry, but trust me when I say it won't be for me. Just continue enjoying my humiliation and you'll get what you need.'

Macallan nodded and wanted to boot her own arse.

'The shock was like a physical illness, and it's pointless trying to explain how I felt at the time. I was angry in a way that frightened me. When he came home that evening, I confronted him and he was distraught. He cried like a child – and that's the only time in my life I've ever seen him like that. We talked and argued for hours, trying to find out where we were both heading. I'll never forget the moment when I realised that Thomas was listening at the door. He was always doing that. Can you imagine that? All in one day. All that truth shared out among us. A young boy trying to take all that in. All his shattered illusions.'

Macallan saw it coming now. The pieces were falling into place – the awful truth that this family had carried like an unidentified virus.

'My son was like a broken doll. It was too much for him. He never told his sister, and he never talked about it, but from that day he was damaged in a way that only Jonathon and I could see. He hated his father yet hardly ever put it into words or anger. People thought he was weak, and although he qualified in law himself, he's a poor excuse for a man. But is that his fault? My daughter managed to hate us just for being who we are, and she left home as soon as she could manage.'

Macallan needed to hear her say it. 'What are you telling me, Mrs Barclay?'

'Surely you can see it, Chief Inspector. Despite his

denials, I was convinced that Jonathon was responsible for the attacks on those women until this latest incident. Then my son came to see me yesterday, and I saw something terrible in his eyes. He said he wanted to speak to his father and then he cried in my lap, sobbing as if he'd break, and I realised what he'd done.' She leaned forward to make sure Macallan understood what she was saying. 'You need to speak to my son.'

Macallan tried not to show her panic. 'Do you know where he is now?'

'I've no idea, but he intended visiting my husband last night.'

Macallan felt her anger rise again. 'I hope that's all of it this time, or I'll come for you and finish the job.'

She ran from the house and headed straight for the prison, calling O'Connor from the car.

'Where the fuck are you, Grace?' he asked.

'Listen to me and don't speak. We need to get a hold of Thomas Barclay and detain him. I'm heading for the prison to see Jonathon Barclay; why don't you join me there? I'll explain it when I see you.'

'Grace?'

She put the phone down and pressed the accelerator to the floor.

71

O'Connor managed to arrive at the prison just behind Macallan, who'd waited for him, wondering if they were about to have a very public confrontation. She knew if her gamble went wrong she was risking a career she'd almost given up on once and could destroy again, but even if it went her way, O'Connor was going to look weak and humiliated and that was almost as bad.

She'd let him in on the game now because he had to be, and she supposed she would just have to live with the aftermath, but when he stepped out of his car and she saw his expression, she felt her shoulders slump. Pissed off was an understatement, and she realised this was going to be harder than she'd thought.

He walked over to her, his face tight and controlled, and she saw that he was hurting badly – his ego had been damaged, and that was something he wouldn't forgive quickly.

'Whatever you're doing, you've done it without me, and that's a betrayal in my book,' he said coldly. 'You of all people. I can see why the boys over the water turned their backs on you – it all makes sense now.'

O'Connor had realised that he could never be Harkins, but his real mistake was that he hadn't applied the same reasoning to Macallan. He was a better politician than she was, but that was all. He felt sick as he realised he could have ten careers and still not compete with her. It came naturally to Grace – she was born for it, and he just acted the part. He was a good manager, but he could have done the same job in an oil company or bank. Macallan and Harkins were the real detectives, and he lacked the balls to be what he really wanted.

Macallan unfolded her arms and felt the words land like blows, but she raised her chin and refused to let him see the wounds he'd just inflicted.

'How the fuck would you know what happened over the water? We were fighting a war while you were playing with yourself in a nice safe office in Germany. What I'm doing here is getting the truth, and if you don't like it then fuck off back to HQ while I sort the mess.' Her chest heaved with emotion. 'Maybe then I can call them and get a real detective to attend.'

His stunned silence brought her relief and she was able to choose her next words carefully, her anger settling almost as quickly as it had risen. She'd faced the worst of men and her gift when she needed it was cold resolve.

'I never expected that kind of comment from you, John,' she told him, folding her arms again. 'You're vain and self-centred but a good man for all that. Now I'm going in so make your mind up.'

O'Connor blinked first. He was intelligent enough to realise that she could well be right and that he needed to avoid throwing away whatever was left in his hand. The reputation he'd built carefully and without too much exposure to stress-testing could go up in a bonfire that his competitors in the force would gladly help fuel, and that realisation cut out any fight he had left. An awful truth had been exposed – that he had been tested but hadn't passed muster, and his instincts told him that if Macallan was right then he had to hang on to the slipstream.

And if she was wrong he could shovel the earth over her decomposing professional corpse.

He followed her into reception without a word, but he watched her back as he did so and imagined plunging something sharp between her shoulder blades. The first chance he got, he promised himself he'd do a number on her.

72

Jonathon Barclay was brought into the interview room, and Macallan saw that he'd become old in the short time he'd served. The hair that had always been so carefully styled was now cut short without care, his face was puffy and his skin had no colour apart from the grey tones reflected from the walls of the room. He tried to smile and failed but seemed relieved to see anyone who wasn't part of the inside of the prison.

Macallan noted the tremor in the hands and wondered what it must be like for a man like Barclay in this place. She'd put Jackie Crawford somewhere similar, and she shivered at the thought of what he must have suffered for killing a terrorist 'past his sell by date'.

O'Connor stayed silent and let Macallan play her hand, settling into the experience of being relegated to appear like the junior officer in the room.

'I know the truth, Mr Barclay. Not all of it but enough to know that you didn't commit the crimes you were convicted of. You're certainly not an innocent man but that's another matter.'

O'Connor stiffened but remained quiet, remembering he was there by invitation only.

'I've spoken to Diana, and I know about your son. I believe he's the killer and that all this was some form of revenge. You could have taken this sentence for him and the world would have forgotten you. And not many on my side would have cared to be quite frank.'

O'Connor shifted uncomfortably at that comment. By rights he should had taken a strip off her for suggesting the police would have countenanced this, but she was right. She seemed to be right about everything, and he cursed her, but he knew she might be holding the only lifeline available to him so he had to play his cards right.

'But as I'm sure you know, another girl has been killed,' Macallan continued, 'and it has to stop here and now. When did you know it was him?'

She leaned backwards and placed the palms of her hands on the table and waited. It was all or nothing.

Barclay studied the back of his hands and Macallan allowed him time to form the words.

'I wasn't sure till he came to see me last night. I knew someone was out to destroy me when the car was stolen and the DNA came back. Obviously I knew it was planted but would you have believed me, Chief Inspector? Despite all the claims I've made against the police in the past, I knew it wasn't you, but some of your colleagues might have been less sensitive about such a course of action. As you know I've mixed with some serious people, and a few of them aren't short of imagination and resources, so there were also candidates among the people I've defended or perhaps let down in the past, and that means quite a number of people, so I've had to come to terms with just what my life amounts to.' He looked down and shook his head at some unexpressed thought.

'It could have been one of them, but there was a problem with the why. The worst that's happened is the odd failure to secure a not-guilty result, but given that they were all as guilty as sin, that was a difficult one to accept. The truth is that I've led a life that's gathered enemies and I just couldn't be sure which one it was, but there's no point in hiding anything now; I'll put all my cards on the table.'

He seemed to gain energy from his revelations. He was in control of the answers Macallan needed, so he played the script at his own pace.

O'Connor watched the exchange silently; he could have been watching from another room, and Macallan and Barclay played their roles as if he was invisible. He knew not to take part or break the spell that had formed like a spider's web before his eyes.

'The car could have been a coincidence, but when the DNA came back I knew that someone had serious intentions. It wasn't coincidence any more.'

'So you'd nothing to do with your car going AWOL?' Macallan interrupted, but Barclay was already anticipating the question and he smiled.

'Of course not, but it was a smart move – just what a guilty man would have done and why would you have thought otherwise? The problem was that you were so busy convicting me before the trial that you were looking but not seeing.'

O'Connor watched the investigation's failures being unwrapped on the table in front of him. He was the SIO and whatever had gone wrong would be picked over like the bones of a predator's kill. The papers and the executive floor would want a human sacrifice to make sure they avoided damage to their own careers.

'My son doesn't own a Merc, though I know he hires them from time to time. Still I couldn't be sure when so many people have cause to dislike me.'

Macallan sighed. She wanted to groan but held it back. O'Connor's hand clenched.

'I put it to Thomas, but he just laughed in my face, said he didn't know what I was talking about. I'd always known that he despised me, but you never really understand the depths of such hatred or what form it might take.'

His eyes glinted with renewed fire over his drooping, inflamed rims. 'What was I to do? Accuse my own son with no evidence whatsoever, when the evidence was stacked against me? He hadn't admitted it so there was always a possibility it was someone else from my past wanting to settle an account. Whatever happened I knew that whoever was behind it had done a good job, and all my past indiscretions would be made public.' He smiled but his eyes remained dead and Macallan briefly wondered about his sanity.

'When you showed me the photographs of the girls I'd been with, that was confirmation that the culprit had gone to the lengths of following me so he could tie me to the victims. Pretty fucking thorough in my opinion.' He sighed and shook his head.

'There was nowhere to go with a defence. What was I to do – suggest it might be my son because he hated me, or an unknown villain from the past? I don't think my adoring public would have gone for that one, and certainly not Lothian and Borders finest or the jury. I knew enough about how they act in these kinds of cases.'

Barclay leaned forward and delivered the truth. 'My son came to see me last night and admitted what he'd done, and why he'd done it. I asked him why he'd killed again when he could have left me to rot, and that's when I realised how sick he is. He said he enjoyed it – apparently that had surprised him and he couldn't stop. His intention was to ruin me and he'd achieved all that. He's just waiting for you now.'

Barclay watched the faces of the detectives and grinned, realising they still didn't quite get it.

'There was another problem, Chief Inspector, and that was that my relationship with my good friend Mick Harkins would come out and seal my fate one way or another – so I decided to keep quiet about that. I had no choice. The likelihood was that a deep investigation into my past would expose what I'd been responsible for, and considering some of the men I'd betrayed to your colleague, I could be pretty sure that I'd suffer in ways I'd rather not think about.'

Macallan opened the last door. 'I knew there was something between you and Harkins. I also know that he removed a page from your notebook, but I don't know why – I thought it might be a fit up – but given what you've said, I don't think that's what you're going to tell me.'

Macallan was angry. She wasn't sure why but she knew they were being still being played; still behind in the game, and it was clear that Barclay was enjoying the power in what he knew. It was as if he was back in the High Court, lacerating the police witnesses stranded in the isolation of the witness box.

'I thought you might have worked it out by now but obviously I gave you too much credit. Some years ago I foolishly experimented with cocaine, as so many of my class were doing at the time. I was with a girl from an agency one night and I'm afraid things got out of hand; unfortunately she became upset and called the police. There'd been a struggle, and if I'm being honest she'd suffered some serious injuries. She brought it on herself, but I concede that a court might not have understood my side of the incident.'

O'Connor wanted to shut his eyes, but he was trapped like Macallan, and all they had left was the endgame. Barclay was pulling all the strings and this was his last big grandstanding moment.

'Mick Harkins was the CID officer called in and … let's just say that we worked out a compromise. You people tend to call it a deal. He knew a good opportunity when he saw one. He fixed it with the girl's pimp and made the unfortunate events go away. I became a source of information. Let's face it – could it get any better than an A-list lawyer, the man who defends the men who matter, the ones you struggle to put away? No, let's call it what it was: I became his informant. I was mixing with the biggest and best criminals in the game so think what I was able to give him! Money wasn't in the deal, and the only thing I insisted on was that I would never be officially registered as a CHIS, as you describe them nowadays. So like the police to use four words where one would do the trick. Who do you think gave you the Drews? How did Mick Harkins get so many headline arrests? The best part for Lothian and Borders Police was that he never had to pay me a penny. He controlled me, and I controlled him.'

He sat back and enjoyed the impact of his words. Macallan blinked; O'Connor was already seeing a ton of shit pouring over the force – and that he'd be buried beneath it. The ACC would relish using Harkins to get to O'Connor. Guilt by association; that was enough. Harkins had handled an unofficial source, which was a serious matter on its own, and he'd allowed it to run. Fine if the results worked out, but a hanging matter when it went wrong, and O'Connor saw exactly where the buck would come to a grinding halt.

'I told Harkins about the entry in the notebook, and he decided to get rid of it without question. I had a powerful weapon because Mr Harkins was clearly terrified that our relationship would become public; in fact, he knew that our deal could have put him in here with me. There was a touch of the Cold War in the situation: mutually assured destruction. The question of guilt or innocence didn't come into it – as far as he was concerned, I was guilty as convicted, and I told him nothing to change his mind.'

O'Connor tried to put it all together but decided it was too much. They needed to get back to HQ and try to work out an escape plan. What had seemed like a triumph and the beginning of a new chapter in his career and personal life had turned into a bridge collapsing under his feet. He couldn't turn back, and the way ahead meant a long fall. He spoke for the first time.

'So you betrayed some of your clients. Christ, you represented the Drews for years. They'll feed you to the fucking dogs.' O'Connor saw the worms pouring out of the can as he said it, and a vein in his neck throbbed out in panic. The Drews would be screaming about their human rights, and dozens of trials might be compromised. There were more people than O'Connor involved, including Macallan, but he was the man on the bridge and Harkins' boss, and Harkins had been allowed to run free for years, so the force would be marked in the same shit storm.

'We have to go, Mr Barclay, but we'll come back once we can locate your son.'

Barclay half raised his hand. 'Not yet, Superintendent. You'll probably have my son before the day's out, and if I'm not mistaken he expects to be caught. That's the problem. I miscalculated, and it seems not for the first time, thinking that whoever did this would stop after my conviction. I was wrong. He wants to take the whole thing a stage further and destroy himself. That way he can be sure there's no way back for me in either reputation, professional career or any pretence that I was part of the establishment.'

O'Connor looked as if he was about to ask a question, but Barclay was back in character as the commanding advocate. The court was his for the moment, and he flicked his forefinger up in a little gesture that told O'Connor to wait for the punchline.

'I'm not finished, and I'm afraid neither is he. When my son came to see me, he wanted to talk, to look me in the eye and admit to me what he'd done and why. For the first time in my life I've spent a lot of hours regretting what I've made of myself, and it might seem strange, but I needed the release of confession. I'm not a Catholic, but it felt right. Another mistake unfortunately.' He paused for a moment and saw the detectives trapped by the words, waiting for the final act of the drama – a terrible revelation that that was only moments away.

'By way of an explanation, I told him about the girl I hurt all those years ago and how Harkins became involved with me. He blames me for almost every-thing that's made him the vain, pumped-up failure he is and for what I brought home to his mother, and now he blames the police for not stopping me in my tracks. When I say the police, I should say Harkins. I think his original plan involved something else and perhaps even you, Chief Inspector, but now I believe you need to rescue Mick, because if I'm not mistaken, my son's been stalking him – or at least trying to find him – since last night.'

Macallan saw it coming, and she was already running the options through her head. Where was Mick?

'He's changed the final part of his game, and I think he's trying to find Harkins to play it out, which shouldn't be too hard given the man's drinking habits. Give Mick my best if you get to him first; no doubt I'll be seeing you on the outside. There's the rub – I think my time in here is limited now. It's an ill wind.' But he said it to a closing interview-room door.

Macallan and O'Connor were already on their way out and running for their cars.

73

Harkins pulled his collar up as the rain killed the warm places below his coat. He sheltered in a pub doorway, trying to work up the energy to leave the warmth behind. The rain had lightened for a moment but it was just getting ready for another downpour.

Any variety in his life had ended when he'd walked away from HQ for the last time, and he felt surrounded by a hostile world, remembering those last days in the squad that had nearly taken him over the edge.

He was sure people knew what had finally kicked the life out of Mick Harkins and his career. The other detectives seemed to have become distant, and he didn't want to talk to them, even to slag them off, as had always been his custom. When they did talk to him, he was sure they noticed his clouded eyes, the imperfect attempts at shaving and the worry grinding in his chest. The fear of discovery was sapping his appetite and shooting waves of nervous energy through his body when all he wanted was sleep.

He was being tortured by some of the same demons who'd visited Thomas Barclay, but there was nowhere for him to go without the job, and bars were the only places that could at least put him near other human beings who would have no way of knowing or judging what he'd done. No one who knew him wanted to be seen in his company – retired police was still police – and he was losing weight rapidly, the space around his collar now wide enough to let the pissing rain run straight down his back.

He stood on the edge of the pavement, squinting into the spray thrown up by the passing wheels. He wondered how it had happened: he was young, then one day he was middle aged, and now he was fucked.

The bookies was on the other side of the road, and he cursed as a flash set of wheels splashed the filthy street water over his legs and shoes. He peered into the driving rain, which had started again with a vengeance, and took no notice of the car revving its engine at the side of the street. He stepped out onto the road as he fumbled in his raincoat for a half-squashed cigarette packet and was barely aware of the roar of the engine before he became airborne and then hit the tarmac.

'Fuck!'

When the car hit him, the pain was an explosion – then almost as quickly it drained into the cold, damp ground below, and with it went all sensation. He was just aware that the freezing droplets of rain were making him blink, and that he couldn't move his head to avoid them. He was sure he was dying, but he felt surprisingly calm. Like most people, he'd wondered how his last moments would be, but there was almost an anticlimax in the experience.

With the pain gone his mind adjusted to the situation. A uniform bent over him and mouthed something, but it was a silent movie, although he could guess what was being said. Christ knows he'd been there often enough himself as a young policeman – a thousand years ago now, it seemed. All you could do was tell the poor sod to be calm and that help was on its way. Well, he was calm but didn't think much could sort his situation. He imagined his own young face on the policeman, and if he could he would have wept. Then he saw Grace trying to get to him. She was crying, her face lacerated with pain, and he realised what she'd become to him. His chest heaved with the effort of staying alive and he said it in no more than a whisper: 'Jesus Christ, this isn't how it should end.'

74

Macallan walked through the hospital corridors, wondering what she would say. She got to the room and saw Harkins through the glass. He was motionless in the chair, staring out of the window, and from what she'd been told, he didn't have much option but to stare. They said there was a chance he might never walk again, but it was early days, and Harkins was a stubborn bastard who would give it a go if even partial recovery was a possibility. The fact he'd survived was a minor miracle on its own.

'Mick?'

He looked round slowly. Harkins could only do slow for the time being.

'Grace. Good to see you. Didn't think you'd come.' He managed a half-grin, but it was tired and the hard man looked feeble.

She told him she understood. He did what he did, and it had gone wrong. Other people did things and survived – it was all in the lap of the gods, and it just depended whether they were having a good day or a shit day. She told him he was a good cop no matter what and that the world was just fucked up.

After an hour she kissed his forehead, walked out of the hospital and headed back to HQ. She knew the fiscal was struggling with charges against him, but what else could they do to him? He was in the worst kind of prison so she thought they should leave him be. She certainly wasn't going to judge the man.

She had an appointment with the deputy chief to get to, and she had no idea whether it was going to be bad or worse than bad, but she could at least take comfort that Thomas Barclay was locked up like a bit player from *One Flew Over the Cuckoo's Nest*. His father was free and hiding from everyone though mostly his ex-clients, but they'd managed to contain some of the information about his relationship with Harkins, so it all depended on whether they put Mick on trial. If they did, then it would surely all come out – and the casualties would no doubt mount up.

75

She knocked at the door, walked into the over-large office and felt her feet sink into the carpet. It was an ill-divided world. The secretary brought a tray in and tea was served right on cue, but the censure never came and Macallan's world changed again.

'You'll be promoted to Superintendent and will take over as lead officer for the MCT. How does that suit you?'

'I'm shocked, sir, and didn't expect this. What about Mr O'Connor?'

'We think his skills lie elsewhere; he'll take over as head of complaints and internal investigation. The force has taken a beating, but we'll survive. We always do. John took some flak, as we all did, but he's a good man and we should never forget that. You took risks and it could have failed, but you're high profile and that reflects well on the force. The story Jacquie Bell did on your career has put you in a good place, and we can use that. John O'Connor might feel like you've replaced him, but he'll just have to live with that, so let's all get on with it and keep up the good work with the MCT.'

She left the room realising that she could never aspire to high office because they all spoke the same crap. The truth was that O'Connor had taken all the flak, even though there was little he could have done to prevent what had happened. She knew that there were people who would always despise her for what she was, and one of them was now in charge of complaints and discipline. 'Fucking wonderful,' she muttered.

She walked into the squad room and her new empire, picked up the phone and booked a flight to Belfast. She'd said that she would never go back, but she wanted to see Bill Kelly before it was too late. She wanted to tell him how much he meant to her – and she wanted to walk round the city in the daylight, when there were no shadows and the dead were just that.

76

Macallan leaned over the chair where Bill Kelly had fallen asleep mid-conversation. He looked old and she could tell his time was near. She ran her hand over his forehead one last time and left. They'd said all that needed to be said to each other, and she was glad she'd seen him, even the way he was. He wasn't frightened, just tired, and managed to wisecrack that some old PIRA boys would probably lift a glass to him after the funeral. She held his wife and left their home to walk into the city.

She wandered through the town past City Hall, but it looked normal and people were just going about their business. The war was long over for everyone but the diehards who just couldn't live without the cause – deluded men and women who couldn't see the world moving on without them. If proof was needed then the dissidents just needed to tune into Ulster's favourite double act – McGuinness and Paisley.

She pushed open the doors of the Crown Bar and sucked in the heavy smells of good beer and real food. The customers were just people talking and living their lives.

Macallan ordered a half of Guinness and thought about how far the city had come and what people could achieve together even after the horrors of the Troubles. The Europa opposite was testament to that – it had been the most bombed hotel in the world at one time, but there it was, lights flashing as if nothing had ever happened.

Darkness fell and she walked along Donegal Pass, onto the Ormeau Road and past the Markets, where years before she would have been taken, her body left on display on some waste ground. But nothing came out of the shadows; it was just night in the city.

Macallan knew that a chapter of her life was closing. The dreams would still come but not so often, and they had started to become blurred, like her memories.

She walked up Newtownards Road and headed for the HQ building of PSNI and what had been the RUC. She touched her face nervously a couple of times as she was checked in by the security men at the entrance. Even by police-building standards, it was uninteresting to look at, but it had witnessed so much in its time. Like so many of her colleagues and friends, some of them murdered by the Provos, she'd spent long days and even longer nights in that building never knowing who was next. The small garden of remembrance was there, commemorating so many dead officers – so many families torn apart in the dirty war – and Bill Kelly had made her promise to go back for a visit. It might hurt, but he knew better than she did that she needed to leave the past where it was.

'Don't expect a champagne reception, Grace,' he'd said, 'but you need to face up to it. The PSNI is part of the service, and you might well need them again in your career. I've called the boss in Major Crime and he'd be happy to meet you. You've grown quite a reputation you know, bit of a celeb.' And he'd managed a grin.

She waited at the counter for her pass and a Major Crime DCI came along and shook her hand warmly. She didn't know him, and she was thankful for that. For him it was just a courtesy visit from a senior L&B detective who'd served in Northern Ireland.

She shivered as she walked along the corridors, remembering how excited she'd been when she first joined the Branch. She chewed the fat with the DCI for half an hour before he suggested they head out for dinner, and she was trying to think up an excuse to avoid it when her phone went off and startled her.

'Macallan.'

It was her office calling – one of the detectives in the MCT.

'Sorry, ma'am, a body's been found. It's a murder.' Her shoulders straightened and she felt that familiar adrenaline beginning to course through her. 'I'm on my way.'

She bid farewell to the DCI and began her journey back to Edinburgh to find out what life held in store for her next.